Sparking old flames . . .

The doorman entered and deposited the luggage—including, Andrea noticed, a duffel bag that didn't belong to her.

Suddenly she felt strange and nervous. Did Bill intend to stay overnight in her apartment? Or was he booked into a hotel? She knew she couldn't send him away if he expected to stay with her. Not when he'd put her up in his apartment in Washington. Not when he'd done her so many kindnesses.

But she also knew that if he stayed it could be a dangerous, explosive situation. After Atlanta, she didn't trust either of them to keep a nice divorced distance.

"Are you going to invite me to stay," he asked bluntly, "or do I go out and find a hotel room?"

Dear Reader:

Romance offers us all so much. It makes us "walk on sunshine." It gives us hope. It takes us out of our own lives, encouraging us to reach out to others. Janet Dailey is fond of saying that romance is a state of mind, that it could happen anywhere. Yet nowhere does romance seem to be as good as when it happens *here*.

Starting in February 1986, Silhouette Special Edition will feature the AMERICAN TRIBUTE—a tribute to America, where romance has never been so wonderful. For six consecutive months, one out of every six Special Editions will be an episode in the AMERICAN TRIBUTE, a portrait of the lives of six women, all from Oklahoma. Look for the first book, *Love's Haunting Refrain* by Ada Steward, as well as stories by other favorites—Jeanne Stephens, Gena Dalton, Elaine Camp and Renee Roszel. You'll know the AMERICAN TRIBUTE by its patriotic stripe under the Silhouette Special Edition border.

AMERICAN TRIBUTE—six women, six stories, starting in February.

AMERICAN TRIBUTE—one of the reasons Silhouette Special Edition is just that—Special.

The Editors at Silhouette Books

SONDRA STANFORD
Bird in Flight

Silhouette Special Edition

Published by Silhouette Books New York

America's Publisher of Contemporary Romance

With gratitude for abiding friendship,
admiration for a talented author,
and enduring affection—
this is for
MARGARET MAJOR CLEAVES

SILHOUETTE BOOKS
300 E. 42nd St., New York, N.Y.   10017

Copyright © 1986 by Sondra Stanford

ISBN: 0-373-09292-X

First Silhouette Books printing February 1986

America's Publisher of Contemporary Romance

Printed in the U.S.A.

Books by Sondra Stanford

Silhouette Romance

Golden Tide #6
Shadow of Love #25
Storm's End #35
No Trespassing #46
Long Winter's Night #58
And Then Came Dawn #88
Yesterday's Shadow #100
Whisper Wind #112
Tarnished Vows #131

Silhouette Special Edition

Silver Mist #7
Magnolia Moon #37
Sun Lover #55
Love's Gentle Chains #91
The Heart Knows Best #161
For All Time #187
A Corner of Heaven #210
Cupid's Task #248
Bird in Flight #292

SONDRA STANFORD

wrote advertising copy before trying her hand at romance fiction. Also an artist, she enjoys attending arts-and-crafts shows and browsing at flea markets. Sondra and her husband live happily with their two children in Corpus Christi, Texas.

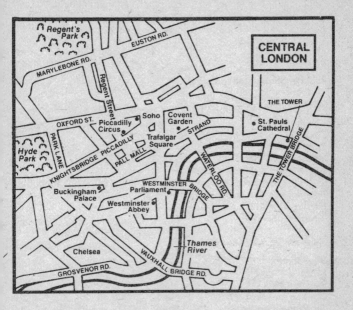

CENTRAL LONDON

Regent's Park

EUSTON RD.

MARYLEBONE RD.

Regent Street

OXFORD ST.

Soho

Covent Garden

Piccadilly Circus

St. Pauls Cathedral

THE TOWER

PICCADILLY

Trafalgar Square

STRAND

PARK LANE

Hyde Park

KNIGHTSBRIDGE

PALL MALL

WATERLOO RD.

THE TOWER BRIDGE

Buckingham Palace

WESTMINSTER BRIDGE

Parliament

Westminster Abbey

Chelsea

Thames River

GROSVENOR RD.

VAUXHALL BRIDGE RD.

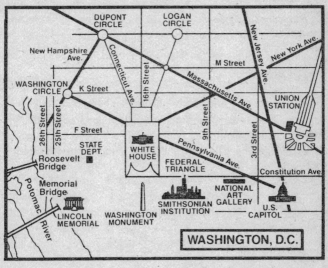

WASHINGTON, D.C.

DUPONT CIRCLE

LOGAN CIRCLE

New Hampshire Ave.

Connecticut Ave.

New Jersey Ave.

New York Ave.

M Street

16th Street

Massachusetts Ave.

WASHINGTON CIRCLE

K Street

UNION STATION

4th Street

26th Street

25th Street

F Street

9th Street

3rd Street

STATE DEPT.

WHITE HOUSE

Pennsylvania Ave.

Roosevelt Bridge

FEDERAL TRIANGLE

Constitution Ave.

Memorial Bridge

NATIONAL ART GALLERY

Potomac River

LINCOLN MEMORIAL

WASHINGTON MONUMENT

SMITHSONIAN INSTITUTION

U.S. CAPITOL

Chapter One

The final curtain call ended, the applause faded at last and the houselights went on. Almost as one, the theatergoers started to rise from their seats. An energetic bustle ensued as the patrons murmured to one another, slipped into coats and began straggling up the aisles.

The play had been a comedy, a light one, but replete with dry British wit. "Well, what did you think of it?" the young woman asked her companion as he helped her into her fur jacket.

"I thoroughly enjoyed it," Bill Sheridan replied. He smiled easily. "You made an excellent choice."

In fact, after the week he'd just spent at the Paris conference where the atmosphere had been heavy with gloomy discussions of nuclear weapons, the latest crises in Iran and Lebanon and world hunger, the undemanding silliness of the play had been precisely what he'd needed to help him unwind.

Bill had arrived in London only this afternoon, and the next couple of days promised to be almost as exhausting as the conference he'd just left. He would spend innumerable hours in still more meetings before he returned to Washington later in the week.

But tonight was his to relax and enjoy himself. Rosalie Chapman was always a charming companion. She was the daughter of a now retired ambassador to the United States, and they had met two years ago at a reception in Washington. Since then, whenever he happened to be visiting the London bureau of the *Washington Patriot*, they usually spent an evening together. Bill knew there had been speculation in Washington and London circles about a romance between them, but the truth was they'd never actually had enough time together to become anything more than warm friends. Rosalie was a beautiful young widow who enjoyed raising horses, and even had they become serious about each other, Bill had the impression that she would never leave England. As for himself, once burned, he deftly evaded becoming seriously involved with any woman.

All the same, he was happy that Rosalie had been free tonight. Her blond good looks were easy on the eye, and she had a terrific personality. He always enjoyed himself whenever he had the chance to see her.

Bill put his hand on Rosalie's waist, and they slowly wended their way up the aisle. When they reached the lobby, he smiled down at her and suggested, "How about us finding a place to have a late supper? Maybe it was all that talk about food in the play, but suddenly I'm starving."

Rosalie laughed at him and said something, but her reply escaped him. Intent on maneuvering their way through the crowd, Bill had glanced away from her. As his gaze swept the lobby, he suddenly turned to stone.

It seemed impossible, but there she was, standing only a few feet away. Bill felt a hundred different emotions roll over him in a gigantic wave. Elation, despair, joy, resentment, hopelessness. And pain. There was even that, after all this time! In one swift blow he experienced all the highs and lows and in-betweens all over again, as though it were only yesterday.

Forgotten were the play, the woman at his side, his sense of time, place or circumstance. Mesmerized, he simply went on staring, his eyes and soul drinking in the unexpected sight.

Her strawberry-blond hair was shorter than it had been the last time he'd seen her on television. The cut suited her, adding an attractive fullness to her face. She was dressed in black satin, and that became her, too, giving her an air of sophistication she'd lacked before.

She was speaking to the man at her side, but as though she suddenly sensed that she was being watched, she turned her head slightly and her gaze met Bill's.

The familiar green eyes, fringed by long, thick lashes, widened with shock and disbelief. Color surged to her cheeks, then drained away, leaving her face alarmingly white. Her lips parted and appeared to tremble. She seemed every bit as stunned as he was.

As for himself, Bill felt as though a mountain had just fallen on him. His lungs were constricted so that he was unable to breathe or move.

"Bill?" Rosalie's voice seemed to float toward him from far away. "Is that someone you know?"

With an effort, Bill drew in a sharp, ragged breath, expelled it slowly and finally heard himself say in a stranger's voice, "Yes. I know her. Quite well, as a matter of fact."

"Then why don't you go speak to her?" Rosalie suggested.

Not like this! Everything inside Bill resisted. *Not so publicly.* Yet he knew he had no choice. It would be churlish simply to leave without even greeting her. He couldn't do it.

Yet his footsteps were slow and laborious as he and Rosalie made their way through the crowd. What was there to say, he wondered dismally, after all this time?

They reached the other couple, and Bill saw that she appeared to have regained her composure. Her shoulders were straight, her head held high. Her gaze was cool, and an inner distance turned the irises a cloudy jade, effectively concealing her thoughts.

Yet he knew her so well. There was a strained set to her jaw, and when he glanced briefly at her hands, he saw that though they were clasped tightly together, they were shaking.

She spoke first, politely, as though greeting the most casual of acquaintances, and Bill had to admire the way she carried it off. Her voice was velvety smooth, as though this meeting were of no particular moment whatsoever.

"Hello, Bill. Fancy meeting you here."

"Hello, Andie." Bill managed a cardboard smile and was relieved that his own voice sounded so normal. "You're looking well."

"So are you." Andie smiled back, but hers, like his, didn't reach her eyes.

Bill wrenched his eyes from her face, sharply aware that they weren't alone, that they had to carry through with the farce of social convention. He turned to include Rosalie and introduced them. "Rosalie Chapman, Andrea Wade Sheridan."

Rosalie's ready smile froze. "Sheridan?" she repeated sharply, picking up on the name at once.

Andrea nodded and, as though speaking of the weather, said without any particular inflection in her voice, "Bill and

I were once married." Before anything awkward could develop from the announcement, she touched the arm of the man beside her and continued evenly, "I'd like you to meet George Vinton."

The two men shook hands. Though they were about the same age, both in their mid-thirties, there the similarity ended. Bill was tall, and his strong shoulders and long, lean legs were displayed to advantage in his evening attire. His black hair was full and well-cut, and his face was saved from being merely handsome by sharply chiseled features and a cleft chin. Vinton was stocky, with curly sand-colored hair and a bushy beard. He looked as though he were uncomfortable in his formal clothes.

His name was nevertheless recognizable and respected. "Nice to meet you." Bill forced a friendliness in to his voice that he was far from feeling. "I was impressed by the superb job you did with that documentary on Brazil."

"Thanks." Vinton grinned. "Andie didn't do so badly herself."

"Indeed." Bill inclined his head toward Andrea. "Your reporting was magnificent, as always, Andie," he said graciously. "Are you here on business now?"

Vinton answered for her. "We're putting together a piece about the British labor unions."

"What about you?" Andrea asked. "Are you here on business or for pleasure?"

"Both," Bill said. "I just finished an international news publishers' conference in Paris, and I stopped over to visit the London bureau for a few days before going home."

"I see. Well, when you get back, be sure and say hello to my baby brother for me, will you? I've been away quite a bit, and I haven't had a chance to see him in a couple of months."

Bill smiled at the old joke. Randall Wade was Andrea's twin brother, but because she was about three minutes older, she'd always teasingly called him "baby brother." Randy was one of the *Patriot*'s top reporters.

"I will when I see him," he promised, "but it won't be for a couple of weeks. He's flying down to Atlanta to cover a mayor's conference, and after that he's taking a little time off to work on that farm of his. You know 'farmer Randy'. He steals every possible moment he can to spend there."

"Do I ever!" She laughed. "It's gotten so bad that he never visits me anymore! If I want to see him, I have to be willing to feed chickens and cows or ride a tractor."

Bill grinned. "I know. The last time I went out there, I helped nurse a motherless kid goat!"

As their laughter died away and their gazes still clung, Bill was suddenly unnerved by the mental picture of the last time they'd been together.... That awful night, after their final quarrel, she'd looked at him with an anguished expression and had said softly, with no further trace of anger, "I just can't be what you want, Bill. We have to end this now before we're both destroyed." And he, hurt beyond healing, had agreed.

Strangely enough, now it was he who felt a powerful compulsion to get away. Abruptly, he nodded and said, "It's been nice seeing you, Andie. Take care."

Her smile was brittle, as plastic as his own. "You, too," she replied.

Once they were out of the theater, Bill took Rosalie's arm and asked, "How are your shoes? Can you walk?"

Rosalie stared at him in confusion. "Can I walk?"

"In those heels? If you don't mind, I'd really like to walk a bit before we get that meal I promised you."

"Ah." Rosalie smiled with swift understanding. "Of course we can walk. You need to blow away some cobwebs from the past, hmm?"

Bill's lips formed a thin smile. "It was a shock seeing her."

"How long has it been?"

"Three years. Ever since the divorce."

"She's very beautiful," Rosalie stated.

"Yes. Very."

They had reached Regent Street. While other pedestrians sauntered along and gazed at the newly displayed Christmas decorations, Bill walked swiftly. Rosalie had to hurry to keep up with him. For a little while she put up with it, but finally she tugged at his arm. "I said I could walk in these shoes, Bill, not sprint."

Bill, apologetic, stopped at once. "Sorry. I'll get a taxi."

"Fine." Rosalie nodded. "Why don't we go back to my flat instead of to a restaurant? I'll make you an omelet."

"Thanks," he said simply.

A half hour later they entered her Chelsea flat. While Bill poured drinks, Rosalie prepared the eggs. They talked of horses and plays and Paris and avoided the subject that was bothering him.

Bill felt better after he'd eaten, and while he helped Rosalie carry their dishes back to the kitchen, he said, "Forgive me. I've been rotten company."

"Don't be silly," she replied softly. "It was just one of those things." She paused, then asked, "Do you still love her?"

"Of course not!" Bill exclaimed vehemently. "Three years is a long time. It's just that seeing her brought back a lot of memories, that's all."

"What caused the breakup?" Rosalie asked curiously. "Was it another man?"

Bill shook his head. "No. Nothing like that. It was her work, her ambition. And her reluctance to be close to anyone...to me, anyway." He sighed. "It's all in the past. There's no point in rehashing it now."

He slid his arms around Rosalie's waist and bent to kiss her. "Let's talk about something more pleasant," he said in a low voice. "Will you take a chance on going out with me again tomorrow night? I'd like to make it up to you for being such bad company tonight."

"I'd love it." Rosalie entwined her arms around his neck.

Bill kissed her once more and then began to draw away. "It's late. I'd better be going."

Rosalie kept her arms where they were. "You could," she suggested, "stay here tonight."

Bill went still, his blue eyes searching hers. Rosalie was beautiful and very desirable. He ought to feel happy that she wanted him. If only he hadn't seen Andie tonight. The trouble was, he had.

He shook his head. "I appreciate the offer," he said huskily, "but it just wouldn't be any good for either of us."

Rosalie sighed and withdrew her hands from his shoulders. "I guess I expected you to say that."

"Maybe some other time..." he began, feeling awkward and not knowing how to go on.

Rosalie shook her head and lifted a finger to his lips. "Get over her first," she told him. "If it's meant to be, one day it'll happen."

"I guess you're right. Will you still go out with me tomorrow night, though?"

She smiled. "Of course."

Bill left the flat. Unable to shake his restless, unsettled mood, he walked for at least an hour before flagging down a taxi to take him to the Ritz.

Andrea bade good night to George in the hotel corridor. With deep relief, she entered her own room and closed the door. She'd felt a desperate need to be alone ever since the incident at the theater. She could think of nothing except the incredible coincidence of running into Bill.

Yet it really wasn't all that improbable. She knew he made frequent trips to London. She'd made a couple of them with him during their marriage. She also knew that he enjoyed the theater as much as she did. It was no more surprising to run into him here than in Washington, D.C., or New York. But the shock lingered and her hands were unsteady as she unzipped her dress, stepped out of it and flung it carelessly across the back of a chair.

He looked wonderful, she thought as she took off her panty hose and unhooked her bra. But then, he always did. All these years later, she could still remember her reaction to his slow, friendly smile and the mischievous, frank admiration in his eyes the first time they'd met. She'd just started working at the *Washington Patriot*, and as she'd emerged from his father's office, Bill, hurrying in, had crashed into her. He'd caught her quickly before she could fall to the floor. But in the end, they'd both fallen...in love.

Andrea padded barefoot across the room and reached into a dresser drawer for her nightgown. It slid smoothly over her head and fell silkily across the tips of her breasts, swirling around her waist and hips. She went to the bed, turned back the covers, but instead of slipping immediately between the sheets, she sank to the edge of the bed and stared into space.

When she'd first seen Bill tonight, it had been as though she'd suffered an almost physical blow. For an instant she'd been unable to breathe, to think, to react in any way. Then she'd realized that he was coming toward her with a woman at her side. From somewhere deep within her, she'd summoned the necessary resolve to get through the ordeal of having to talk with him. Though she'd been trembling inside, alternately going hot and cold from sheer nerves, she was proud that she'd remained poised on the outside. She'd managed a polite smile, small talk, and most miraculously of all, she'd refrained from going for his beautiful companion's jugular. She was still appalled as well as astounded at the hot streak of jealousy that had shot through her. She couldn't imagine what had come over her. Until now, she'd never thought of herself as a jealous person.

There was no doubt that Bill had been as stunned as she at their unexpected encounter. His cobalt-blue eyes had been dark with surprise, and she'd had the feeling he hadn't been any happier about the occasion than she. He probably would have preferred to avoid her, but that would have been rude. And they were civilized people, of course, living in a civilized society. They'd had a civilized marriage, a civilized divorce. There'd been no choice for either of them except to do as they had tonight, exchanging brief, cool pleasantries as though they'd never been important in each other's lives.

She'd never known any other man who had more beautiful and penetrating eyes than Bill Sheridan. His eyes could turn cutting in a flash when he was angry, and they could be as bright as a summer sky when he laughed. And, she recalled, Bill's eyes could turn smoky-blue when he was caught in the depths of desire.

Andrea groaned. Now why did she have to think of that? For years she'd forced herself not to think of the nights she'd spent in his arms, and after tonight, seeing him in the company of such a beautiful woman, she had even more reason to maintain that rule. While still a very young child, she had learned never to long for the past, that the wise course was to put it behind her. The ability to concentrate on the present had always been her greatest protection.

She crawled beneath the heavy covers and flipped off the beside lamp. She would think about tomorrow's work schedule, she decided firmly, until she fell asleep.

The tried-and-true formula almost worked. She was in the twilight state between waking and sleeping when she awoke with a sudden start. A horrible sense of disaster rolled over her like a black fog. Her heart pounded and her mouth went dry.

Trembling, Andrea sat up in bed, turned on the light and looked at her watch. It was shortly after midnight. After a moment, she got up and went into the bathroom for a glass of water, trying to tell herself she'd only been having a nightmare.

Yet she didn't think she had actually slept, much less been dreaming. She'd had these dreadful sensations a few other times in her life, and they'd always portended tragedy. It had happened just before her father's death when she'd been fifteen; a few days before Randy had broken his leg playing football; and only hours before a fire had broken out in the dormitory of her boarding school. A couple of other times the feeling had come before more minor events, but the sensation itself had never been wrong. Something awful had happened, or was about to happen. It was just that she had no way of knowing whom or where it would strike.

She felt an urgent need to talk with Randy, just to assure herself he was safe, but Bill had told her he'd gone to Atlanta. It would be early evening there, and if she knew her brother, he'd be out hitting the high spots of the city with other reporters and wouldn't be in his hotel room until late. Besides, she had no idea where he was staying. She could spend half the night trying to track him down and still not reach him.

Anyway, the premonition, if that's what it was, might not have anything to do with him. That was the trouble. She could never tell. Maybe the feeling concerned Bill. Seeing him tonight had made such an impression on her that it might have triggered her subconscious into warning her that something threatened him. She toyed with the idea of trying to locate him.

On the heels of that thought came sane logic. She could easily find out where he was staying by calling the night editor at the *Patriot*'s London bureau, but it was very late to be disturbing Bill over nothing more substantial than the state of her nerves. He'd probably call her paranoid, and she wouldn't blame him.

Yet when she turned out the lights and tried once more to fall asleep, Andrea remained wide awake and the irrational anxiety that had taken possession of her refused to be banished.

By morning, Andrea was exhausted. She'd only slept in snatches all night, and when she saw the darkened hollows under her eyes in the bathroom mirror, she grimaced. It was going to be a long day.

She ordered a tray of tea and croissants and began to dress for her appointment.

According to most standards by which the world measures such things Andrea Wade Sheridan, at twenty-seven, was successful. She had one best-selling book behind her about the turmoil in the Middle East; a new one, *Floods along the Rio Grande*, about illegal aliens crossing the Mexican border into the United States, had only last week hit the best-seller lists all over America, and in addition, she had become known and respected for the three television documentaries she had done. She was admired for her hard-hitting, poignant, yet unsentimental portrayals of the effects on ordinary human life of often cruel political processes. She had money in the bank, a good address in New York City, and she had been privileged to travel all over the world. She had met many important people, and she was well liked by her colleagues in the journalistic profession. Whenever she found time to socialize, which was seldom, her list of suitors included a famous defense lawyer, a U.S. senator and a television talk show host. She ought to have been happy with her life, yet Andrea knew she was not.

There had been a few periods that she could label as genuinely happy. One was a two-year stretch when she and Randy had lived with their grandmother in Wyoming; another had been the first six months of her brief marriage to William Sheridan.

But this morning she didn't want to think of Bill...or of the inexplicable anxieties of the night. She had work to do, and she was grateful for the distraction it offered.

In the hotel lobby she met Kent Andrews, the cameraman who was to accompany her on her interview. He was about her own age, tall and lanky with a crop of carrot-red hair, a sprinkling of freckles on his face and an easygoing, casual manner. They had become fast friends a couple of years ago when they'd first worked together on a documentary with George. Kent reminded Andrea a lot of her brother, and their relationship was somewhat like that of siblings. Kent confided in Andrea about his numerous girlfriends; she groused to him whenever she was having a particularly difficult time with her work; and though they squabbled occasionally, there was also an unfailing bond of loyalty between them.

"I hope this big shot of yours is worth the trouble," he greeted her morosely. "It's pouring cats and dogs out there. I can think of better things to do at this hour of the morning. Like going back to bed."

Andrea grinned knowingly. "Who is she this time?"

"Are you kidding?" Kent retorted. "George has kept me so busy on this trip, I haven't had time to meet anyone. I've tried to explain to him that he's ruining my love life, but does he care?" He grimaced. "Last night while he was squiring *you* to a play, I was in a stuffy meeting hall filming angry miners."

"That's really tough." Andrea grinned and said, "Come on, Kent, keep a stiff upper lip like the British do." She glanced at her watch. "We'd better get moving or we'll be late, and lowly little commoners like us don't keep members of Parliament waiting."

They were to meet their subject at his club, and as the taxi carried them through the drenched streets, Kent looked sideways at Andrea and said, "I had breakfast with George. He told me you had a very interesting evening last night."

"George always did talk too much," Andrea snapped, tight-lipped.

"Actually, he was a little concerned about you. He said you seemed pretty shaken up when he left you at your room. Are you okay?"

"Of course I'm okay! Bumping into one's ex-husband isn't that big a deal, you know. The earth is still spinning as far as I can tell, and," she added as she peered through the swirling raindrops that lashed against the window, "I suppose the sun is still up there somewhere."

"There's no need to get sarcastic," Kent said dryly. He scrutinized her face. "The planet may still be in orbit after seeing your ex, but the meeting sure didn't do any wonders for your beauty sleep."

"Do I look *that* awful?" Andrea asked anxiously, thinking of the camera's merciless lens.

"You've looked better," Kent stated bluntly, "but you'll do. I'll just make sure not to zoom in for a real close-up."

"Thanks," she said gratefully.

"So...tell me about it. I'm dying of curiosity."

Andrea shrugged. "There's not much to tell. Bill was there with a gorgeous date and we did the small talk routine, that's all. It was over in five minutes."

"Maybe the meeting was. Your feelings for him aren't."

"What do you mean?" Andrea asked sharply.

"I mean the way you hold other men off. I've seen you operate, remember, pal? The only men who ever get near you are ones like George and me, because we're just friends and don't threaten you emotionally."

"Nonsense." Andrea turned and stared at the rain-washed window again.

"Is it?" Kent went on relentlessly. "You have an occasional date, but I've never known you to go out with anyone more than three times."

"You don't know everything about my personal life!" Andrea snapped.

"Don't care to, either," Kent answered laconically. "It would probably bore me to death. I think you never let real romance enter your life because you've still got it bad for Sheridan."

"You're crazy, you know that? Just because I'm more fastidious than you in my romantic life doesn't mean I'm pining away over Bill!"

The taxi squealed to a halt beside the curb, and Kent shrugged and said calmly, "Have it your way."

While Andrea paid the driver, Kent unloaded his equipment beneath the building's awning, and in a short time they were inside the blessedly warm and dry lobby.

Kent might as well have stayed in bed all morning after all. The man they'd come to see, while willing to speak to Andrea quite candidly on the subject of the unions, declined to appear before the camera or even to be quoted by name.

Dismayed, Andrea exerted all her charm and persuasiveness to get him to change his mind, but he was adamant. At last, accepting defeat, Kent hauled his equipment out of the room and departed while Andrea remained to salvage what she could.

Back in her hotel room an hour and a half later, she brooded over her notes as she typed them. Above all things, she hated interviews of this type and generally managed to avoid them. Much of the punch of the man's statements had been eliminated by the stricture not to use his name. If there had been time to line up an interview with another, more open subject, she would have done so, but George intended to complete the segment that afternoon.

At noon, taking the story with her, Andrea set out on foot for the pub where she was to meet the rest of the crew for lunch. It was the first moment all day that she'd had completely to herself. She tried to take pleasure in it. The morning rain had ended; the day was raw and cold, but that mattered little to her. Soon it would be Christmas. As she sauntered along the street, Andrea gazed into shop windows and told herself that before she left London she would find the time to get in a little gift shopping.

She paused before a men's clothier's window and admired the display. There was a suede coat that would look magnificent on Bill.

Andrea swallowed hard and hurried on. Kent had accused her of still being in love with Bill, but it couldn't be true! She wouldn't allow it! She'd only been surprised to see him. *Yes,* a small voice whispered. But why couldn't she stop thinking of him now?

Deliberately she thought of her brother instead. That suede coat she'd just seen certainly wasn't Randy's style, but the sweater that had been displayed next to it was. Tomorrow, if she had time, she might come back and buy it.

Andrea looked forward to spending Christmas at Randy's Virginia farm. It would be so cozy, so homey, so intimate, the way she imagined real family Christmases were.

She rounded a corner and found herself in front of a travel agency. A poster of a jet in flight was in the window. Andrea halted abruptly as the dark fog of fear engulfed her once more. She gasped, blind to everything around her, the traffic on the street, the noontime pedestrians jostling past her, and her own horrified reflection in the glass.

All morning she'd been able to hold her vague apprehensions at bay, but now they closed about her with clammy, ghostly fingers, choking and suffocating her.

This time she could no longer thrust the misgivings to the back of her mind and she hurried away. When she reached the pub, she went immediately to a telephone and called the *Patriot*'s local office. She was past caring what Bill thought. She had to know that both he and Randy were all right.

"Mr. Sheridan, please," she said to the female voice at the other end of the line.

"I'm sorry, but Mr. Sheridan isn't in just now. May I help you?"

Andrea nibbled at her lips. "This is Andrea Sheridan," she said. "Can you tell me what time you expect him back?"

"Probably within a couple of hours. Would you like to leave a number where he can reach you?"

"I'll be out all afternoon. Tell him I'll...I'll call back later. But in case I miss him again, would you please ask him to tell you if he knows where my brother, Randy Wade, is staying in Atlanta? It's very important that I reach him."

"I'll be happy to do that," the voice replied courteously.

"Thanks." Andrea hung up the phone and made her way toward the table where other members of the film crew were already assembled. But though she managed a lighthearted greeting, her heart was heavy and she was cold with a dread she couldn't shake.

Chapter Two

Waitress, three more lagers here, please," Bill requested. Then he returned his attention to his two luncheon guests.

It had been a grueling morning at the office as Bill, Ed Carlton, the London bureau's managing editor, and John Seevers, the editor-in-chief, went over business matters with a fine-toothed comb. They had discussed policy, budget and personnel matters; new procedures to be implemented, old ones to be discarded. Even over lunch they had discussed business, but now, as they finished the meal, the talk became general while they all enjoyed a well-earned break and a second lager.

John Seevers, a young man of about thirty, had only recently become a father. Knowing this, Bill asked about his wife and baby. Seevers beamed with pleasure and proudly whipped out snapshots of the new arrival. Bill duly admired them and then sat silently as Ed Carlton, a grandfather and therefore an "expert" on fathering, began to offer the younger man unsolicited advice about colic, traveling with a baby and even how to cope with a new mother's mercurial moods.

Though he laughed and smiled in the right places, Bill tuned out. For at least the thousandth time his thoughts returned to Andie. Last night she'd looked so breathtakingly lovely that just remembering made his heart race. It was a good thing Rosalie had been there. And Vinton. Otherwise he might have made a complete fool of himself by sweeping her into his arms.

Now Bill was deeply grateful he'd been restrained by circumstances from such an idiotic impulse. Anyway, hadn't he already made a big enough fool of himself over Andie? Once in a lifetime ought to be enough for any man. He'd loved her too much, wanted too much and had expectations Andie had not been prepared to fulfill. She'd chafed beneath the burden of his love. Inevitably, she had soared away, a frightened bird flying toward freedom, while he had been left alone in the abandoned nest.

When John left the table to speak to someone he knew, Ed leaned across the table and, intruding upon Bill's brooding thoughts, asked, "Why don't you stay over through the weekend? Betty wants you to spend a couple of days with us."

Ed and his charming wife had a lovely country home in Sussex, where they'd always made Bill welcome, but since his father's death almost four years ago, he'd never had the time for such pleasant side trips. Now he shifted restlessly in his chair and cupped his hands around his mug. "There's nothing I'd like better, Ed, but I have to get back to Washington for an important meeting. Tell Betty I'll try to make it next trip, and when I do, I expect one of her delicious steak and kidney pies."

Ed grinned. "That'll please her." He sobered and shook his head. "Though nobody ever loved her cooking more than your dad." He sighed, adding sadly, "I still miss him."

Bill nodded and said softly, "So do I."

"He'd be proud of you, Bill," Ed went on. "The way you've picked up the reins. I know it hasn't been easy for you. In your heart, you're nothing more than a fire engine chaser."

Bill chuckled. "You've got that right."

Bill's father had been the owner and publisher of the *Washington Patriot*, having inherited it from *his* father. Now it was Bill's turn to run one of the world's finest daily newspapers. It was a job he took seriously. Not a day went by when he wasn't concerned with the welfare of the paper—with circulation numbers, advertising figures, being on top of the most important news stories—nor did he ever forget how many lives were dependent on its continued success. All the same, not only did he miss his father and wish he were still alive and in charge, but he also missed his own less exalted position in the firm. He'd genuinely enjoyed his work, first as a reporter, or "fire engine chaser," as Ed described it, and later as a political journalist. There was nothing more thrilling than being where the news was happening.

Now, though, all that fun belonged to others. Bill had to content himself with his weekly column on the editorial page and spend most of his time in the office, grappling with the multitude of details involved in running a large corporation. No longer was he just one of the guys, and he missed that as much as anything else. The closest rapport he had with his former colleagues these days was with Ed Carlton, an old-time pro, and his former brother-in-law, Randy Wade. Despite Bill's divorce from Andrea, the two men had remained good friends, and there had never been any question of Randy leaving the paper just because his sister was no longer married to the boss. When Bill had been kicked upstairs, Randy had taken over his position as the *Patriot*'s chief political reporter, and even if they hadn't been personal friends, Bill would have wanted to keep him on as one of the paper's most valuable and talented journalists.

John rejoined them, and the three men left the restaurant to walk back to Fleet Street. It was a cold, damp afternoon, but at least the rain had ended.

When they entered the office, Judy, the receptionist, stopped Bill as he passed her desk. "Oh, Mr. Sheridan, I have a couple of messages for you. One of them is urgent."

Bill frowned and took the slips of paper. The one labeled urgent was from Dave Sullivan, his managing editor in Washington. Dave had requested Bill to call him immediately. Wondering what had gone wrong this time, Bill glanced with less interest at the other note until he saw the name of the caller.

"Andrea Sheridan called?" he asked, not believing the evidence of the written words.

Judy nodded. "Yes, sir. She said she'd be out all afternoon, but would call again later. However, she wanted me to ask, in case you're not in when she does call back, if you know where her brother is staying in Atlanta? She said it was very important that she reach him."

Bill shrugged. "I don't have the slightest idea, but I guess somebody in the Washington office knows. I'll ask Dave when I talk to him. Put through the call for me, will you, Judy?"

"Yes, sir."

"Why don't you use the phone in my office?" Ed offered.

"Fine." Bill went in and shut the door. He sat down in the swivel chair behind the desk and while he waited, puzzled over Andie's call. Funny, they hadn't seen each other or spoken in over three years. Last night they'd met unexpectedly, and today she'd phoned him. He knew it must be really important, or she wouldn't have called today. He wondered what could have happened between last night and this afternoon that made it essential for her to get in touch with Randy.

Bill shrugged aside the question as the desk telephone rang. It would be his call to Washington. He scooped up the receiver.

"Sheridan here. Is that you, Dave?"

"Yeah, it's me." Dave's voice sounded grim. "Brace yourself, Bill. I hate like hell to tell you this, but I figured you'd better know right away." He paused for a fraction of an instant, as though giving Bill time to prepare, and then said in a rush, "It's Randy Wade. He's missing. The plane never made it to Atlanta."

As the words sank in, the muscles in Bill's neck tightened and his entire body went rigid. He was no longer even aware of breathing...just of the anguish that ripped through him. His knuckles whitened as he gripped the receiver so hard he might have been trying to crush it. "My God!" he groaned. Then he pleaded, "It can't be true!"

"I wish it weren't," Dave said despondently. "But we've checked and double-checked, and the answer's still the same. He just never got there."

Bill slumped in his chair and closed his eyes, as though by doing so he could block out reality, block out the dreadful news.

He was silent so long that Dave finally asked, "Bill? Are you okay?"

Bill sucked in a ragged breath. "Okay? *Okay?* Are you kidding? I feel like I've been stabbed and you ask me if I'm okay?"

"I know." Dave's voice was also unsteady. "We're reeling from the effects of it here, too. It's like a morgue in the Rumpus Room," he said, using the common nickname for the newsroom.

Bill shook his head, still having a hard time taking it in, and then he took another deep breath. This time the action seemed to clear his head. He sat up once more, leaned toward the desk and picked up a pen. "All right," he said sharply. "Tell me all you know."

"Very little, I'm afraid. He was in the company plane. You told him to take it if he wanted," Dave reminded him.

"Yes." Bill's dark brows knitted together. "Get on with it."

"There was a bad storm over Tennessee and northern Georgia and the Carolinas. Rain and lightning and strong wind gusts. As a matter of fact, it's still going on. The authorities think he must have got caught in it, and I'm inclined to agree with them because he filed a flight plan. He should've gotten to Atlanta around six yesterday evening."

"All right. Now, listen. Have your staff contact law enforcement people along the route he should have taken," Bill said decisively. "Also the fringe areas, where he might have been blown off course. Alert them all, so they'll be on the lookout for a downed plane."

"The FAA has already done that, Bill," Dave explained patiently. "Up until this point search parties couldn't go out because of the storm and the darkness. Now that it's daylight, they've started looking in spite of the weather. There's nothing more we can do except sit tight and say our prayers. One thing, though. The authorities have asked our help in locating and notifying Randy's family. They didn't have any luck at it. I know his mother lives in Italy, but so far we haven't been able to find out what her name is. I figured maybe you knew. As for Andie, I put a couple of people on it after I couldn't reach her in New York, and we've finally learned that she's in London working on a TV project. Will you find out where she's staying and go tell her yourself, Bill? It's a hell of a thing for you to have to be the one to tell her, but I don't see any choice. Besides, in a way it might be better for her to hear the news from you than from someone else."

Bill felt a chill climb his spine. "It's almost as though she already knows," he murmured.

"What?" Dave's voice was sharp. "Have you seen her, then?"

"Yes. Last night. We ran into each other at a theater. She asked about Randy and I told him he was going to Atlanta. Then today, while I was out to lunch, she called here and told Judy she needed to reach him and wanted to know where he was staying."

Dave gave a low whistle. "I've heard twins sometimes have a strange mental telepathy thing going for them. I guess maybe it's true."

"It's true in Andie's case, all right," Bill said unhappily. Until Dave brought up the subject, he'd forgotten that strange ability of hers to sense danger—especially to someone she loved. One incident that had occurred while they'd still been married came to mind. Her brother had gone on a skiing trip with some friends and Andie had begun to worry about him for no apparent reason. Bill had tried to convince her that she was being silly, but later that same night Randy had called to tell them that he'd just been involved in a car accident, though he was unhurt.

Another time, Bill had been the focus of her anxiety. She'd been away on one of her many trips out of the country when Bill, upon leaving a restaurant late one evening, had been held up at knife-point. He'd wrestled with his assailant and come out the winner, suffering only a slight cut on his arm. Even though Andie had been thousands of miles away, she'd somehow sensed that something was wrong. When he'd gotten back to their apartment, the phone had been ringing and the caller had been his anxious wife.

She hadn't always picked up on such things, but now, with a sinking heart, Bill knew that this was not one of the times when she was blissfully unaware. Somehow, she knew something was wrong. She'd even sensed that it concerned her twin. That was why she wanted to reach him.

Bill felt sick with dread at the thought of having to confirm her worst fears. "God, I hate to have to tell her, Dave! They've always been so close. This is going to crush her."

"I know," Dave agreed sadly. "But it's not something that can be kept from her. You just can't spare her this, Bill."

"If only I could." Bill sighed. Then confronting the unpleasant duty that lay before him, he added, "Well, it has to be done. I'll find her, Dave, even if I have to tear this town apart."

"What about the mother? She needs to be notified, too."

"She's married again since I was part of the family. I'm not sure what her name is now. I just remember Randy saying she was married to some Italian count. Andie will know, though, so we'll get in touch with her from here. You keep tabs on the search and call the bureau the second you have any news."

"Will do," Dave promised. "And Bill?"

"Yeah?"

"I'm really sorry."

"Yeah," Bill said softly. "Me, too." He cradled the receiver and got to his feet. In two strides he was at the door, which he flung open so recklessly that it thudded against the wall. The sound reverberated throughout the outer office, and heads swiveled toward him.

"I want everyone who isn't involved in something vitally important to drop what they're doing and start calling hotels." Bill barked the command. "We've got to find Andrea Sheridan. Or George Vinton. Or anybody connected with their film crew. They're doing a documentary on the labor unions. Find out where they're shooting today as well." The staff remained still, awaiting further instructions. Infuriated by their lack of action, he bellowed like a lion, riled and in pain. "Move it, and find them, or I swear you'll have to answer to me."

Hands fumbled for telephones and grabbed for directories, and only Ed Carlton, who'd been waiting for his own office to be freed, dared to approach this suddenly unapproachable bear of an employer. He touched Bill's shoulder and said in a low voice that was in marked contrast to Bill's shouting, "Take it easy, old chap. You don't need to threaten anyone to get a job done. A polite request is all that's required."

Bill was instantly contrite. "I'm sorry," he murmured.

"What's the problem?" Ed asked gently.

Bill rubbed his forehead and fought to keep his voice steady, but it cracked with strain despite his best efforts. "It looks like Randy Wade's gone down in a plane. And I'm elected to find Andie and tell her."

"I see." Ed didn't attempt to offer futile words of sympathy. He merely said quietly, reassuringly, "We'll find her for you, I promise."

Bill nodded. "Keep one line open, in case she tries to call here again."

While George and Barney, the assistant producer, consulted about the exact angle of the next shot, Andrea reviewed her lines and shivered. The air along the waterfront was bone-chilling. She was eager to be done for the day, and dreamed longingly of getting back to the hotel and drinking hot tea before indulging in a long, hot bath.

It had been one of those impossible days. First there'd been the unsatisfactory interview during the morning. Next there had been a mix-up over where everyone was meeting for lunch, and George and a lighting technician had ended up going to the wrong place. After everyone had checked back at the hotel and found each other again, valuable shooting time had been wasted. Then, just as they'd been about to begin taping along the riverfront with Tower Bridge in the background, Kent had pulled a muscle in his leg. He had been in such pain that they had packed him into a taxi and sent him back to the hotel. The other cameraman was away on assignment in Liverpool. Finally Barney had agreed to man the camera. Barney was competent, but he wasn't as talented with a lens as Kent.

"Okay," George said at last, "let's try it." He glanced anxiously at the gray sky. "It'll be dark before long, so let's get it right."

Andrea moved into position near the rails and tucked her notes into her coat pocket. Her hair whipped in the wind, but there was nothing she could do about it. She only hoped she wouldn't end up looking like a mop when the segment was run.

George shouted, "Action," and she began her speech.

The first part went well, and as Andrea neared the end, she continued speaking the words she had memorized. "...and if a compromise isn't reached soon, it's virtually certain that there will be an explosive situation here. As one member of Parliament put it, the union—"

"Cut!"

Andrea bit off the remainder of her words in frustration. *Now what?*

George stomped over to her, his bushy hair rippling in the wind and his beard quivering with indignation. "I don't believe it! I just don't believe it!"

"What?"

"'As one member of Parliament put it,'" George mimicked. "What's his bloody name? That's what I'd like to know, and so will the audience!"

Andrea sighed. She should have known George would notice the omission at once. "You know his name as well as I do," she answered with a grimace. "But he wouldn't let Kent get him on tape this morning, and he refused to let me quote him by name."

"And you bought that?" George bellowed with furious incredulity. "Since when is anonymity your style, Andie? If he wouldn't cooperate, why didn't you line up another source?"

"There wasn't time. You wanted to tape this segment today. If you'd like to put it off, I'll try to talk to someone else tomorrow."

"That'll mean this afternoon was totally wasted!" George said gloomily.

"Not really." Andrea was eager to make amends because she was as frustrated and disappointed as George, and she'd been planning how she could work around it. "Look, while I was in the taxi coming over I made some notes." She fished some crumpled papers from her purse. "We can go ahead and tape this part this afternoon," she went on, tapping the paper. "That skirts any direct quotations. Later we can splice in the interview segment once I get what we need."

While George studied her notes, Andrea tossed her head and brushed her hair away from her face. As she did so, her gaze swept beyond Barney and the camera, and she stiffened with disbelief.

Coming toward her with long, purposeful strides was her former husband, and there was a frightening intensity, a grim set to his features that sent alarm signals clanging at her nerve ends.

"You know, your idea might work out all right," George said. "What do you think if we—" He broke off as Andrea gasped softly, and then he looked up to see what had caught her attention.

Though Andrea was speechless as Bill joined them, George wasn't. "We're busy here," he snapped irritably. "Andie doesn't have time to chitchat." As an afterthought, he added, "How'd you find us, anyway?"

"I called the hotel and talked to a cameraman. He told me." Bill answered the question, but his eyes never wavered from Andrea's face.

A tense silence fell. Andrea and Bill gazed at each other for what seemed to be an endless moment, and it was impossible for her not to feel the underlying strain. There was an odd pallor to his face, and his blue eyes were smoky, hazed over by some deep emotion. Only once before had she ever seen him with quite this same anguished expression...just after his father had died.

At that instant, she saw compassion burn through the intensity of his gaze—and suddenly she knew.

Her lips parted and trembled. Her throat was raspy and she had trouble voicing the terrible words. "Randy! S— something's happened to Randy." It was not a question. It was a statement of fact, of knowledge that struck through to her very soul.

Slowly, Bill nodded. He stepped closer and gripped her icy hands. "Andie. Darling, I'm so very sorry, but...the plane is missing. Randy never made it to Atlanta."

A buzzing started to build in Andrea's ears, and then a loud roaring like an angry ocean. For a long moment she stared at Bill, before his face began to waver and blur. Then merciful darkness descended over her, and as the world spun, she slumped.

For the first and only time in her life, Andrea fainted— and it was Bill who caught her in his arms.

Chapter Three

Andrea's hotel room was crowded. She was half reclining on the bed, resting against the pillows at Bill's insistence. Bill himself sat beside her, holding one of her hands and cradling the telephone receiver between his ear and shoulder while he talked with his local office. George, Kent, who was feeling much better, and a couple of the other film crew members stood nearby, talking to one another in hushed murmurs.

A knock sounded at the door, and George detached himself from the group and went to open it. A waiter entered the room bearing a laden tray.

Andrea felt strangely detached from all that was going on around her. It was as though she were watching a play. Kent was pouring hot tea from a silver pot; George was lighting a cigarette and looking about vaguely for an ashtray. Barney joined Kent and surveyed the contents of the tray while Bill listened to the person on the other end of the telephone. The others in the room continued to speak softly to each other, and now and then one of them would give her a compassionate glance. They all seemed to know their parts and their lines perfectly.

Except herself. She didn't quite know what was expected of her. Was she to cry? But there were no tears in her stinging eyes or her aching throat. Better to laugh, and tell them she knew this was all just a horrible joke!

But the laughter didn't come, and neither did the tears. Andrea remained dry-eyed, her face set and unemotional as though it were chiseled in stone.

She hadn't spoken since she'd revived from her fainting spell. She'd come to and found herself being supported by Bill and George as they'd carried her to the taxi that Bill had kept waiting. She remembered listening carefully as Bill explained what Dave Sullivan had told him, but she couldn't form any words in response either then or now. Randy, her adored Randy, was missing, maybe dead. No words could express the depth of her grief.

Ignoring his sprain, Kent approached the bed and offered her a cup of hot tea. "Drink this. It'll warm you," he said softly. "There's sandwiches and biscuits, too."

Andrea shook her head and spoke for the first time. "Nothing to eat," she said hoarsely. But she accepted the tea gratefully. Inside, she felt cold...cold as death.

Bill hung up, and Andrea's tortured gaze flew to his face. "Anything?" she pleaded.

He shook his head. "Not yet," he said gently. "Dave hasn't called again, and he would if he had any news. It just takes time, honey."

Andrea nodded mutely and stared down into the cup of tea. In the liquid amber mirror, she saw her reflection and was jolted. It was a face she'd seen many times in her travels...the stoic mask concealing an anguish and despair so

immense that it robbed the features of even the tiniest spark
of animation. It was as though the body went on moving
while the person within had almost ceased to exist.

She knew she had to make an effort of some sort, anything that might pull her back from the abyss that plunged
her toward black, hopeless desolation. Slowly she lifted her
eyes to Bill's concerned face, and forced herself to ask, "Did
they check the airline schedules?"

Bill was watching her closely. When he nodded, Andrea
sensed that as well as answering her question, his gesture
indicated silent approval of her struggle to cope with the
reality of the situation. "Yes," he said. "We're booked on
the first plane to Washington tomorrow morning."

Andrea looked at George. "I don't know what to tell
you...about the film. I don't know when I can get back. If
I can."

"Don't worry about it," George said gruffly. "We can
work around you for a few days. You or Bill can call and let
me know what's going on. If everything is all right, you can
come back."

"And if I can't?" she asked in a hollow voice.

"You will," George insisted with a forced heartiness.

Andrea shook her head. "Maybe you ought to go ahead
and replace me."

"Let's give it a couple of days," George said quietly.

"Thanks. I—I don't know how to thank you all for your
k—kindness." Andie's voice broke and she made a hasty
effort to hide it by sipping at her tea. "You're so go—good
to me."

Kent sat down on the opposite side of the bed from Bill.
"Don't be silly, kid," he said gently. "That's what you've
got friends for. We've got enough to keep us busy the next
few days without using your pretty face. If it comes down
to it, Barney can always do the rest of the interviews, and we

can edit out his voice later and work you in as the moderator. Think positively. Randy's a tough guy, so don't you dare give up on him!''

Andrea managed a smile. "He *is* tough, isn't he?"

"The toughest," Bill seconded firmly. "Kent's right. We're not about to give up on him. Now," he went on, "finish that tea and let Kent pour you another cup. You're still shivering." He patted her knee and asked, "Where's your address book? I'll put in that call to your mother."

While Bill dealt with English and Italian telephone operators, the others departed one by one, promising Andrea they would look in on her later. Wearily, she closed her eyes, suddenly glad that they had gone. It was such an effort to talk, to pay attention, to respond politely, when all her mind could do was dwell on Randy....

At the same time, she was quietly, deeply grateful for Bill's presence. How much worse it would have been without him! Unasked, he'd taken charge. He had the Washington office monitoring the search, and she knew he spoke the truth when he said the moment there was any news, Dave Sullivan would call; the local office had helped locate her and gone on to arrange their flight back to the States. Now Bill was efficiently dealing with the trying task of placing an international call to her mother. But more than all the practical help he'd given her, Andrea was grateful to Bill for being there when she needed him. No one else in the world, least of all her mother, understood quite how much Randy meant to her. Moreover, Bill loved him, too. They still had that in common.

"Hello? Yes." Bill's voice rose a trifle, as though he were speaking over a bad connection. "I wish to speak to Contessa Luciano. Bill Sheridan calling.... No, that's Sheridan." He gave Andrea a tiny smile of encouragement, then returned his attention to the call. "Yes, I'll hold."

Andrea wondered if her inner coldness would ever end. The tea had warmed her only momentarily. Now a peculiar numbness was stealing over her. How, her heart cried silently, could she possibly ever manage the rest of her life without Randy? He was her brother, her twin, her playmate and confidant. Randy was the only person who had ever truly loved her without qualification or reservation. Bill had loved her, too, once, in a different way—until she'd killed his love. But with Randy, she'd never needed to be concerned about approval. He'd always been on her side, just as she'd been for him.

"Carrie?" Bill said finally. "Yes, it's Bill Sheridan here. Yes, it has been a long time. No, I'm not in Rome. I'm in London with Andie. Listen, Carrie, something has happened. I'll let Andrea tell you."

Bill handed the receiver to Andrea. She drew in a deep breath, then said, "Mother?"

"Andrea, darling, how are you?" The wire was crackly and full of static, but Carrie's high-pitched, little-girl voice overrode it. "What on earth are you doing in London with Bill? Have you married each other again?"

"What?" The question, so unexpected, so at odds with reality, dazed Andrea for a moment, knocking her off base. Then she said in a rush, "No, of course not! Bill is with me because...because..." Andrea broke off, then started over. "Mother, brace yourself. I have some very bad news."

"Bad news? My dear, you're always so serious and melodramatic," Carrie chided. "What is it this time? Did you get banned from one of those dreadful countries you're always visiting because you were unflattering to the government, or did you—"

Andrea cut in. It was the only way to deal with Carrie, the eternal little girl, the superficial social butterfly who had never dealt with anything more weighty in her life than the next party or the new season's wardrobe. "Mother, please, it *is* serious! I want you to listen to me!"

"Well, all right," Carrie said, sounding miffed. "Though I feel it my duty as your mother to point out that your manners are deplorable! I honestly don't see how any daughter of mine could—"

Andrea interrupted again without compunction. "Mother, for once in your life shut up and listen!" There was a stunned silence at the other end of the line, but at least this time Carrie remained silent long enough for Andrea to say what she had to. "Mother, Randy is missing. They think the plane he was flying crashed."

Carrie gasped, and this time the silence lasted even longer. Her voice quivered when she finally spoke. "But he... Randy's a very good pilot, isn't he? Maybe he just went off somewhere to have a good time and forgot to tell anyone he was going."

Andrea sighed. Carrie had never been brought to understand how different her children were from herself. Because jaunting off for pleasure was for her such an ingrained habit that it was like breathing, she expected the same irresponsibility from others.

"No, Mother, it wasn't like that. He was on assignment for the paper, and they believe he ran into a bad rainstorm."

"Oh, dear," Carrie said helplessly. "Oh, dear."

"Bill and I are flying back to the States tomorrow morning. You'll come, too, won't you? You can reach me through the *Patriot* and I'll meet your plane."

"Oh. I hadn't thought...I, well, to tell you the truth, Andrea, I don't see much point in it, do you? I mean, as long as he's missing, what good would it do if I were there? Anyway, tomorrow evening we have a reception planned for the ambassador, and I think I should carry on until I know something definite. Don't you?'' she asked appealingly. ''I think it always helps to stay busy and keep one's mind off one's troubles. But of course the minute it's necessary, I'll go at once.''

Andrea caught her bottom lip between her teeth to keep back the cry that burned her throat. *Why can't you be a real mother just this once?* she begged silently. *Why can't you, especially now, care about Randy? And about me?*

But she knew from experience that this was the hand she'd been dealt, that it was useless to wish otherwise. Carrie would never change. Perhaps she couldn't.

''You're right, of course,'' she said at last. ''There wouldn't be any point in your coming now, since there's nothing you could do. And of course you can't possibly disappoint the ambassador.''

Bill looked sharply at Andrea, accurately filling in the gaps of the conversation for himself. Abruptly he got up and crossed the room to the table where the tea tray was. He didn't want Andie to see the disgust and fury on his face.

He poured himself a cup of coffee and stood at the window, looking out. It was dark and had begun to rain again.

He'd never met anyone quite like Carolyn Wade Hamilton Luciano, and he marveled that anyone so immature and utterly selfish could ever have produced such fine people as Andie and Randy. He'd heard the stories of how the twins had been shuffled around all their lives. There had always been plenty of money, but the children had never had what most kids accepted without a second thought—a secure home.

In the early years their parents had been too busy traveling to be bothered with babies, and the children had been deposited first with one relative, then another, and sometimes left for months with only a paid housekeeper to watch over them. By the time the twins were eight, the family had been permanently broken by divorce. Carrie had soon married again, and the children had gone to live with their paternal grandmother for a while. But after a couple of years, ill-health had ended that arrangement, and the children had been shifted again between their parents' homes in California and Paris until they were old enough to be conveniently tucked away in boarding schools. They'd been only fifteen when their father had died. After that the boarding school, and later on, college, had become their permanent homes except for brief summer visits to their mother's home in Los Angeles. A couple of years ago, Carrie had divorced her second husband and married once more, this time to a titled Italian.

Bill heard Andie hang up. "How'd she take it?" he asked, turning toward her, although he already knew the answer.

Andrea shrugged. "As well as you'd expect her to," she said flatly. "She has a dinner party planned for the ambassador tomorrow night. She'll carry on bravely as long as there's no news." She pressed her lips together to still their trembling and looked away.

"I'm sorry, honey," Bill said gently.

Andrea swallowed hard. "I thought for once she might have—" She broke off and then said angrily, "Who am I kidding? We're talking about Carrie here."

Yes, Bill thought grimly. They were talking about a mother who, as far as he'd ever been able to determine, had never celebrated a single one of her children's birthdays with them, and precious few Christmases. The couple of times he'd met Carrie, he'd had to struggle with his dislike of her. She'd constantly criticized and belittled Andie, the way she wore her clothes or did her hair, her lack of the social graces, which to Carrie meant that Andie didn't fawn over people...and once she'd even had the nerve to criticize the way she wrote her articles! As though Carrie, who had a master's degree in social climbing and snobbery, were a qualified critic of one of the most talented, insightful writers on the contemporary scene!

His own mother had been so different that it was inconceivable to Bill how a woman like Carrie could even exist. Up until the day she'd died seven years ago, his mother had been warm, loving and supportive, not only to his father and himself, but to the patients she'd nursed at the hospital where she'd worked for over thirty years. She had worked because her job gave her a sense of satisfaction, yet despite the hours that it had taken her away from home, not once could Bill ever remember feeling neglected or unwanted. She'd always had time for him, and he'd adored her. To this day he wondered what Carrie did each day to fill up all the empty, meaningless hours.

"Look," he said, deciding it was wisest to try to get Andie's mind off her mother, "you need to eat. There are some sandwiches here, or we can order up anything else you'd like."

Andrea shook her head stubbornly and said, "I'd choke. Oh, Bill, please call the office. Maybe they've had word and tried to reach us while I was talking with Carrie."

Bill thought that was highly unlikely, since no more than ten or fifteen minutes had elapsed, but to appease Andie, he went to the phone.

It was a long night's vigil. Throughout the early evening hours, the film crew came and went, ostensibly to see if there'd been any word, but actually to offer whatever support they could to a friend in trouble. Bill wondered what it was about Andie that inspired such loyalty from others, as well as from himself, when at the same time there was something in her character that maintained a certain distance from everyone—except her brother. It was that very distance, one he'd found impossible to bridge and intolerable to live with, that had finally caused the breakup of their marriage. He hadn't understood it then, and he still didn't.

By eleven, when everyone except Bill had cleared out, Andie looked exhausted, and Bill felt anxious about her. "Try to get a little sleep," he suggested quietly. "We have a long trip ahead of us tomorrow."

There were dark shadows beneath her eyes, and her face, already pale, grew paler as she looked at him and asked hesitantly, "You—you're not leaving, too, are you?"

For the first time all evening, Bill smiled broadly. "No," he reassured her. "I'm going to pack your things and then stretch out beside you and try to get some sleep myself. So move over and don't you dare snore!"

"Snore!" He had the satisfaction of seeing that her indignation brought a bit of color to her cheeks. "I don't snore!"

Bill shrugged. "When we used to share a bed, you did."

"I never!" Andrea snatched up a pillow and threw it at him. "You're making that up, William Frederick Sheridan, so take it back!"

Bill chuckled and tossed the pillow back at her. "Actually, you were quite terrible now that I come to think about it. Besides snoring, you gritted your teeth, growled in your sleep, stole the covers, and your feet were always cold as ice!"

"I'll concede the cold feet, but that's all!" Andrea retorted. "The rest of the description fitted you, Freddie, my dear."

"Don't call me Freddie!" Bill snarled menacingly.

He lunged for her and Andie rolled out of the way just in time, laughing. "Freddie, Freddie, Freddie! You take it back about my snoring and I won't call you that anymore!"

Bill grinned at her. "Deal." He went to the wardrobe and took out her suitcase. A moment later he was emptying the contents of a bureau drawer into it.

Andie moved over to the closet, removed a blouse from a hanger and folded it neatly. "What about your bags?" she asked suddenly. "Don't you need to go back to your hotel for them?"

Bill shook his head and emptied another drawer. "John Seevers did it for me. He's coming over in the morning and will drive us to the airport." As she removed a dress from the closet and brought it toward the suitcase, he saw that the trauma of shock and the weariness of a long day were closing in on her. Her face had gone white again and her shoulders drooped. Bill took the dress from her hands and ordered softly, "Go lie down and get some rest."

Andrea shook her head and swayed. "I can't sl—sleep. I'm so scared, Bill! I can't—" A harsh sob caught in her throat and cut off her words.

Bill dropped the dress into the half-filled suitcase and pulled her into his arms. "I know, darling," he murmured. "I know."

He led her to the bed, and still fully clothed, she lay down. Bill was about to reach for a blanket when she grasped his hands. He paused to look at her and saw that her eyes were brimming with tears. "Please, Bill," she begged in a choked voice, "please...hold me?"

Bill nodded and lay down beside her. He switched off the light, pulled the blanket over them and gathered Andrea into his arms. She smelled sweet, as he remembered from the past, of spring flowers, yet she was trembling and her skin was cold to the touch as though she'd just come out of a winter storm.

"It's going to be all right, love," Bill whispered. He kissed her forehead, then lightly brushed his lips across hers. "It's going to be all right."

And he wished with all his heart that he believed it.

Chapter Four

In the wee hours of the morning Andrea lay snug and warm within the familiar curve of Bill's body. Beneath the blanket that covered them, his arm was draped carelessly across her hip. His face was nestled against her throat, and she could feel his soft breath against her skin.

They had talked long into the night about mutual friends, politics, things they'd done in the past three years. Andrea had been unable to speak of Randy except to worry aloud from time to time why it was taking searchers so long to find him. Bill had followed her lead, understanding without being told that for the moment, she couldn't bear to discuss her twin or how much he meant to her.

Andrea had been unable to sleep, and Bill had kept watch with her until an hour ago, when he'd dozed off. Now, restless and a bit stiff from staying in one position for so long, she gently removed his arm so that she could crawl out of bed without disturbing him. He needed whatever sleep he could get.

As she moved, Bill shifted, too, and sighed. His arm came around her again and his hand closed about her breast. Andrea drew a sharp breath at the unexpectedly intimate contact. Old sensations she'd thought long since gone abruptly welled up inside of her, and in dismay she caught her lower lip between her teeth. She'd had ample time these last few years to get over such feelings for Bill. This simply couldn't be!

She tried once more to free herself from his embrace, but this time she found herself being cradled even more firmly. Bill's hand moved from her breast to her arm, and then she was being pulled over onto her back and, finally, toward him.

The enveloping darkness made Bill's form an insubstantial shadow beside her, but the strength of his arms as he drew her to him was anything but fleeting. He was real flesh-and-blood man with the unmistakable heat of desire pumping through his veins.

He was also no longer asleep, although his voice was drowsy and heavy as he murmured, "Don't leave. I like holding you. You're so soft and warm." His hand caressed her breast through the fabric of her blouse while the other slid from her waist to her back in a soothing circular motion.

Weakness flooded through Andrea as the sensations, so long suppressed, ignited an answering desire. "Oh, Bill," she moaned softly.

Bill kissed her then. His lips, so full and sensual, burned hers with searing passion. Andrea was transported on the wings of time, back to when their love was fresh and new and their need for each other was all-consuming. She responded now because it was impossible to do otherwise.

Long starved for the sweet taste of each other, they both gave and received, their lips sensitive to the other's entreaty.

A moment later Bill's searching fingers undid the top buttons of Andrea's blouse. The garment fell open and her skin tingled at the touch of his hand on her soft flesh.

Andrea quivered, her entire body tense with the need for release from the emotions that had been aroused. But reason got the better of her, and sighing, she tugged herself free from Bill's arms.

"This is insane," she whispered, her voice shaking. When Bill reached for her again, she pleaded, "No, please don't. We're forgetting that we're divorced now."

Bill chuckled softly. "We don't seem to have divorced the feelings we could always arouse in each other. That part, at least, was always good between us. I want to make love to you again, Andie."

Andrea glanced away. "That's just it!" she protested. "Sex was too good between us, and if we make love now, it'll just complicate everything else. I don't think it would be very wise. Besides, we're forgetting the circumstances that brought us together like this." A sudden sob rose to Andrea's throat. She sat up and murmured in horror, "How...how could I possibly have forgotten Randy for a single instant?"

Behind her, Bill's voice was soft and muffled. "I guess we both did for a second there. You're right. It wouldn't be wise. I guess it just felt so good to wake up with you in my arms again that I forgot myself."

Andrea swallowed hard. "We...we both did. But it was all my fault."

"How's that?" Bill switched on the bedside lamp and sat up beside her.

Andrea turned to look at him. Like her, he was still fully dressed, wearing the same clothes he'd worn the previous day. His blue shirt was open at the throat, the collar crumpled and limp. His hair was tousled and his face was darkened by the faint stubble of his beard. Rumpled and disheveled as he was, he still held a powerful attraction for her.

She forced her glance away and said in an emotion-laden voice, "Bill, I don't know how I could have borne it through the night without you. I needed you more than anyone else because you care about Randy, and I suppose because you once loved me. I needed the comfort of being in your arms. I'm deeply grateful to you, and I'll never forget this as long as I live. You were only being kind to me and then things got a little out of hand. It's all my fault and I'm sorry. You have enough reason to hate me already without this, without my refusal, but I can't—I just can't—"

"Don't be ridiculous!" Bill growled harshly. He swung to his feet and paced restlessly to the window and back to stare down at her with stern eyes. "In the first place, I don't hate you and never did, even when I was most angry with you. In the second, my ego is not that fragile, you know. If I could live after you walked out on our marriage, I believe I can accept the temporary disappointment of this. Yes, I wanted very much to make love with you just now, but my timing was abysmally off. And as you pointed out, it probably wouldn't have been wise to get involved that way with each other again. So forget it."

"Bill, I..." Andie stopped, miserably aware that she'd only made the situation worse.

"I said forget it!" Bill snapped. "Look," he added, agitatedly rubbing his neck, "we'd better finish packing your things. And you—" this time his eyes were impersonally critical as they swept over her wrinkled clothes "—need to spruce yourself up. Why don't you freshen up while I order coffee?''

"All right," Andrea agreed. "But first, will you call the bureau? Maybe they've had some word." She glanced at her watch. It was ten after four. "It's been hours since we last heard."

Bill humored her and sat down on the edge of the bed to dial the office, but they both knew it was futile. Andrea was as aware as he that should any news come in from Washington, the London branch would notify them immediately.

He spoke into the telephone for a few moments, and when he cradled it, he said gently, "There's been no word, but it's nighttime there, honey. They can't resume the search until daylight."

"You're right. I'm being unreasonable." Andrea swallowed her disappointment. "I'll take my bath now."

Bill touched her arm and said softly, encouragingly, "Maybe there'll be news by the time we get to Washington."

Bill was being kind again, and it brought tears to her eyes. "Yes," she said stoutly. "There's bound to be news by then." Quickly, she moved away from him and went into the bathroom.

In spite of her tension, the hot bath did its soothing work. The water lapped gently around Andrea's body, washing away some of her fatigue and shock. Beyond the door came the reassuring sound of Bill's footsteps as he moved around, packing the rest of her belongings.

Almost all her life Andrea had taken pride in her self-sufficiency, but last night that old friend had deserted her. She had been utterly defenseless, and only Bill's stalwart presence had kept her from completely falling apart.

The incident between them a few minutes ago, though, had shaken her defenses in a different way. Bill's casual touch had so quickly turned sensual and her body had treacherously and instantly responded! The strong physical magic that had always existed between them obviously still lurked below the surface, ready to flare to life again at the first provocation. It was something they would both have to guard against as long as they were thrown together, because to give in to it would only create a whole new set of problems, problems neither of them needed. Never again did she want to go through the pain of parting. Once had been enough.

Becoming aware that she was wasting time, that she had a plane to catch and a long journey home, Andrea stepped from the bathtub and reached for the fluffy white towel on the warming rack.

A few minutes later, dressed in a pair of gray wool slacks and a soft pink blouse, she applied her usual light coat of makeup. Her pallor stole through, and she couldn't help but notice that her eyes were dulled with fatigue and fear. The mirror showed an exhausted woman who'd just gone through a severe shock.

Andrea reached for the blusher and added a touch more to her cheeks, determined not to wear her heart on her sleeve for the rest of the world to see.

Her hand stilled and she stared at her reflection. Suddenly, and seemingly from out of nowhere, she realized why she'd ended her marriage to Bill. She'd always tried to protect herself from being hurt by building an imaginary wall around her heart. Even with Bill she'd never completely let down her guard and for that reason—her inability to really trust the man she loved—she had ended the marriage.

The saddest part of all was that she had loved him beyond reason, and she'd known in her heart that he had loved her, too. But it was a love that had been doomed. Bill could never understand why she'd been so restless, why it had been impossible for her to fit into the sort of groove he'd expected from his wife, and she'd been unable to explain. How could she when she'd never quite understood it herself? So they had fought. And once the arguments began, the end had been inevitable. There'd been a demon inside that had driven her further and further away from him, even when she'd yearned for just the opposite. Finally the day had come when she'd packed her bags and left him—and that time, Bill had not tried to stop her.

There had been many times since when she had acknowledged, in the secret place of her heart, that in her obsession not to be wounded, and by wounding Bill first, she'd possibly made the worst mistake of her life. It was so devastating a thought that she had never been able to dwell upon it for long.

Andrea heard voices in the room beyond and emerged from the bathroom to find that John Seevers had arrived. He'd brought Bill's shaving kit and a change of clothes, and Bill immediately took possession of the vacated bathroom.

During her marriage to Bill, whenever they'd been in London they'd usually spent at least one pleasant evening socializing with John and his wife, so now Andrea smiled warmly and said, "It's nice to see you again, John. I really appreciate your getting up so early to drive us to the airport." A coffee tray rested on a table near the window, and she went to pour each of them a cup.

"You know I'm quite happy to do it," John said. "I'm really sorry about your brother, Andie."

"Thanks. I know you are." Andrea's voice was thick as she turned to hand John his coffee.

"Is there anything more I can do for you?" he offered.

Andrea nodded and said seriously, "Yes, there is. You can sit down and talk to me right now to keep my mind off...other things. How's Lydia?"

"She's fine. We have a baby now, you know."

"No, I didn't know. Boy or girl?"

"A son," John said proudly. "Would you like to see a picture?"

"Of course."

While Andrea admired John's photos and murmured the expected comments, a deep sadness came over her. Bill had wanted children, too, but she'd held off. Now it was too late.

And Randy. Her heart constricted. Though they were twins, he was her opposite in so many ways. He'd always maintained that once he found the right woman, he would settle down and raise half a dozen children. In anticipation of that eventuality, last year he had plunked down most of his hard-earned savings to buy that farm of his. And now...

With difficulty, Andrea got a grip on her emotions by forcing herself to concentrate on what John Seevers was saying.

A few minutes later Bill rejoined them, wearing a dark-blue suit. Andrea had little luggage, so without waiting for a bellboy, they carried it to the elevator themselves.

On the ground floor, Andrea stopped at the desk to check out while John went to bring his car around. Bill and a porter carried the bags out to the curb.

The luggage had been stowed in the trunk of John's car and the men were standing next to it, their backs to the hotel, as Andrea emerged from the lobby. They spoke in low voices and were unaware of her presence.

"...able to reach Rosalie and explain why I couldn't see her last night?"

John Seevers nodded. "Yes. She said she understood perfectly and would be looking forward to your call."

"And the flowers?"

Again, Seevers nodded. "Two dozen white roses, like you said."

"Fine."

Unbidden, a fresh pain assaulted Andrea. Not once last night or this morning had she dreamed Bill was thinking of another woman, that he'd broken his date with Rosalie Chapman in order to stay with her. She felt betrayed. All the while he'd given her his undivided time and attention, he'd wanted to be with the other woman. Suddenly Andrea was both embarrassed and angry; embarrassed that she'd felt the need to lean on Bill, and angry that in spite of his current interest in Rosalie Chapman, he'd wanted to make love to her, Andrea, only a couple of hours ago! When she remembered her own response to his touch, she felt humiliated.

The anger and resentment ran deep, and in an odd sort of way, it was exactly what she needed. Its hot energy superseded the numbing grief that had held her in its grip since the previous afternoon. It brought a flush of color to her face and pumped adrenaline into her veins, rejuvenating her mind and body.

Pretending she'd heard nothing, Andrea said loudly, "I'm ready. We'd better hurry, don't you think?"

A few minutes later, they were on their way. The early morning streets of London were quiet and almost empty. Hyde Park was an oasis of peace. Later the thoroughfares would be clogged with red double-decker buses, cars, trucks, black taxis and tour coaches. The park would come alive with cyclists, joggers and people walking to work. But for now the city was still drowsy and hushed. Only a few lights gleamed in shop windows and flats as the new day began to unfold.

Andrea shivered and wondered what news the day would bring.

The long flight was uneventful. Andrea spent most of those hours of enforced idleness gazing blindly out the window at the clouds and thinking about Randy.

She didn't talk much to Bill, and once or twice she could feel his puzzled gaze upon her. She hadn't been exactly cold to him—after all, he'd done much to help her. Besides, as long as they were together through this crisis, they needed civility. Their relationship was fraught with enough pitfalls as it was. No, it was more of a withdrawal into herself, a quietness and a conscious reserve in her demeanor as she continually reminded herself that she had no claim upon him anymore, that he no longer belonged to her and that once this situation ended, they would go their separate ways. She could not afford to invest her emotions in Bill. She needed them for Randy...and for herself.

Now, wedged between Bill and Sara Borden, Bill's personal secretary, as they drove from Dulles Airport toward the city, she sat numb and silent while the soft voices of the other two floated over her head.

It was an unseasonably mild afternoon for late November, the sort Washingtonians and tourists alike took advantage of with long walks on the Mall. The Potomac glinted beneath the sun like a newly minted silver coin, and thrusting into the clear blue sky like a beacon of hope was the grandeur of the Washington Monument.

But Andrea was unable to appreciate the fine weather, nor could she summon the smallest shred of hope in her heart, for Sara, her soft brown eyes brimming with compassion, had greeted them at the airport with the news that Randy had not yet been found.

"The problem," Sara explained as she drove, "is that down south they're still having rainstorms and that's hampering their search efforts."

Bill put his arm around Andrea's shoulders, and she didn't resist. Once again a chill was seeping into her bones as well as her heart.

"What are the weather forecasts down that way?" Bill asked.

"Promising," Sara said quickly. "By late afternoon they should be moving out. Our people have done what we can, Bill. We're keeping in touch with officials, of course, but we've also contacted every newspaper, radio and television station along the route he most likely took and have asked them to publicize it so that people will be on the lookout."

Andrea closed her eyes. All this time gone by and still no one had found Randy. Even if he'd initially survived the crash, if he'd suffered injuries, not to mention exposure to the cold and the rain...well, she knew the odds as well as anyone else. Renewed fear iced her veins.

Bill saw Andrea shudder and knew how she must feel. He felt sick at the lack of news, too. Poor Randy. It would be a miracle if he were still alive.

But he could do nothing for Randy; his immediate concern had to be for Andrea. She was so exhausted as well as traumatized that she was in danger of a nervous collapse. She hadn't slept on the plane and had only picked at her food.

His original intent on arriving in Washington had been to go straight to the office and join the staff in monitoring the search efforts. It was where he'd felt certain Andie would wish to be. But now he could see that she wasn't up to it, and frankly, neither was he. His own reserves of energy were about exhausted and they both needed sleep.

Sara's searching glance went to Andrea and then beyond to Bill. As though she'd read her employer's mind, she asked, "Do you want me to take you home or to the office?"

"Home," Bill replied firmly. "We're beat, and we've got to get some rest. Naturally I expect to be called if there's any news."

Sara nodded, and for the remainder of the drive no one spoke.

The condominium apartment was the same one they had shared during their marriage, and it gave Andrea a strange feeling to be entering it again. Though she was worn out, both mentally and physically, nevertheless she stopped in the center of the living room and looked around with interest.

"Nothing has changed," she said slowly, scarcely believing the evidence of her eyes. The cushiony egg-colored sofa was still there, as was the glass cocktail table. The books in the bookcase appeared familiar, and the walls and tables were devoid of decoration. There was still an incomplete look to the room, as though it belonged to someone who'd never found the time to give it a personal stamp, hadn't quite known how or had the courage to try. It had the bare, stripped-down-to-essentials appearance of her own apartment in New York.

Bill shrugged. "There never seemed to be much point. I only sleep and occasionally eat here."

"I see. I'm surprised you haven't remarried, Bill," she said sarcastically. "To some nice little homebody who lavishes all her attention on homey touches, meals and having babies."

Bill clenched his jaw, suddenly furious with her. "You taught me a valuable lesson," he said harshly. "Not many women want that sort of life these days, and I don't care to make a second mistake."

He saw Andie wince, but in spite of the circumstances, he was beyond caring if he'd hurt her. She'd hurt *him,* by reminding him of how foolishly unfounded his hopes had once been.

"I'm sorry," she said huskily. "For what I just said. And for our marriage not working out."

Bill sucked in a deep breath. "Yeah," he said curtly. "Sure you are." He turned his back to her, picked up her suitcase and carried it into the bedroom.

Andrea followed and said urgently, "You don't believe me, but I truly am sorry, Bill. The failure was all my fault, not yours, and I never wanted it to make you bitter toward marriage. Of course there are women who still want the sort of marriage you deserve to have." She took a breath and plunged on. "What about that woman you were with at the theater in London? The one you sent roses to?"

Bill dropped the suitcase with a thud and swung around to glare at her. "Oh, so that's what brought out your claws, is it? And why you were so cool and indifferent toward me on the plane? You overheard John and me talking, didn't you?"

Andrea nodded and glared back. "I was very angry with you. You tried to make love to me this morning, and all the time you were thinking of her! It's inexcusable!"

Absurdly, Bill's heart soared. Andie was jealous! He could scarcely believe it. He stepped forward and, overcoming her resistance, pulled her into his arms. "Believe me, honey," he said gently, "this morning in bed I was only thinking of you. Of us. Of how it used to be."

"But you told John to send her flowers...."

Bill sighed. "We had arranged a date and I had to let her down. The flowers were just a means of apologizing for standing her up, that's all."

"You shouldn't have broken your date on my account," Andie murmured stiffly. "I could have managed without—"

"Shut up!" Bill snapped. "Where else would I want to be at a time like this, except with you? We may be divorced,

Andie, but that doesn't mean I don't have feelings for you. If you're in trouble, of course I care! I want to help you any way I can. Wouldn't you have done the same for me?"

"Yes. But—"

"No buts," Bill interrupted. "Look, honey, the truth is I'm just too damned tired to get into an argument with you. About anything. And you're not in shape to go another round in the ring, either."

Andrea managed a wan smile. "You're right," she said wearily.

Bill smiled back. "Good. I'm glad we got that settled. Now why don't I rustle up some food for us? You've hardly eaten a bite since yesterday."

"I couldn't," Andie said huskily. "There's a knot there"—she touched her midsection—"the size of a melon."

Bill softened and tucked a strand of her hair behind her ear. "I know, honey. But you need something to keep up your strength."

In the end he persuaded her to swallow a little soup and half a slice of toast. Afterward, when she would have helped him straighten the kitchen, he stopped her and said gently, "I'll get this. Why don't you go take a hot shower and then get into bed?"

Andrea shrugged and said listlessly, "I don't think I'll ever sleep again. My mind won't stop thinking."

"You're a walking zombie and you've got to get some rest," Bill said, taking her by the arm and leading her into the bedroom. There he opened her suitcase himself and fished out a silky pink nightgown, which he thrust into her hands. "While you're bathing, I'm going to call a doctor friend of mine and have him send over some sleeping tablets for you."

"No," Andrea protested. "I don't want anything like that. What if somebody calls with news about Randy? I want to be alert."

Bill sighed. She had a valid point. All the same, she had to get some sleep. They both did. "All right," he said, relenting. "No pills as long as you do what you're told."

Thirty minutes later Andrea, clad in the revealing nightgown, her hair, moist from the shower, curling in tendrils, crawled into the king-sized bed. It was the same bed she'd shared with Bill during their marriage, and old memories came rushing back. There had been many delightful nights of passion here, some so glorious that they hadn't even bothered to sleep at all. And when they had, there'd still been the morning after, sweet and cozy as they'd awakened nestled in each other's arms.

Just then, Bill came into the room and halted abruptly near the door. His blue eyes took in the sight of her in his bed, and for a long moment they were both speechless as they stared at each other.

At last Bill said somewhat gruffly, "I never thought I'd see you there again."

Andrea swallowed. "I know. Are you...?" She paused and her heart thudded as she tried again. "Are you coming to bed now, too?"

Bill shook his head and smiled a little grimly. "I'm not made of stone. I wouldn't trust myself the way you're dressed, and you made it plain enough this morning that you didn't want anything to do with me. No, I'll crash on the sofa tonight. I just came in to see if you're all right and whether you'd changed your mind about the sleeping pills."

Andrea felt an odd disappointment that she couldn't quite understand. She didn't want to start a new series of complications after all these years apart, and yet being here in "their" bedroom, in "their" bed, and with Bill gazing at her with a hunger he couldn't entirely conceal, she knew that it would only take one small move on his part for her to open her arms to him.

But Bill did not make that move, and Andrea found that his stilted demeanor froze something inside of her. She ached for his arms to close about her, for his lips to caress hers, for his body to warm hers, yet she could not have stated those needs for the world. If he rejected her, she would have to leave, for this place was already haunted by the ghosts of the lovers they had once been; and if she left, where else could she go? Back to New York to sit alone by the telephone in her own apartment?

"I'm fine," she said, hoping he couldn't see how disturbed she was. "And no, I still don't want any pills." At her words, Bill nodded crisply and began to turn toward the door. Suddenly panic and loneliness washed over her, and Andrea asked quickly, almost shyly, "Could you...would you mind staying with me until I fall asleep?"

Bill felt his rigid resistance snap. Blatantly sexy though she looked there in his bed, "their bed," with her blond hair spilling across the pillow and the lacy top of her gown provocatively tracing the fullness of her breasts, Andie also looked nervous and unsure of herself. Then it dawned on him that it could be no easier on her to find herself back in their marriage bed than it was on him to see her there. Added to the awkward situation was her anxiety over Randy. He could no more ignore her plea than stop the beating of his own heart.

"Sure," he said with forced casualness. He sat on the edge of the bed and clasped one of her cold, trembling hands in his. "Now close your eyes and try to sleep."

Andrea obediently closed her eyes, but after a moment she sighed and murmured, "Bill?"

"Yes, honey?" His voice was gentle.

Her cloudy green eyes opened. "Do you think Randy knew how much I really loved him?"

"Of course."

"Of the pair of us, he was always the good one."

Bill smiled. "I don't know. You've had your moments, too."

Andrea returned the smile. "It's kind of you to say so, considering everything, but even at my best I was never like Randy. He was always the peacemaker. He wasn't quarrelsome like me."

"In his personal relationships, true, but get him on the subject of politics or the slant of a news story, and he could argue his point for hours."

"Only when he believed he was right." Andrea sighed again. "I'm glad you two stayed good friends, Bill. That you didn't let our divorce mess that up."

"Me, too," Bill answered softly. "Me, too. Now close your eyes again and go to sleep."

This time when her eyelids fluttered down, they stayed that way. As the minutes ticked by and Andrea's soft breathing grew steadier, Bill quietly watched her. His throat choked with emotion. She was so beautiful, this woman he'd once loved so passionately, and just now she was as vulnerable as a baby. He felt a fierce protectiveness toward her. Andie had always been such a quicksilver mixture of moods. Sometimes she'd leaned on him like the proverbial clinging vine, but at other times she'd behaved so arrogantly and independently that it hadn't seemed as though she needed him at all. Or cared how he felt. There'd been times when she'd seemed to love him to distraction, and others when she'd been cold and distant, even cruel. Through it all, he'd loved her, and after the divorce it had taken a long, long time before he'd gotten her out of his system.

Or had he? Renewed desire and tenderness swept over him as he gazed down at her face. Though he might no longer love her, there was clearly a part of him that still cared deeply, and a thousand divorce decrees could never change that. Andrea had once been his wife, and he realized now that she would always belong to him to a certain extent because she lived inside his heart. Years had separated them, and when she went away again their futures would distance them, yet no power on earth could make him forget her completely or cease to think of her from time to time with a wistful longing and a wish that things might have been different.

Andrea had fallen asleep at last, and there was no further need for Bill to remain at her side. He gazed at her for one moment more, then impulsively leaned forward and brushed her soft lips with his before he left the room.

For a time he prowled restlessly through the living room and kitchen, more affected than he could even admit to himself because Andie was in the apartment they'd shared together. Visions of the past came to torment him . . . Andie in the kitchen, in tears of frustration over a burned pot roast; seductively lovely in a black nightgown; leaning over a typewriter, her lower lip caught between her teeth as she labored late at night over a piece of writing. There were other pictures, too . . . Andie and her suitcase at the door as she was about to leave to do an investigative article in Nicaragua; quarrels that left them both so bitter that they hugged their own sides of the bed in an effort to make no physical contact when their minds could not meet; her vehement objections to buying a suburban home.

At last Bill forced himself to stretch out on the sofa. His body ached with the strain of the past two days, and his eyes were gritty with the need for sleep. Still, his thoughts raced on like a speeding train through a dark tunnel.

Shortly after their marriage Andie had quit her position at the *Patriot*. She'd been obsessed with the notion that as the wife of the publisher, people might no longer take her seriously as a journalist. Bill had understood that, in part. She'd wanted no question of nepotism to affect critics' judgment of her work.

But Andrea couldn't be content merely to go to work at another paper, or perhaps to write an occasional free-lance article. She'd had some deep-seated compulsion to prove herself, so she'd begun her travels. At first the trips were brief, always resulting in a thought-provoking article for some major news magazine; but then she'd decided to do an in-depth book on the strife in the Middle East, as war and terrorist acts affected the lives of ordinary people. It became a bestseller as soon as it was published, for Andrea had a knack for placing world and political events in a personal context that touched hearts and minds in a powerful way. The professional in Bill recognized and respected that. Nevertheless, the weeks and sometimes months that she'd been away had played havoc with their relationship.

Bill knew he'd reacted badly to the situation. He'd resented her long absences and couldn't cope with her inexplicably strong need to prove herself at the expense of *his* needs. The quarrels had begun, growing progressively fiercer until they had reached the point where all Andie's brief visits home had resulted in verbal warfare. There'd been nothing to do except end their relationship.

Bill finally fell asleep, and his dreams, strangely enough, were warm and peaceful, offering what reality had denied him. He was with Andie, a soft, melting Andie he'd never met before, and they were both smiling as they watched children playing in a garden. He knew they were *their* children, and he felt an unusual happiness that pervaded every atom of his body.

But when he awoke at dawn he realized it had only been a taunting illusion. He was no longer married to Andie and there were no children. She had never wanted them.

Shaking off the lingering dregs of sleep, Bill got up. Tiptoeing into the bedroom where Andrea was fast asleep, he collected fresh clothes and went to take a shower. He was annoyed that being with Andie again had brought out subconscious hopes and desires he thought he had long since dismantled and forgotten.

The best way to get Andie out of his head, temporarily at least, was to get out of her vicinity. Although she was asleep, her mere presence seemed to fill the entire apartment. Bill shaved and dressed quickly and soon let himself out the front door.

The morning sun was breaking through the gray-blue sky as he drove toward the office. Bill's thoughts turned from Andrea to her missing brother, and suddenly an anger born of anguish seized him.

Damn you, Randy! his mind raged bitterly. *You go and probably get yourself killed and bring Andie back into my life, and all for what? So we'll both have to live without you as a friend and a brother? So we'll have to deal with unresolved feelings about ourselves and a marriage that long ago ought to have been decently forgotten?*

Bill's throat tightened in a mingling of fury and grief. He wasn't sure he could ever forgive Randy for putting him and Andie through this. His fingers curled around the steering wheel as the pain of loss wracked him. His head bowed slightly beneath its impact.

He was going to miss his old friend terribly. As for Andie, he didn't know how she would be able to survive it. He had better reason than most to know that Randy was the only person in the world she had ever been capable of loving without reservation.

Chapter Five

From the depths of her slumber, the sound of a bell summoned Andrea. She was dreaming of Randy and herself as they'd been as children. They were playing in a meadow, skipping along and laughing. It was a peaceful place, their meadow, strewn with wildflowers and clover, and the jarring bell was an intrusion upon their pleasure.

The bell would not stop ringing, yet it seemed to have no source. Andrea sighed and turned over, but the dream began to recede as she floated up to consciousness.

Rousing slowly, Andrea became aware that the sound she heard was a telephone. She opened her eyes, but for an instant she was disoriented. Her gaze fell upon the soft blue draperies, the tallboy against the wall and the closed bedroom door. Then, she remembered. Randy was missing, and she had come to Washington with Bill. Now she was in "their" apartment, "their" room, "their" bed.

And the telephone was still ringing.

Fully awake now, Andrea sat up. For a moment, she debated with herself about picking up the phone. Bill should be doing that. After all, this was no longer her home. But where was he? She knew he'd slept in the living room, but if the insistent ringing of the telephone had wakened her, surely it had also wakened him. Yet the thing was still jangling.

To silence it, Andrea finally decided to answer the call herself. She leaned across the bed and lifted the receiver.

"It's about time!" came the aggrieved voice. "I was beginning to think you'd gone out."

"Bill?" Andrea frowned down at the bedspread. "I was still asleep." She turned quickly and squinted at the clock on the bedside table. It read a quarter past eleven. "I can't believe I slept so long!" she gasped. Then a thought struck her and she demanded, "Where are you, anyhow?"

"At the office. I've been here for hours. I left you a note in the kitchen, but if you just woke, you won't have seen it. Listen, darling…" He paused half a heartbeat, then rushed on, "I've got incredible, wonderful, miraculous news!"

"Randy!" The one word on Andrea's lips was a hope and a prayer.

"Right." Bill's voice was warm and joyous, pouring over her like a pitcher of sunshine. "The call just came in. He was found in northern Georgia in a remote forest area, and as far as they can tell, he's not too badly injured."

"Thank God!" Andrea breathed. "Oh, thank God!" Something caught in her throat, and the last words ended on a sob of elation and intense gratitude.

"Hey," Bill said gently. "You've been good and brave up to this point, so don't go falling apart on me now."

"I won't." Andrea gulped and took a deep breath. "It's— it's just that I'm so h-h-hap…"

"I know." Bill's voice went husky. "I've got a bit of a lump in my throat, too. Now," he added briskly, "dry your eyes and pay attention. We've got plans to make."

Andrea lifted a corner of the sheet and dabbed at the moisture on her cheeks. She sniffed and, in a more normal tone, said, "All right. I'm listening. How soon can I see him?"

"In a few hours, I hope. Right now a helicopter is carrying Randy to a hospital in Atlanta. I've already chartered a plane for us so we can get there as quickly as possible. What I want you to do is take a taxi and meet me here at the office. We'll leave for the airport from here. And don't forget to bring our suitcases."

"Will do," Andrea replied. "Lucky we're still packed; I'm not sure I'd have the patience to bother." Laughter spilled out over her words. "I probably won't even need a taxi. I may just float on a cloud. Or sprout wings."

"I think you're a little giddy," Bill teased. "Sure you haven't been raiding the liquor cabinet?"

Andrea giggled. "Who needs an artificial high like that? It would only be a poor imitation of what I'm feeling right now."

"I know." Bill was no longer teasing. "I feel the same way, honey. Now, how soon can you manage to get here?"

"I'll be there so fast it'll make your head swim. All I've got to do is throw on some clothes and I'll be on my way."

"Fine. Oh, one more thing, Andie."

"Yes?"

"Try not to sound so downcast, will you?"

Andrea laughed again. "I'll do my best," she promised.

"All right." Bill chuckled softly. "See you in a little while."

Always efficient, today Andrea outdid herself. She contacted the doorman and had him order a taxi; within fifteen minutes, dressed in a cheery red woolen suit, she left the apartment.

A scant forty-five minutes from the time Bill had called, her cheeks rosy from the cold and her excitement, Andrea entered the wide glass double doors of the building that housed the *Washington Patriot*.

She was immediately assaulted by an unexpected sense of homecoming. The plushly carpeted reception area, with its profusion of potted plants and deep, comfortable sofas, was much the same as she remembered. Only the young receptionist behind the desk was new.

The taxi driver deposited her baggage near the door, and Andrea paid him before turning to speak to the girl.

"I'm Andrea Sheridan. Mr. Sheridan is expecting me."

The girl's face brightened at once. "Of course. You can go right in, Mrs. Sheridan, but may I tell you first how happy I am over the good news about Randy?"

Andrea smiled. "Thank you. It's fantastic, isn't it?" she said as she headed for the corridor.

She took the elevator past the second floor, which housed the editorial department where she'd once worked, and continued to the third, where the administrative offices were located. Sara's desk, in the outer room, was deserted, so Andrea breezed past it to the door that opened into Bill's private office.

He was standing with his back to the door, gazing out the window as he cradled the telephone receiver against his shoulder. His dark hair was softly burnished by the sunlight that streamed through the windows, and his white shirt-sleeves were rolled to the elbows. Beneath the shirt, Andrea could see the play of muscles in his back as he shifted position.

"Get a few more bids on the job first, Charlie," he said. "I think we can come up with a better price than that."

A potted ivy sat on the window ledge, and restlessly Bill began to touch first one of its leaves, then another. For the first time since Randy had been declared missing, Andrea's mind was free to consider something other than her brother's safety. Now, unexpectedly, swift compassion for Bill rushed through her. He had a heavy responsibility running the *Patriot*, and she knew it was not the kind of job he would have preferred. Printer's ink was in his blood all right, but his talent lay in covering the news; he was a reporter, not an administrator. His father had wielded his authority as a publisher with natural skill and an ease born of a love for the job; Bill had been thrust into it by inheritance and a deep-seated sense of duty. For the first time, just by the set of his shoulders and his slightly bowed head, Andrea got the impression that Bill was a very lonely man.

As though sensing that he was no longer alone, Bill turned, and when he saw Andrea standing in the doorway, his eyes lit up like blue fire. He motioned with his hand for her to enter the room. Andrea stepped inside and softly closed the door while he spoke again into the phone. "What? No, handle that however you think best. I've got to go now. Andrea's here. Yes, I'll tell her."

Bill dropped the receiver into its cradle and swiftly strode around the desk. Andrea didn't pause to think, merely followed her impulse and rushed toward him, exuberantly flinging herself into his arms.

Bill crushed her to his chest with equal fervor. Andrea put her arms around his shoulders, and they beamed at each other with unabashed delight.

"He's really all right," Andrea stated.

Bill nodded. "He's really all right. A few minutes ago I talked to the hospital in Atlanta, and Randy's there. They couldn't let me speak to him because he's being treated right now, but the nurse I talked to assured me he's not badly injured and that he's in good spirits. She promised to give him your love and tell him we're on our way. What was it your friend Kent said the other night in London? Randy's tough.''

"Yes," Andrea said softly. "He is. And so are you. You're magnificent."

"Me? How's that? I wasn't the one who found him."

"No. But you found me, and your strength held me up through the ordeal. Bill, I . . . I couldn't have made it without—"

"Hush," Bill growled. His lips formed a tiny smile. "You've said all that before, remember? You must be getting old and forgetful, sweetheart. You're starting to repeat yourself."

His face was inching closer to Andrea's, so that she was having difficulty concentrating on what she wanted to say. His gentle teasing wasn't helping matters, either. It summoned up the good times they'd once shared, when they'd always seemed to be laughing and joking and each day had been a bright, new, shiny coin that they would spend together.

But this was now, and they no longer belonged to each other. They needed to remember that. Still, right this instant, Bill's firm lips were so near, so tantalizing, so distracting that she could think of nothing else.

Using all the self-discipline she possessed, Andrea fought the inclination to bridge the space between their lips. "Bill, please," she pleaded. "Let me say how grat—"

Bill sighed, lowered his head and kissed her. It was the only way to shut her up. Besides, she was irresistible. She always had been.

Bill's mouth grew soft and gentle as it captured hers. Andrea's bones melted, and her blood heated, lava hot. Inexorably, she was plunged into the river of time, floating back to when her entire existence had centered around this man, when her body had thrived on the joy of his touch. Then every kiss had been magic, every caress a bewitching sorcery.

As it was now. Her fingers slid up from his shoulders to entwine themselves in his hair. Her lips parted beneath his, and Bill felt his own body harden with desire. It was as natural and swift a reaction to her response as a soul being uplifted by an exquisite sunrise. He had never, in all this time, been able to drive the memory of Andie completely from his heart. Now he didn't even try. He only knew that she could still affect him as no other woman ever had.

Their kiss grew more ardent, more demanding, and Bill became all feeling. Once again after years of deprivation, he was holding the only woman who could send him over the brink of passionate delight. Lowering the last shield guarding his heart, he allowed himself to revel in the sensation.

At last their lips parted and, somber and wondering, they gazed wordlessly at each other.

Andrea found that she was trembling. "I—we..." she began huskily.

Bill smiled tenderly and touched his finger to her lips. "Shh. Just let it be," he whispered. He pressed his cheek to hers, holding her to him, enveloping her shaking body with his warmth. Then his gaze fell on the doorway across the room and he murmured, "Put on a bright smile, darling. We've got company."

He released her, and Andrea turned to see Dave Sullivan and Sara Borden standing in the doorway.

Dave chuckled and came into the room. "Sorry we barged in without knocking," he said with a big grin, not looking sorry in the least. "When we heard you'd arrived, we just couldn't wait to see you, Andie."

"Dave!" Andrea exclaimed. "It's wonderful to see you." When the older man opened his arms, Andrea accepted his bear hug.

"I just had to tell you how glad I am that Randy's safe," he added.

"Thanks, Dave. I know you are."

"The same goes for me," Sara said as she, in turn, embraced Andrea. As they smiled at each other, she added, "I have to say you look in considerably better spirits than you did yesterday."

"It's amazing what a difference a day makes, isn't it?" Andrea laughed. "The past couple of days were the worst of my life." She shuddered, then glanced toward the man at her side and said, "The only thing that kept me going was Bill, and he won't even let me thank him properly."

"Seemed to me you were doing a pretty good job of it when we came in," Dave said dryly.

Andrea felt her face blushing crimson. They'd been caught in the act, and now there was nothing to do except brazen it out. "It's what's known as a friendly divorce," she said, keeping a straight face. "It's the 'in' thing to have, you see. Right, Bill?"

Bill's hand slid around her waist easily. "I understand that some divorces are even so friendly that the couples go so far as to—Ugh!" Andrea's elbow had just poked his midsection. While Sara and Dave hooted with amusement, Bill gave her a reproachful look. "You didn't let me finish. I was going to say that some divorced couples even go on double dates together."

Andrea glanced at him. "Double dates?" she echoed in disbelief.

Bill nodded. "They sort of vet each other's new romances and offer advice on whether they're suitable replacements or not. Do you think we ought to try it sometime?" he asked with deceptive innocence.

"Not in a million years," Andrea declared vehemently.

"Hmm. Too bad," Bill said with a thoughtful air. "You were giving me some advice last night, and it seemed to me I ought to be allowed to return the favor."

Andrea's eyes narrowed, warning Bill he was pushing too far. "I may have offered some general advice," she admitted, "but I don't have the slightest intention of checking out your dates for you. Or vice versa."

Bill winked at Dave and Sara. "She's really afraid her own dates couldn't stack up next to my devastating charm."

Andrea grimaced and said to the others, "Isn't it a shame that poor Bill suffers from such a dreadful inferiority complex?"

They all laughed. Mercifully, the uncomfortable moment ended when the telephone rang. Sara moved to Bill's desk to answer it, and a moment later she told him, "It's your call to Italy."

"That'll be Carrie," Bill said. He motioned for Andrea to take the call. "While you're telling her the good news, we'll go down to the Rumpus Room. Meet us there when you're done. All your old friends want to see you before we leave for Atlanta."

Andrea nodded and began speaking to her mother while the others filed out of the room.

Ten minutes later she stepped into the elevator, on her way to join the others. Carrie had been relieved and delighted that Randy was all right. When Andrea asked if she would be coming to see him, however, her mother had sighed and expressed her regrets: it just wasn't convenient at the moment. If Randy had been seriously injured, she'd assured

Andrea, nothing could have kept her from her son's side; but as it was, she had other obligations that must take precedence. There was to be a party on a Greek shipping magnate's yacht, and she was a cohostess. Since a few members of royalty and even a couple of world leaders were to be guests, it might have important consequences politically. Surely Andrea must understand just how great her responsibility was for this event.

Andrea had swallowed her resentment and assured her mother that she did indeed understand. Which she did. She understood that Carrie would always find other people more important than her own children. It was a painful truth, and it cut deep into Andrea's soul, but it was a reality that both she and Randy were better off facing. If you didn't count on anything from Carrie—not moral support or love or even her physical presence at appropriate times—you couldn't be disappointed or hurt.

On the second floor, Andrea pushed open the door that led into the editorial department, better known as the Rumpus Room. One huge, vast room, filled with desks, filing cabinets and computer terminals, was home to the journalistic staff. Smaller private offices lined the back of this room and were occupied by various editors.

Andrea expected to see everyone busy at their desks, just like any other normal working day. But the moment she entered, pandemonium erupted. Though her mother might have lacked what she considered suitable enthusiasm over Randy's safety, the gang here did not. Instantly she was mobbed by old friends eager to hug her, kiss her cheek and express their joy that one of their own had been found alive and well.

Tears sprang to Andrea's eyes as the bedlam continued, and as first one and then another greeted her, she saw that she wasn't the only one in the place with moist eyes. It occurred to her that this was a family. These people genuinely cared about Randy and about her, and they were unashamed of their own overflowing emotions.

Someone held up a huge banner that read "We love Randy!" and others thrust gifts for him into Andrea's arms. "Speech! Speech!" several yelled.

Suddenly Bill was at Andrea's side, and his arm went around her shoulders. "Are you okay?" he asked, noting the tears that were streaming down her face.

She nodded and tried to speak. "Y-yes. But I...I'm overwhelmed! Did you plan this?"

Bill shook his head and smiled gently. "No. It was entirely the staff's idea. Like the banner says, they love Randy, and they just wanted you to know how happy they are. From what I've gathered from Dave, this has been a pretty gloomy department the past couple of days." He removed the gifts from her arms, placed them on a desk behind them and handed her his handkerchief. "Mop up those tears, darling," he suggested in a low voice, "and give them their speech. Then we need to head for the airport."

Andrea managed to say a few words of gratitude. Afterward she couldn't remember what she'd said, but she knew it must have been all right because it had brought loud applause. A few minutes later, charged with dozens of well-wishing messages for her brother, she left the room with Bill and Sara.

As they waited for the elevator, Sara exclaimed, "I almost forgot in all the excitement, Andie. Somebody named Lisa Weber has been calling and asking about Randy ever since the story broke in the paper. Do you know her?"

Andrea shook her head. "Never heard of her. Have you, Bill?"

Bill shrugged and shook his head, too.

"She sounded really anxious about him," Sara said.

"Maybe she's his latest girlfriend," Andrea ventured. "Since I haven't seen him in a few months, I wouldn't know whom he's dating now. Did she give you her telephone number?" Sara nodded, and Andrea went on, "Then call her when you get a chance, will you, and tell her he's all right?"

"Will do," Sara promised.

The elevator arrived, Bill and Andrea bade the secretary goodbye and stepped into it.

It was dusk when they walked into the hospital in Atlanta. Bill inquired at the information desk, and a few minutes later they were escorted, not to Randy's room, but into an office.

The man behind the desk rose and extended his hand to Andrea. "Mrs. Sheridan. Mr. Sheridan. It's a pleasure to meet you. I'm Dr. Ross. I wanted to speak to you before you go in to see Mr. Wade."

"Is something wrong, Doctor?" Andrea asked anxiously. "We were told that my brother wasn't seriously injured."

"That's correct," the doctor said with a reassuring smile. "His appearance is a lot worse than his actual condition, and I wanted to emphasize that to you before you saw him and perhaps became alarmed."

"His appearance?"

"He's bruised and scraped on his face and arms," Dr. Ross explained. "He's also wearing a bandage around his head where he sustained a nasty cut. As to the main injuries, he's got several broken ribs, and we think he may have suffered a slight concussion. Also, we've found that his lungs are slightly congested, and that's causing him to run a fever. No doubt it's due to his lengthy exposure to the heavy rains and the cold."

"Pneumonia?" Bill asked.

"No. Just a bit of congestion, as I said. It's not too serious at this point. We're giving him antibiotics to fight the
infection and hopefully that'll take care of the problem. He
is in some pain because of the ribs, and we've got him on
painkilling medication, so he'll probably be quite drowsy
when you see him. But essentially he's doing fine. He's a
very lucky young man to have come through all he did no
worse the wear than that."

"I agree," Bill said with a smile. "And we appreciate the
care you're giving him. Any idea how long he'll need to be
here?"

The doctor shrugged casually. "Only a few days, barring
complications. I would like to see the congestion cleared up
before we release him, just to be on the safe side." He smiled
at Andrea and said, "I know you're eager to see him, so if
you'll come with me now, I'll show you to his room."

"Thank you, Doctor."

Dr. Ross led them down a maze of corridors, and when
he reached Randy's room, he paused outside the door. "You
can go in now, though I'd advise you not to stay overly long
and try not to excite him too much. He really could use all
the rest and sleep he can get." He looked meaningfully at the
piles of gift-wrapped packages they each carried.

"Low-key and short," Bill promised.

Andrea's first sight of Randy would have been most
alarming if she hadn't been forewarned by the doctor. His
eyes were closed and his breathing had a raspy, labored
sound to it. His face, arms and hands were a mass of swollen, blue-black bruises, nasty burned areas and ugly
scratches. A wide bandage swathed his forehead, so that
only the very top of his reddish-brown hair was visible. He
wore a green hospital gown that lent a sickly cast to the few
unscathed areas of his skin. All the same, he looked won-

derful to her, and a tremulous gladness filled her. He was alive! Miraculously alive!

"He's sleeping," she whispered to Bill.

"You heard the doctor. He needs his rest," Bill whispered back. "Let's go downstairs to the cafeteria and have something to eat. Maybe he'll be awake by the time we come back."

Andrea nodded. "All right." She deposited the gifts she carried on a chair and then, unable to resist, tiptoed to the bed and gently touched Randy's hair. She just had to prove to herself he was actually, physically here. She wanted to bend down and kiss his cheek as well, but she was afraid that would wake him. Besides, where could she kiss him without hurting him?

Bill put his pile of gifts on the window ledge, and the two of them crept out of the room.

Thirty minutes later they returned to find Randy awake. He grinned weakly as they walked in and, referring to the pile of gifts that cluttered the room, said, "I figured Santa Claus must have come early this year."

"Oh, Randy!" Andrea burst into tears as she flew toward him.

"Hey, hey, no salty tears, sis," Randy protested. "They'll sting my scratches." All the same, he put his arms around her as she bent down and pressed her face next to his, and they both trembled with emotion.

After a long moment, Andrea withdrew, mopping fiercely at the tears on her cheeks as Bill clasped Randy's hand. The two men gazed somberly at one another, silently communicating what they could never have expressed aloud.

At last Bill asked, "How do you feel?"

Randy grinned. "I've had better days. On the other hand," he added thoughtfully, "I've had worse days, too."

"Yeah." Bill nodded and, in a masterpiece of under-statement, said, "We've had a couple of unpleasant days ourselves."

Randy's green eyes, so like his twin's, surveyed them both, and then he said lightly, "I guess you have, at that. You both look like hell."

"Well, thanks!" Andrea sniffed. "Your mug isn't ex-actly pretty right now, either!" But her actions belied the affront in her voice. She was stroking his shoulder because all she wanted was to keep on touching him, to convince herself that the nightmare was over, that he was really here.

Randy had been heavily sedated, which made his speech somewhat slurred and slower than normal. Still, he seemed to have a need to talk about the accident. "It was the wind," he told them. "This huge surge of wind. All of a sudden the plane was spinning around like a top and then I went down. I'm sorry about the plane, Bill."

"Who cares about the damn plane?" Bill snapped, sounding almost angry. "It's insured. All that matters is that you're alive."

"I don't know why I am, either," Randy mused. "When I crashed, I was thrown out. Otherwise I'd have been killed for sure, because then the plane burst into flames." He shuddered. "I remember this big ball of fire and me getting up from the ground and running. And then I guess I must have passed out because the next thing I remember is wak-ing up cold and in pain, with the rain pounding my face."

"They said a hunter found you wandering in the woods."

Randy nodded. "I'd been walking off and on ever since the crash, looking for a way out of the forest. I had no idea where I was, and I was beginning to think I'd never break away from the trees and find any civilization. As it turned out, I was only half a mile or so away from a country road when we just stumbled right into each other!" He grinned suddenly. "He had some sandwiches and a thermos of coffee on him, and I polished it all off before he led me out to the road where his truck was parked. I'm here to tell you a sirloin steak never tasted better than those egg sandwiches of his!"

"Everybody at the office sends you their love," Andrea told him. "They're the ones who loaded down Bill and me with all these gifts. Do you feel like opening them now?"

Randy yawned and shook his head. "I don't think I have the energy. I can't seem to stay awake."

"That's because of the medication they're giving you. You need all the sleep you can get," Andrea said. She glanced toward Bill and added, "I think we ought to leave now."

"So do I," Bill answered. "We could both use a good night's sleep ourselves." He glanced down at Randy and added, "We'll be back to see you again in the morning."

"Okay." Randy's hand tightened around Andrea's. "I'm glad you're here," he said, for the first time sounding choked up. "Both of you."

Sara had booked them a suite at one of Atlanta's finest hotels. After leaving Randy, Bill drove the rented car there and they were soon checked in.

The suite consisted of a sitting room and two bedrooms. Bill placed Andrea's suitcase in one of the bedrooms and his own in the other. Andrea went to the window of the sitting room and glanced out at the night lights of Atlanta.

It was only a little past ten, and when Bill returned to the sitting room, he said, "Do you want to watch TV? I guess the news is on."

Andrea turned from the window and shook her head. "I'm too tired," she told him. "I think I'll take a bath and go to bed."

"I had the same plan in mind," Bill said. He stretched and stifled a yawn. Then he smiled at her, adding, "Sweet dreams."

Andrea flashed him a quick grin. "Oh, they will be tonight! No doubt about it!"

She went into her bedroom and closed the door. Bill made sure the sitting room door leading to the corridor was bolted, then flicked off the light before going into his own bedroom.

Five minutes later he was naked and standing beneath the spray of hot water in the shower. He yawned again. Lord, he was tired. He supposed that the trauma of the past few days was catching up with him. He had a suspicion that he'd sleep just fine tonight.

So would Andie, probably. He grinned, remembering the glow in her eyes as she'd sat on the edge of Randy's hospital bed. And the exuberant kiss she'd favored him with this morning. He wouldn't take a million dollars for either.

Face it, he told himself as he rubbed soap across his chest, there was a part of him that still had a soft spot for that woman. He'd found that out these last few days. When she was sad, he was sad; when she was happy, so was he. True, he would've been glad solely on his own account, because Randy was his friend; but seeing Andie's joy magnified his own somehow. He had a hunch it was better not to analyze why.

Bill yawned once more and laughed at himself. Now he had a hunch he'd better finish this shower before he fell asleep on his feet and drowned.

Hastily, he rinsed away the soap, stepped out and dried off. Then he slipped into a pair of pajama pants, padded out of the bathroom and crawled straight into bed.

His eyelids had just closed when a disembodied voice pierced the darkness.

"Bill?"

"Hmm?"

"Are you asleep?"

"Obviously not. What is it?"

"He didn't look too bad, did he? His face won't be scarred or anything, will it?"

"I wouldn't think so," Bill replied. "He was pretty banged up, but none of the injuries looked severe. Give him a month and he'll be the same old handsome Randy he's always been, pursued by all the girls."

He heard Andie giggle. "I hope so. Oh, we forgot to tell him about the one Sara mentioned. Lisa somebody."

"We'll tell him tomorrow," Bill said.

"Right. Well...good night."

"Night."

Silence fell over the room. Bill stretched out full length, relaxed and expelled a long sigh. The bed was extraordinarily comfortable. Given half a chance, he could probably sleep straight through for a week.

A tiny sound disturbed the peaceful blackness, and then Andie's voice floated toward him once more. "Do you think Randy was just drowsy from the medication, or could it have been something more serious? After all, the doctor said he might have suffered a slight concussion."

"It's just the medication," Bill assured her. "Stop worrying and go to sleep."

"You're right. Night, again."

"Good night, Andie."

Bill turned over on his side and burrowed deep beneath the covers. His body heat was warming the bed, and a delicious languor was stealing over him. He suspended all thought, drifting down, down...

A loud whisper came from the doorway. "Are you still awake?"

Bill sighed and gave up. He opened his eyes, flung back the covers and got up. He crossed the room and, with unerring instinct, reached out through the darkness, clasped his fingers around Andie's arm and forcibly led her toward the bed.

"What're you doing?" she asked, sounding startled.

"I'm putting you to bed, Jack-in-the-Box." At the edge of it, he ordered, "In you go."

"No. I don't think—"

"Stop thinking and just get in," Bill told her. "If you don't, I'll put you there myself. It's the only way either one of us is going to get any sleep tonight."

"I promise I won't come back to bother you anymore," Andie said. "I'll go back—"

"I . . .said . . .get . . .in . . .the . . .bed!"

His frustration and fast-fading patience must have gotten through to her. Andie hesitated half a moment more and then capitulated. Bill crawled in beside her and pulled the covers over them. Then, without a word, he wrapped his arms around her and drew her close. She felt soft and cuddly in her silky nightgown, and tired as he was, his senses appreciated the sweet, clean scent of her. He pressed his cheek to her hair.

"Bill?" Andie's voice was muffled.

"What now?" He sighed wearily.

"This . . .this wasn't what I was after," she said thickly. She wriggled, trying to free herself from the intimate contact with him.

Bill refused to let her go, but his voice had a cutting edge to it when he said, "Don't you think I know that? I'm well aware that you don't want me. You've made it plain enough that I hold no great charm for you. If I had, you wouldn't have kept running away from me and from our marriage the way you did. Now relax. I know you're just tense and keyed up. Neither of us has had much sleep lately, and sometimes it's just good to have the warmth of another human being beside you."

It *was* good, and Andrea was grateful that Bill understood. In the other room she'd felt cold, restless, wideawake. Now she felt snug and warm and comforted.

Nevertheless, Bill's comment disturbed her, and she couldn't just let it pass. "I appreciate your understanding," she said softly. "And your thoughtfulness. But there's one thing you're wrong about."

"What's that?"

"I always did find you charming. There was nothing wrong with you or our marriage, Bill. Don't ever think that. It was my fault. The lack was in me."

"It doesn't matter anymore, Andie," Bill murmured. "It stopped mattering a long time ago. So let's get some sleep now, okay?"

Andrea felt unaccountably hurt. Didn't it matter to him? On reflection, she realized that if it was true, if none of it still mattered to him, she had no one to blame but herself. She'd been a poor excuse for a wife. She'd been too afraid.

But Bill couldn't know that. She'd been scrupulously careful to hide that side of herself beneath a layer of selfish independence.

Chapter Six

Andrea awoke wrapped in a cocoon of warmth, with an inner sense of well-being. At first she questioned such contentment, since it was far from the norm. Then she remembered.

Randy was safe. Alive and safe, thank God. And so was she, nestled here in Bill's arms.

She knew she ought to fight the seduction of this pleasure. The comforting security of having Bill's body cuddled next to hers was a treacherous lie—an insidious threat to her peace of mind, and to the independence she had achieved for herself these past three years.

Yet she found herself not wanting to fight it. It felt so wonderful to be curled within the arc of his body, to feel the weight of his arm draped across her hip, to experience his soft breath against the sensitive flesh of her neck. Every fiber of her being was alert and tingling. Andrea smiled to herself. If she were a cat, she thought, she would be purring.

At the time she'd left Bill, it had seemed to make sense; but now, in this still moment of an early morning, she was less convinced. All her life people had dumped her—her parents, various relatives, even school friends, as children will. Everyone she'd ever cared about except Randy. And with Bill, she'd expected the same.

When Bill had first proposed marriage, Andrea had been reluctant to accept. After observing her mother's numerous marriages and her father's two, she scarcely saw much point in it. In today's throw-away world, marriages were disposed of as easily as cellophane wrapping from a grocery store package. Going through the formality of a wedding ceremony seemed futile. Nothing was sacred anymore, nothing was forever, so why bother?

Yet she'd married Bill anyway. She'd even endured all the hoopla that accompanied a large, fancy wedding—because he'd wanted it, and because she'd been hopelessly in love with him.

But as so often happens, the passion and delight of the early months had gradually deteriorated as daily problems and disagreements surfaced. Only a few short months after the wedding, Bill's father had died unexpectedly. Bill had sunk into an understandable period of mourning, and Andrea had done her best to be supportive and loving. At the same time, the magnitude of his new responsibilities as the head of a large enterprise had rested heavily on his shoulders. Through no fault of his own, he was suddenly confronted with duties that demanded endless amounts of time and energy. There had been precious little left over for a bride.

Though she hadn't thought so at the time, Andrea wondered now if that hadn't contributed significantly to her sense of insecurity. Whatever the underlying causes, their marriage had soon turned stormy.

Within a month of Bill's assuming the title of publisher at the *Patriot*, Andrea had handed in her resignation. Bill had thought it foolish of her, but even in that brief period of time, her relationship with her co-workers had changed. Before, she'd just been one of the gang, like Randy, even if she had been married to the boss's son. But once she was the boss's wife, there was suddenly a wariness, a diffidence that hadn't been apparent in the past. Her colleagues were still friendly, but a little reserved as well. That was when she'd known she had to leave, for everyone's sake. Also, she'd realized that if she were to continue getting critical acclaim for her work as a professional writer, it had to be independently of her husband's newspaper. Otherwise, the taint of nepotism would forever cling to her.

She began to travel, gathering research for articles and books. This had caused even more trouble between herself and Bill. He hadn't understood her need to go so far afield, to spend so much time apart from him, and Andrea had never had the courage to enlighten him. She was serious about her work, of course, but it had been more than that. In all her life, she'd rarely spent more than two or three months in any one place except boarding school, and even then there'd been holiday trips away. For as long as she could remember, she and Randy had been accomplished world travelers, flitting from place to place to meet parents or other relatives, going to or from their current schools. It was an integral part of life for her. Andrea had therefore felt the need to put some distance between herself and Bill before he grew tired of her the way others always had. She'd believed that the separations would keep their love alive.

She couldn't have been more mistaken. Bill had bitterly resented her travels. As a result, when she had been home they'd spent more time quarreling than ever before. Finally, he'd issued an ultimatum—stay home and be a wife, or call it quits.

The rest was history.

Dwelling on that period of extreme unhappiness was self-defeating, however. Especially now that Bill seemed to be awakening. She'd just heard him sigh softly, and now his lips were moving, warm and soft with sleep against her ear.

She lay within the confines of his embrace as electrifying sensations shot through her. His lips traveled to one exposed shoulder, and his hand, which had been relaxed against her rib cage, slid upward to her breast. If she dared to let herself respond, she might not be able to stop.

"You always did taste good," Bill murmured drowsily as his mouth sought her throat again. "Sweet, like honey."

"Maybe we ought to put you on a no-sugar diet," Andrea countered swiftly.

Bill growled and pulled her over so that she lay on her back. Then he propped himself up on one elbow so that he could look down at her.

"What? Are you insinuating that I'm overweight?" he asked with a scowl.

Andrea's eyes betrayed her determination to stay in control of herself. Slowly she scanned the breadth of the golden chest hovering above her. Lean and rockhard; there wasn't an ounce of spare flesh covering the superbly developed muscles. Crisp, black wisps of hair swirled down the center, drawing her gaze in spite of herself.

"Don't be silly," she chided at last. "It's only that the temptation of sweets should usually be resisted."

"It's awfully hard to do," Bill said thoughtfully as his gaze left her face and descended to the swell of her breasts, "when the delectable dessert is so easily within reach."

As he spoke, his finger traced the top of the lace-edged bodice of her gown, tantalizing her as it ever-so-lightly brushed against her breast.

Andrea's mouth went dry. If he kept it up, she knew that this time she would be lost. "I think—" she tried to sound firm and decisive "—I'd better remove the temptation."

She made a move to get up but abruptly found herself a prisoner between the bars of Bill's strong arms. Andrea lifted her gaze to his face and saw a resolve and determination far stronger than she'd been able to muster. And desire. Blazing, compelling desire. His eyes smoldered with a disturbing intensity.

"Bill," she croaked from a scratchy throat, "you know we decided not to—"

His mouth silenced her. It was a forceful kiss, aggressive and demanding. Andrea's lips parted beneath its powerful insistence, and their tongues met in wild excitement.

Bill's arms slid beneath her, lifting her to him, crushing her breasts to his chest while his hands caressed her back and followed the flaring contour of her hips.

Flushed with the strong surge of emotions that were overtaking her, Andrea clasped her arms around his neck. She was tired of resolve, of trying to be strong. It had been so long, so terribly long, and she was heartily sick of deprivation. Bill was here; she was in his arms and he wanted her.

As though he sensed her capitulation, Bill lifted his head and the corners of his mouth curved into a devilish grin. "Well," he said, "go ahead and get out of bed. Isn't that what you want to do?"

It was a ridiculous question, and one to which he already knew the answer. Andrea's body was on fire, burning with the need he had aroused in her.

"Damn you, Bill Sheridan!" she snapped in a spurt of angry indignation. "How dare you do this to me and then mock me!"

Bill laughed softly and swooped down to plant an impertinent kiss on the tip of her nose. His lips came to the edge of her mouth and he murmured, "Are you saying you'd rather stay?"

"You're a rat, you know that?" she grumbled while her fingers crept up of their own accord to wind through his dark hair.

"I may be a rat," he conceded genially, "but at least I'm a rat that knows what it wants. Do you?"

Their eyes met, and his gaze was piercing as it questioned her.

Andrea sighed and nodded. "I know I shouldn't anymore, not after all this time, but heaven help me, I want you, Bill. I want you to make love to me."

"Why?" His voice was soft and low.

Andrea smiled, and this time it was her turn to tease. She shrugged. "Because I like your blue eyes."

Bill's lips quirked. "What else?"

She pretended to think about it. "Because your birthday is in August?"

Bill chuckled. "What else?"

"Oh, I know! Because your middle name is Frederick. I've always been partial to men called Freddie-e-e-e-e!" She was suddenly being tickled in the ribs and tried desperately to free herself from the assault. "I take it back!" she gasped.

"Promise?"

"Promise."

"All right," he said grimly. "The truth."

"Because you're the sexiest man I ever met, and you're a great lover!"

"That's more like it." Bill grinned. "Even if you don't mean it."

Andrea was suddenly serious, and her voice was thick and unsteady as she whispered, "Oh, but I do. I mean every word."

"Ah, Andie." Bill sighed. "You always did go from one extreme to the other, casting me down, then building me up. I never have known what to believe about how you really felt about me."

"Didn't you?" she asked in genuine surprise. "I loved you. Right up to the bitter end and beyond."

"And I loved you," he said sadly. "So why didn't we make it together?"

Andrea shook her head. "I don't know. Maybe sometimes love just isn't enough."

"Maybe we should have tried harder."

"Maybe." Andrea gazed at him soberly. "It was all a long time ago, Bill."

"You're right. We can't go back. But we have now, don't we?" His finger stroked her cheek, and then he drew her close again. "And you're more beautiful and more desirable than ever. I've missed you, Andie."

Moments later, freed from the restriction of clothing, they embraced and kissed again with tremulous fervor. Bill molded Andrea's soft curves to the hard, angular form of his body, and she fitted perfectly to it as she had before. He soon lost all coherent thought as he inhaled the sweet, enticing scent of her. He touched her in places that he knew would pleasure her, and his heart raced as she gasped and trembled with growing tension.

His own body ached with painful urgency, but he fought for restraint. Beads of perspiration dampened his brow as he aroused her at a deliberately slow, measured pace.

She whimpered as his mouth teased the hardened nipples of her breasts, and his own excitement mounted. He could feel blood sizzling through his head as the pressure increased, but he continued to take his time, reveling in the intimate exploration of her body, thrilling to the magic of touching her.

Andrea writhed in a frenzy of desperation as Bill's tongue and lips tortured her unmercifully. In retribution, she tortured him, too. She nibbled at his earlobe, at his shoulder, and her hands raked his chest and back and hips.

Their breathing grew raspy and erratic, their bodies feverish and moist as their passion rose unchecked. Still, they did not seek relief but continued to climb toward the peak of insatiable stimulation.

All barriers were down. Their lovemaking had always been uninhibited, but nothing like the torrid emotions that they elicited in each other now. They felt completely free, each lavishly bestowing the gift of ardor upon the other. He affirmed her femininity with generous, wordless praise; she paid tribute to his virility by the adoration of her touch.

Finally, Bill could withstand the exquisite agony no longer, and he moved his body over Andrea's. Her green eyes glowed with a light that bemused him. Then she smiled and received him into her, where all was warm and welcoming.

He buried his face in her hair as they began to move in unison. He thought that he had never cherished her as much as he did in this moment. Their troubles together and the years apart faded away as their passion exploded in a burst of fireworks.

As Andrea floated down from the enchanted mountaintop, she heard Bill's heart thudding. Or was it her own? One last rapturous shudder coursed through her as she clung to him, holding him close, holding him still. She never wanted to let him go.

Yet it had to be. They had become one for a joyous moment, but now they were two, different bodies, separate entities. As Bill moved away, Andrea felt her flesh chill.

Bill saw her shiver, and he pulled up the covers and tucked them gently around her.

"I never should have let you go," he told her softly.

Andrea shook her head. "You couldn't have stopped me," she answered.

"But why, Andie? When we have something like this together, even now? Why did you leave me?"

She shook her head again, not wanting to talk about it, not wanting to think about it. "I doubt if I could explain it. Sometimes I'm not even sure I understood myself then. Or if I understand now." She smiled and touched his chin with her index finger. "There's a scratch. Did I do that to you?"

Bill grabbed the finger and gave it a little shake. "I wouldn't doubt it. I probably have battle scars all over me." He grinned. "You were a tigress, Mrs. Sheridan. Or is it Ms.?"

Andrea's eyes twinkled. "I generally answer to either. Even to 'Hey, you.'"

Bill kissed the finger he still held. "Hey, you, Mrs. Sheridan, want to take a shower with me like old times?"

"Hmm. That does sound tempting," Andrea admitted. "But we do have other things to do today. What time is it?"

Bill rolled over to reach for his watch on the bedside table, and Andrea was unable to resist running her hand over his smooth, gleaming back.

Bill groaned. "You're not going to like this," he stated. "I can't believe we slept so late. It's ten after ten."

"Honest?" Andrea was stunned.

"Yep." Bill turned toward her and reached out to cup her breast. "Does this mean I don't get my back massage in the shower?" he asked, pouting.

"Now don't go giving me your sad-eyed Saint Bernard look!" Andrea said smartly. "You know we don't have time for that. We'd never get out of this room!"

For a brief time they gazed at each other, lost in the delightful memory of days when there had been time, when they'd taken long, luxurious showers together, played friskily like a couple of fun-loving seals, before they'd finally ended up back in bed for still more lovemaking.

"Sounds all right to me," Bill declared, a wicked gleam in his eyes.

Andrea tilted her head to one side. "And Randy?"

Bill shrugged and grinned. "He's probably flirting with all the nurses anyhow and won't even realize it if we don't show up."

"Silly!" Andrea scooted out of bed, then turned back to shake a finger at Bill and say sternly, "Get a move on, man! We've got places to go and people to see."

Bill's eyes were frankly scanning her nude form, and admiration blazed in their azure depths. "It ought to be against the law to have a body like yours," he murmured suggestively. "It's certainly given me many a sleepless night."

Andrea laughed at him. "And a few mornings like this when nothing else got accomplished."

"You've decided to be sensible, then!" Bill exclaimed. He unfurled his long limbs from beneath the covers and got to his feet.

"What do you mean?" Andrea asked. The sight of his tall, lean body as he strode toward her was electrifying. She could no more help appreciating it than she could stop being a woman. He was sleek and smooth, and superbly proportioned.

"About the shower," he said. His voice brought her back to the discussion at hand. "And going back to bed. We can still see Randy this afternoon. He's not going anywhere."

He reached for her, but Andrea waltzed away from him, toward the door. "Don't be greedy," she chided. "That was always a weakness of yours."

"Sez you!" Bill grabbed her nightgown from the foot of the bed and tossed it to her. "When you parade around looking like that, what do you expect me to do? Pretend you're my sister?"

Andrea giggled at his ferocious scowl. "Speaking of siblings," she said, "I still have a brother who's expecting us. He *is* the reason we're here, you know." Without waiting for a reply, she turned and vanished through the door.

Bill sighed, shook his head and went to take his solitary shower.

By the time they met again, fully dressed and in the neutral atmosphere of the sitting room, Andrea's mood had altered. Bill picked up on it immediately. She was strangely unwilling to meet his eyes and uncharacteristically talkative.

Instead of looking at him as she shrugged on her coat over a red sweater and black slacks, she went to peer out the window. "It looks like rain. I didn't think to bring along an umbrella or a raincoat, did you?" Before he even had an opportunity to reply, she turned, picked up her purse from the sofa and added, "I've been thinking. Since Randy's suitcase burned in the accident, he doesn't have any clothes. If you don't mind, I thought that before we go to the hospital we could find a shopping mall and pick up some things for him. I've made a list," she went on as she fished inside her purse. "I know it's here somewhere." When she couldn't find it, she rattled on, "Oh, well, I remember most of it. I know he'll need a set of clothes and a pair of shoes for when he's released, pajamas and a robe; oh, and shaving gear, of course. I wonder if we ought to stop at a bookstore and pick him up some reading material, while we're at it. And maybe some candy. Can you think of anything I forgot?"

"What's the matter?" Bill asked quietly.

"Why, nothing!"

"Then why are you so nervous?"

Andrea's laughter trilled across the room, high-pitched and quavering. Briefly, her gaze swept across his face, then flitted away again. "That's ridiculous," she declared. "Why on earth would I be nervous?"

"That's what I'd like to know." Bill crossed the room and clasped her forearms. "Look at me, Andie. What's wrong?"

Andrea tossed her head back in a defiant gesture, and her golden-red curls bounced saucily around her face. Her smile was brittle and forced. "What could possibly be wrong?" she countered.

"That's what I'd like to know," Bill said grimly.

"You're imagining things, Bill." Andrea squirmed free of his hands, as though she couldn't bear to have him touch her, and asked hastily, "Don't you think it's time for us to go?"

Bill's eyes narrowed as his arms dropped to his sides. "No," he snapped. "I don't. Not until you tell me what's happened in the last half hour to make you change toward me? You're acting like I'm a stranger to you."

"Of course I'm not!" But again, she wouldn't look at him. She moved toward the door. "Please, Bill, let's go. It's terribly late."

Bill stood perfectly still. "You don't regret what happened between us, do you?" he asked incredulously.

Andrea went still, too, and her head bowed. Slowly, she nodded, and her voice was soft and unsteady. "Yes," she replied. "I do."

In three strides, Bill was beside her. This time he cupped her face between his hands and gently lifted it until her glittering eyes were forced to meet his. "You don't mean that!"

"Bill, it was wonderful. I'll admit that. But I just wish it hadn't happened, that's all."

"Mind telling me why?" Bill's voice went hard and cold as ice, and his hands left her face.

"Please," she begged. "Can't we just drop it?"

"Sure," he said, suddenly angry. "Sure, we'll drop it. Maybe that's best. I doubt if I'd care to hear the explanation, anyway." He grabbed his own coat and thrust his arms into it. "You're obviously a different person than the one I used to know. That Andrea had her faults and her hang-ups, but at least she had a healthy attitude toward sex. She didn't turn a good thing around and muck it up into something bad."

"I'm not doing that now!" Andrea protested hotly.

"Aren't you?"

"No!" She inhaled deeply. "Oh, Bill, I just believe it would be a whole lot better for both of us if it hadn't happened. We've been divorced for three years! We're different people with different lives now. This..." Wildly she waved a hand toward the bedroom. "This was just an isolated incident, purely physical, and all it's done is to stir up old memories. And what good is dredging up the past?"

"None at all that I can see," Bill said in a hard, clipped voice. "Mostly it just brings back things I'd rather not remember."

"You see? I'm right."

"No, damn it," Bill said savagely. "You're not right. This is now, today, not the past. It was good between us, Andie, and you were just as happy as I was. We still care about each other and we showed it. What's wrong with that? We didn't hurt anybody; we're not being unfaithful to anyone." His gaze became sharp and piercing as his heart sank. Suddenly he felt sick. "At least I'm not," he said slowly. "Is that what this is all about? Are you involved with someone?"

Andrea shook her head. "No. There's no one. Otherwise, I would have never—Anyway," she went on swiftly, "that's not the point. Can't you see? Like you just said, we do still care about each other. In spite of the quarrels we had, we've got some fond memories of the past, too, or we wouldn't still be able to care at all. And that's where the danger is."

"Danger?" Bill was almost amused. He was so relieved to know there was no other man in the picture that he was scarcely even listening to the rest of it.

Andrea saw the glimmer of amusement and was instantly furious...and hurt. "Maybe not to you," she said unsteadily. "I can see you think it's all a joke. But it's not to me."

Bill was contrite. Placing his hands on her shoulders, he said gently, "It's no joke to me, either. But darling, your usually astute thinking appears a bit muddled to me. I'm sorry, but I honestly can't see this danger you're talking about."

"Obviously," she said unhappily. "Let's—let's just forget it." Once again she tried to free herself from his touch.

Bill refused to let her go. "Okay," he finally conceded. "I see your point. You're afraid we'll get emotionally entangled again, aren't you?" Andrea nodded mutely, and he went cold inside. Cold and empty. His voice hardened. "Look, it happened. We can't undo it. I realize I took advantage and I shouldn't have. You were still feeling vulnerable and unnerved, and I was there. It was only a reaction to the strain we've both been under. So leave it at that, why don't you? Believe me, I'm not reading anything into it that you don't want, so stop making such a big deal of it. Now," he added harshly, "let's get the hell out of here. I need some fresh air."

Andrea was hurt by his words. From then on, while they ate a late breakfast and afterward picked up the things Randy needed, she felt shut out. Bill was civil, but she was aware of a distance between them. A wall had been built, and they were on opposite sides.

Yet she'd begun constructing it first, so she could hardly blame Bill for completing it. They *had* been happy earlier. There had been tenderness, then untamed, exuberant passion and finally playful, affectionate teasing. Just like old times...yet new and exciting.

Only when she'd returned to her own, unused bedroom to dress had she realized the enormity of what had occurred. She'd grown miserable and confused when she'd realized that in the end there was no place to go—except back where she belonged. Alone.

When they arrived at the hospital, they found Randy sitting up in bed, balefully eyeing the TV. "'Bout time you got here," he grumbled. "I thought you'd abandoned me to the soaps." He pressed the button on the remote control and the screen went blank.

"We were busy," Andrea said, depositing packages at his feet. "How are you today?" she asked as she kissed his cheek. "Besides irritable, that is?"

"Fair." Randy's eyes were emerald-bright and alert today. He watched Bill deposit more packages on the bed and said, "I hope there's some pajamas in one of those bags. These hospital gowns are downright indecent!"

Bill chuckled. "The better for them to stick needles in your backside. Do they at least send a cute young nurse to do it?"

Randy grimaced. "They did, and I refused to let her near me. They finally sent a grandmotherly type to do it."

Andrea and Bill hooted with laughter. "I didn't realize you had such deep-seated modesty," Andrea sputtered.

"Neither did I." Bill's grin was broad. "All this time I thought you were a sexy charmer with all the girls."

"Lay off!" Randy snapped. "It's pretty hard to be charming and sexy when you're exposed for all the world to see!"

Andrea plopped down on the edge of the bed. "Has the doctor been in?"

"Not yet." Randy reclined against the pillows. "Unless I missed him. I've been down in the X-ray department most of the morning. I keep getting these spasms in my right foot. Yesterday they were more concerned with my ribs and lungs, so they're just now getting around to checking it out."

"Do you think it's broken?" Andrea asked anxiously.

"I sure hope not," Randy said fervently.

"How are the ribs?" Bill asked.

Randy winced. "Painful. They've got me bandaged up so tight I can hardly move." He grinned suddenly, flashing the winsome smile that so effortlessly brought him friends. "Still," he added, "I'm among the living, so I'm not complaining too much."

"Except for exposure, eh?" Andrea teased. But her throat tightened as she patted him on the arm. "I agree wholeheartedly," she said huskily. "Even banged up as you are, you're still the best-looking sight in the world to me."

"Hey," Randy chided softly. "Now don't get weepy, Andie. I thought I taught you how to be tough a long time ago."

Andrea blinked rapidly and said, sniffling. "I am tough...and I'm *not* weepy!" But she turned toward the window and was grateful when Bill began to talk in a matter-of-fact tone, covering her momentary weakness.

"When they spring you from here," he said to Randy, "I want you to take a couple of months off from work. You can rest up and recuperate out at that farm you're so nuts about."

"Thanks, Bill. That sounds great." Randy shifted slightly, and a spasm of pain crossed his face. "Although I guess I won't be able to enjoy being there as much as usual. I can't see myself accomplishing much anytime soon."

"Nonsense. You'll be back to normal before you know it," Bill said briskly.

"Feel like opening your gifts now?" Andrea asked. The gaily wrapped packages they'd brought last night were still on the window ledge.

"Might as well," Randy said. "Let's see what you brought, too."

The gifts from his colleagues cheered Randy immensely. There was candy, of course; an outrageous pair of pajamas with Christmas bells, Santa Claus faces, teddy bears and dolls sprinkled all over them; a bottle of fine whiskey, which brought an appreciative grin to his face; and a comical vinyl inflatable in the shape of a well-endowed young woman wearing a bikini.

Next he opened the packages that Bill and Andrea had brought. He pounced on a pair of subdued blue pajamas and said, "Make yourself scarce for a while, will you, Andie? I want to change into these right now."

"I think you should wear the Santa ones," she teased. "Get into the spirit of the season early and all."

Randy grinned. "You would. No, I think I'll save them for the farm. And total privacy. Now be a good kid and get lost."

Andrea picked up her purse. "Okay. I'll go down to the coffee shop. Want me to bring some back for you?"

"Sounds good," Randy said.

Andrea looked at Bill. He nodded and said more formally, "If you don't mind."

It made her want to scream at him. Mind bringing him a lousy cup of coffee after all he'd done for her these last few days? He had to know better than that!

But the closeness of those days was over now, brought to an abrupt halt because they'd overstepped the bounds of two people merely pulling together through a crisis. Because she couldn't handle the emotional baggage of a casual fling with her ex-husband.

Downstairs, she lingered over her coffee, giving Randy plenty of time to change. The solitude also gave her a breather from Bill's constant, disturbing presence. Finally she knew she'd been gone long enough, so she bought two more cups of coffee and headed toward the elevator.

On Randy's floor, she stopped at the nurses' station to ask if they knew when Dr. Ross would be coming to check on him.

"Probably after lunch," the nurse said. "He was in earlier, but Mr. Wade was in X-ray. Oh," she added as Andrea was turning away, "while he was in X-ray, there was a long-distance call for him. She asked to speak to one of us since he wasn't available, and we told her he was doing fine. We haven't had time to give him the message yet, so would you do it?" She held out a scrap of paper. "Here's her name."

Andrea looked at it. Lisa Weber. The same girl Sara said had called the newspaper.

When she got back to the room, Bill was at the window, peering out. Randy, now neatly and modestly attired in navy-blue pajamas, was propped up in bed, talking on the telephone.

Andrea handed him his coffee, then carried the other to Bill.

"Thanks," Bill said as he accepted it. "That's your mother on the phone."

"Oh."

Bill grinned. It was the first genuinely sharing moment between them since they'd left the hotel. "From Randy's comments, I gather she's offering a long-winded explanation about why she can't rush to his bedside."

"Of course." Ruefully, Andrea grinned back. "She's terribly disappointed, but . . ." There was no need to finish the sentence.

When her brother was off the phone, Andrea wrinkled her nose at him. "Well?"

Randy's mouth twisted with derision. "You know how it is," he said. "She's so dreadfully busy with such dreadfully important people and since I'm not dreadfully half-dead and don't really *need* . . ." He shrugged.

Andrea didn't want him to fall into the same depression that she had had over their mother's lack of maternal concern, so she offered him the piece of paper the nurse had given her and said hastily, "Never mind. A nurse just gave this to me. While you were being X-rayed, a girl named Lisa Weber called and asked about you. Sara told Bill and me that while you were missing she also called the paper several times to get news. Who is she, Randy? Do you want me to call her back, since she seems so anxious about you?"

Randy's scratched, bruised face brightened. His pleasure was unmistakable. "Lisa called? I wanted to talk to her this morning, but I haven't been alone long enough to do it. She lives a couple of miles from the farm, and for the past four months we've been seeing each other every weekend that I've been down there. She's terrific, Andie. As a matter of fact," he confided, "I'm crazy about her. I'm hoping you'll get to meet her soon."

Andrea grinned. "Then I take it you'll return her call yourself?"

Randy nodded, and his grin was infectious. "You bet! This minute, if you two'll get out of here for about half an hour."

Andrea pretended to pout over being kicked out of his room twice in one hour, but her brother wasn't even paying attention. He was already dialing.

At the time, Andrea hadn't really minded; in fact, she'd been pleased that her brother wanted to have an intimate conversation with his girl. What could be more natural, what could better indicate that he was getting back to normal? It was only later that afternoon, when she and Bill were with Randy again, discussing his release from the hospital, that her feelings toward the person named Lisa developed into sullen resentment.

Dr. Ross had stopped in to announce that the X-rays showed his foot to be only bruised, not broken; furthermore, Randy's lungs were responding nicely to treatment. If all went well, said Dr. Ross, he'd be released the day after tomorrow. Randy was ecstatic.

"I'll charter another plane back to Washington," Bill promised. "We'll stop by your apartment to pick up your clothes, and then I'll drive you down to the farm."

"Thanks, friend," Randy said. "You're being awfully good to me, considering how I smashed up your plane."

Bill smiled. "Just say you owe me one," he said lightly.

Randy's face became serious. "I know it."

Bill punched his shoulder in a playful gesture. "You know I was only kidding," he said gruffly. "Forget it."

After a moment, Randy nodded. Then he glanced at Andrea. "Don't you need to get back to London to finish that documentary?"

Andrea sighed. "Yes," she said regretfully. "I do. And now that Dr. Ross says you're out of the woods, I think I ought to go tomorrow. But I hate to leave when you'll be needing someone to stay with you at the farm. I've been thinking. Surely I can hire someone to stay there until I get back and can take over the job myself. I'll call one of the employment agencies in Washington and—"

Randy shook his head and interrupted her. "Not necessary, sis. Or your coming to stay, either. Lisa's going to do it." His eyes twinkled and danced. "And with her brand of kiss-it-better treatment, I'm bound to heal fast."

Bill laughed with him. Andrea plastered a smile on her lips, but inside she felt an unexpected pain that shot through her like a thousand burning needles. Incredible as it seemed, her twin, the dearest person in her life, suddenly didn't need her, didn't even want her! It was such a blow that she reeled beneath its impact.

Somehow, she was able to keep her feelings concealed. Randy, usually so perceptive where she was concerned, missed it entirely as he continued to favor them with praises of Lisa.

By the time she and Bill left the hospital, Andrea's head was throbbing as she seethed with animosity toward the girl.

"Lisa, Lisa, Lisa!" she blurted out to Bill once they were back in their hotel suite. "What a paragon she is! I tell you, if Randy had said one more thing about how incomparable she is, I would've been sick!"

Bill looked at her with mild surprise. "What's eating you?" he asked. "I'd think you'd be happy he's so happy, especially after all he's just gone through!"

"Of course I'm glad," Andrea croaked. "But I don't care to be bored silly by a comprehensive list of all her virtues! Just tell me, how much do *you* care whether she cooks like an angel, won a jillion or two awards in high school for her prowess as a basketball player, or donates half her time to being kind to old folks and animals and performs assorted other good deeds?"

Bill's eyes narrowed. "You're jealous!" he declared.

"I am not!" Andrea's denial was hot and vehement.

"Oh, yes, you are! Until now Randy used to change girl-friends almost as often as he changed his socks, and he certainly didn't talk about them with such unbridled enthusiasm, so you never felt threatened. But now you do. All of a sudden you find that you're not the only important female in his life, and you can't tolerate that!" Bill's gaze was filled with contempt. "Your love for your brother has become possessive, Andie. That's ugly, and it's downright unhealthy as well!"

"That's not true!" Andrea cried. "We've never been possessive of each other, and you know it! That's a rotten thing to say!"

"Then what's the problem?" Bill prodded relentlessly. "Surely you knew it was inevitable that someday Randy would find someone of his own. It's a basic law of human nature. But that doesn't mean he's going to stop loving you. It's just that when he finds the right woman, whether it's this Lisa or someone else, he's bound to turn to her, to start needing her more and needing you less, simply because it's a different sort of love."

"Don't you dare patronize me!" Andrea snapped. "Don't you dare! Of course I'm not jealous of his girlfriend . . .or of his love for her, if that's what it really is! It's just that he's been through a traumatic time and I ought to be the one to be with him, to take care of him and see that he's all right, not somebody he's only known a few months! He...he—'' Her voice broke as the pain spilled over. "He's shutting me out!" She turned quickly and, with her eyes blinded by tears, stumbled toward her bedroom.

She shut the door and leaned against it, fighting the tears. Bill had hit upon the truth, damn him! Now, in private, she admitted to herself that she was jealous. And part of the pain she felt was a deep shame for the emotion that ravaged her.

Without warning she had been abruptly replaced in her brother's affections, shunted aside like last year's cast-off clothing, and it hurt. Oh, God, it hurt!

Randy was the only person who'd always given her love, esteem and a loyal friendship without qualification. And she'd given it back to him. Though other people had come and gone, they'd always had each other, and that underlying security had kept her afloat on the rough seas of life. No matter how transient others might have been, she'd been able to count on him.

Andrea knew she was being unreasonable over this, that she shouldn't feel rejected and abandoned just because her brother cared for someone other than herself. But she did.

Moreover, she hated Bill for seeing through her.

Chapter Seven

This first Saturday in December, Harrod's was packed with Christmas shoppers. Andrea jostled through the milling crowd, taking advantage of an unexpected free afternoon by picking up her own gifts. They included a lovely cashmere sweater for Randy, a crystal vase that the store would ship to her mother, men's cologne for her co-workers and silk scarves for a few women friends.

She'd been back in London for two full working days. This morning Andrea was supposed to have interviewed a young coal miner and his wife, but a family crisis had delayed the couple's journey from the north until tomorrow.

The last two days had been draining, with long hours of work to make up for the time Andrea had been away. Everyone was tired and anxious to finish the project and return home. Tempers had frayed and patience and tact had been discarded. By this morning, when word had come that their taping would have to be delayed for a day, scarcely any of the crew was speaking to each other except by necessity. Andrea had been no better than the rest. Thus, with an un-anticipated day off, she'd decided to get away from the hotel and everyone else for a few hours.

The truth was that she hadn't recovered her good humor since the afternoon Randy had chosen his girlfriend Lisa to play nursemaid instead of his twin sister. She was still deeply hurt over that, though pride had kept her from revealing her feelings to him before she'd left Atlanta.

Worse even than the pain over Randy's unexpected betrayal was the mental turmoil where Bill was concerned. Though she'd been working hard and with a frantic intensity the past couple of days, thoughts of him kept haunting her, disturbing her by day, torturing her by night.

But she didn't want to think about Bill right now, any more than she wanted to think about work or Randy. Though her shopping was basically done, she was reluctant to return to the hotel, so she wandered into the food department of the famous store. Maybe, she thought vaguely, she'd buy some gift boxes of jams and have them shipped home. That sort of thing always made excellent last-minute gifts.

The crowd of shoppers was just as pressing here, but Andrea took it in stride. She was in no hurry. All that awaited her was a lonely hotel room or, even less appealing, the company of irritable coworkers.

Along one counter was a display of decorative cakes for just about any occasion. Andrea was amused by some of them. There was one shaped like a baby carriage, another that looked like a hamburger and even a huge crossword puzzle cake.

As she paused to admire a beautiful white heart-shaped cake that would be perfect for an engagement party, she heard someone calling her name.

"Andie Sheridan? Andie? That *is* you!"

Andrea looked over her shoulder and saw John Seevers shouldering his way through a sea of shoppers.

"Well, hi, John! Fancy meeting you in this crush!"

"Amazing, isn't it?" His face stretched into a warm smile. "I just wanted to tell you how happy we all were at the bureau when we learned your brother was safe."

Andrea nodded. "I was sorry I missed you when I stopped in to thank everyone for all the help we were given at this end. I especially appreciate the trouble you took on my account, John."

"Think nothing of it. That's what old friends are for." John eyed the green bags with gold letters that she carried and said, "I thought you were here to work. Looks like you're trying to buy out the store."

Andrea shrugged. "We got an unexpected day off, so I decided to get most of my Christmas shopping done while I had the chance. What about you? Is Lydia here with you? And the baby?"

John shook his head. "No, they're at home. The baby got two strollers exactly alike as gifts, and I came to return one. While I was here, I thought I'd pick up some of Lydia's favorite candy. Got to spoil the new mother a little, you know," he said with a sheepish grin.

"Well, don't sound apologetic about it," Andrea said. "I think it's nice. Be sure and give her my love, will you?"

"Why don't you do it yourself?" John suggested suddenly. "Since you're free for the day, why don't you come home with me? Lydia would love to have a chance to visit with you."

Andrea tilted her head and grinned. "You mean *you'd* love to have a chance to show off that new baby!"

John chuckled. "So, you saw through me! Well, how about it?"

"Why not?" Impulsively, Andrea decided it was exactly what she'd enjoy most. She'd always liked John and Lydia. Just because John worked for her former husband was no reason to curtail an old friendship. "But only if you call ahead and warn Lydia that I'm coming," she added.

"It's not necessary, but if that's what you want, I will."

"It is. Tell you what, I think I'll run upstairs to the baby department and buy your son a little gift while you get your candy and call home. I'll meet you outside in, say, half an hour?"

Lydia Seevers was a lovely English rose. Pale blond hair fluffed beguilingly about her gentle face. She welcomed Andrea warmly, and the two of them went immediately to the bedroom, where the baby lay in his crib.

Little Christopher Seevers was adorable, with dark hair like his father's and a creamy complexion like his mother's. His plump little arms and legs waved aimlessly in the air as his deep-blue innocent gaze fastened on the gold chain necklace that Andrea was wearing.

"What a sweetheart," Andrea said softly. "Lydia, I'm so happy for you and John."

"Thank you. Would you like to hold him?"

Andrea suddenly looked a little unsure of herself. "I'd like to, but I don't know if I'm very good at it. I've never had much to do with babies."

Lydia laughed at her. "It's not that hard." She leaned over the crib and picked up her child. "Come on back to the other room where you can sit down, and then I'll give him to you."

In the sitting room, Lydia motioned for Andrea to take the rocking chair. When she did, Lydia bent down and placed Christopher in her arms. "Just be sure his neck is supported at all times, that's all."

The moment the infant was in her arms, the strangest sensation came over Andrea. She felt quite soft inside, like a marshmallow. He was so cuddly and warm and smelled so sweet. His trusting gaze focused on her face, and Andrea experienced a strange, primitive feeling of protectiveness. Fiercely, earnestly, she wanted nothing bad ever to happen to this child. In but an instant, Christopher had stolen her heart.

For a time John and Lydia hovered nearby, smiling and accepting the congratulations that Andrea murmured. But as she became more and more mesmerized by the small wonder that she held within her arms, they left her alone and went to the kitchen to make tea.

Andrea was only vaguely aware that they had even gone, for she was utterly enthralled by the tiny creature who was squirming in her arms. She marveled at the perfection of his features—and looked in amazement as one small hand curled around her finger.

Is this what it's like to feel maternal love? she asked herself wonderingly. She was bewildered by the delight that spread through her as she held the infant's silky, puppy-warm body next to hers, the strange ecstasy she experienced as his soft, fuzzy head bobbed against her shoulder when she lifted him. Christopher made tiny gurgling noises of satisfaction, and Andrea found herself laughing gently. She couldn't help it.

Suddenly she understood how people, mostly new parents and grandparents, became so besotted over their babies. This was life, miraculous, glorious life at its finest. It was the thrilling, ultimate completion for two people in love, the creation together of a new and awesomely wonderful human being.

This was what she had denied herself and Bill. Guilt assailed her, and Andrea castigated herself harshly. *Selfish, selfish,* she mocked silently.

Bill had wanted children so much, so very much, and with blind, insensitive cruelty, she'd refused even to contemplate the notion. Blithely, she'd rattled off all the clichés to justify her selfishness—the horrible state of today's world, the threat of an even more dangerous tomorrow, the need to fulfill herself as a person in her own right, to have unlimited freedom to develop and grow in her career.

Not once had she told him the truth.

Christopher began to squirm and fuss. Andrea patted his back and murmured soothing words, but his complaints only grew louder and more insistent.

Lydia reappeared and Andrea was relieved. As she transferred the baby back to his mother, she grimaced ruefully. "I told you I didn't know what to do with babies. I think he knew it."

Lydia did some swift checking and grinned. "Not your fault. He just needs to be changed."

"Oh." Andrea had to laugh at her ignorance and inexperience. She hadn't even so much as thought of *that*!

While Lydia carried Christopher to the bedroom and John remained occupied in the kitchen, Andrea leaned back in the rocker and gazed idly about the room.

It was cheerfully eclectic. The sofa was a dusky rose chintz, with embroidered eggshell-white throw pillows. An oval glass table stood before it, enhanced by a potted chrysanthemum. A wide window opened onto the street, and the waning afternoon light spilled into the room, across a cushioned easy chair. On the walls were groups of framed photographs covering a variety of subjects: Christopher, of course, and John, the sea, an autumnal scene, the prime minister, a pink rose in full bloom, the queen. Lydia was an accomplished photographer.

John returned bearing a tray with the tea things. While he set it on the glass table, Andrea asked, "Does Lydia still do free-lance work for magazines?"

"Not since she became pregnant. She says she'll go back to work someday, but for the time being she wants to be a full-time mother."

"But all that talent!" Andrea burst out in protest.

John smiled. "I know. But she won't stop taking pictures. She'll just take most of them of Chris for a while, that's all."

"Won't she miss it, though? Her work? The challenge?"

"Mostly it's the money I'll miss," Lydia answered with a little laugh as she came back into the room. She sank down to the sofa next to John, who was pouring the tea. "It means it'll take us that much longer to get our home in the country, but we'll do it someday. Right now I feel my challenge is tied up in raising that little bundle of energy in the other room."

John handed Andrea her tea, and she thanked him before asking Lydia, "Aren't you afraid you'll start to feel...well, tied down, as though you're missing out on things?"

Lydia shrugged. "I don't think so. If I do, I'll hire someone to take care of Chris and go back to work, at least part-time. But for now I'm completely satisfied just the way things are. All I need to make me happy is my family."

Later that evening, when Andrea was back in her hotel room and dressed for bed, she remembered Lydia's comment and wondered if any woman, at least in this age of liberated career women, could truly be happy just staying at home and taking care of her family. Her own mother's "career" had been her jet-setting social life, and her family had always ranked last in order of importance. Bill's mother had been a career woman too, with her nursing. Yet from things he'd said, she'd also been a very loving and devoted parent.

Had Bill's mother been an exception? Was Lydia? Andrea was still not convinced that it worked out well in most cases. In her experience, women got too caught up in their own lives to care a whit about their children. They also got divorced, changing partners as easily as hairstyles, thus further eroding any sense of security for their children. Andrea had not wanted to bring a child into the world who would suffer that indifference and neglect. And because she hadn't felt confident enough in herself or her marriage, she'd made the decision never to have children.

All the same, remembering how it had felt to hold little Christopher in her arms, a deep sadness came over her. In a perfect world, her marriage would have been strong enough to survive, she and Bill would be proud parents of happy, well-adjusted children and they'd all be contentedly sharing a rambling, love-filled home in the suburbs, complete with dog and cat.

And they all lived happily ever after.

Andrea shook her head to clear away the cobwebs of fantasy and grimaced to herself in the mirror as she brushed her hair. She dropped the brush with a thud and headed for bed. She wouldn't be having foolish fairy-tale imaginings if she hadn't seen Bill again. If he hadn't been so wonderfully helpful to her when she'd been worried sick over Randy.

If they hadn't made love again.

That was the crux of her current restlessness, the strange underlying anxiety that had nagged at her night and day since she'd left Atlanta. That morning had brought to light a disturbing fact: She still had deep feelings for Bill. She'd managed to submerge them for three years beneath a layer of work and everyday concerns, but she could pretend no longer. After all this time, she wasn't over him. It was as simple as that.

All the same, her honesty with herself had its limits. She'd learned she still cared about Bill, more than was good for her, but she wasn't ready to acknowledge that she'd never stopped loving him. That would be too sad even to contemplate.

Andrea crawled beneath the covers and flipped off the light. But she couldn't so easily switch off her thoughts. They marched forward, a veritable parade of scenes from the past.

When they'd first been married, she and Bill had had such fun and enjoyed each other so much that nothing else had seemed to matter. Bill had laughed at her inept attempts to cook a meal, and he hadn't minded her aversion to domesticity. Oh, she'd cleaned their apartment, because she hated dirt and disorder, but she'd never been able to come up with the homey touches most women found so natural. To this day, a meal on a paper plate in front of the TV was as pleasurable to Andrea as a formal dinner.

In her own apartment, she didn't bother with decorative touches like potted plants or Oriental rugs. As long as the essentials were there, she was content. It was a waste of time, she felt, to spend endless hours shopping for just the right dress for a party or trying to match up drapery color to wallpaper. Nice, neutral things that didn't require any effort had always been her style. She favored blacks, whites, beiges, maybe a navy-blue on occasion, and her wardrobe was tailored and uncomplicated. These days, because she'd become something of a minor celebrity since her books and television documentaries, she bought more expensive clothes and had to take more pains with her appearance, but she still kept it as simple as possible.

Perhaps her lack of interest in such matters was a reaction to her mother's elaborate life-style, but Andrea couldn't bring herself to consider a hairdresser's appointment or a manicure of vital importance. Her hair was trimmed regularly, but she wore it in the simplest of styles, swirling loosely around her shoulders. She kept her fingernails clean, unpolished and fairly short, much to her mother's disgust; but she'd reasoned that since she typed every day, long nails and worry over chipped polish would simply be a nuisance.

In the beginning, Bill had accepted her as she was, plain, simple and unpretentious. But gradually, things had changed. He had begun to talk of buying a house in the suburbs, over in Virginia. He wanted a nice place where they could entertain and raise a family. To Bill it was a natural step forward, a stabilizing element in their marriage. But Andrea saw things differently. What if Bill were to discover, once they were "settled," that she couldn't live up to his expectations after all? Wouldn't he inevitably grow tired of her? From then on their relationship had deteriorated at an ever-increasing speed.

But the thing that had truly made her flutter away like a frightened quail was Bill's strong desire for a family. Alarmed, she'd done the only thing she could think of: she'd put a safe distance between them. She'd begun to travel frequently, sometimes staying away for several weeks at a time, using magazine assignments and research as a convenient cover for her cowardice.

After that, it had simply been a matter of time before they'd reached the end. Andrea knew her inability to be the sort of wife Bill wanted had led directly to the divorce. Their parting had seemed inevitable, like all the other partings in her life.

Since then, she hadn't changed, and neither had Bill, most likely. All things considered they were better off away from each other.

Only now . . . whispered her heart, *now that you've seen him, been with him again, you can't seem to get him out of your mind.*

Three days later, the documentary was finally complete. The film crew celebrated by going out to an elegant restaurant for dinner. Now that the work was done, the fatigue and irritability they'd all been suffering vanished and the mood was festive. Over the meal, they took turns making toasts and congratulating each other on the superb job they'd done.

After dinner, the men decided to continue their celebration by going to a nightclub, but Andrea elected not to join them. She preferred to go back to her room, read for a while and get to sleep early. Tomorrow they would be taking the long flight back to New York.

"Aw, come with us," Kent cajoled. "Who'll we dance with if you don't go? You're the only female we've got."

Andrea gave him an arch look and laughed. "I can't imagine you having a problem finding a dance partner."

"Maybe Kent won't, but how about the rest of us?" George asked. "We're not all lady-killers. We need you, Andie."

Andrea grinned, but she shook her head and stuck to her decision. "You'll just have to manage, fellas. I really just want to take it easy tonight."

At last she convinced them, so they put her into a taxi and bade her good-night. Andrea gave the driver the address, and then leaned back against the seat and closed her eyes. She really was tired. The last two weeks had been hectic, what with two flights across the Atlantic, the concern over

Randy and the long hours of hard work since her return. Normally one good night's sleep and she could bounce back from anything, but these past few days she'd noticed that even though she'd been sleeping well, she hadn't enjoyed her naturally high energy level.

Once she was back in her room and had changed into her nightgown, she curled up on the bed and called Randy to let him know she was coming home.

His telephone was answered by a lilting female voice. For an instant Andrea was so taken aback that she could think of nothing to say. Lisa, of course.

"Hello?" asked the voice for the second time.

"This is Andrea Wade Sheridan. Is my bro—"

"Hi, Andie!" the other girl exclaimed excitedly. "It's so nice to actually hear your voice. This is Lisa Weber."

"I'd assumed as much," Andrea said dryly. She was aware of the contrast between Lisa's warm tone and her own much less enthusiastic voice.

"Randy and I were just talking about you not an hour ago."

"Oh?"

"Yes," Lisa went on cheerfully, apparently oblivious to Andrea's coolness. "He was telling me about how you used to do each other's homework as kids. He did your math while you did his geography."

Andrea chuckled in spite of herself. "You know, Randy and I've traveled all over the globe, but if you showed him a map today, I doubt he could locate Cleveland. And I still can't add two and two. I'm afraid, in retrospect, that we didn't do each other any favors."

"I suppose not," Lisa said, laughing. "How's London?"

"Cold, but at least it's not raining. I just called to tell Randy we're finally finished with our work. I'll be heading home tomorrow."

"Great. I suppose you'll be glad to get home?"

"Very. If nothing else, it'll just be nice not having to live out of a suitcase for a while."

"I suppose that would be tiresome," Lisa said. "All the same, your job sounds awfully exciting compared to mine."

"What is that?"

"I'm a bookkeeper in an insurance office." Before Andrea had time to respond to that, she went on, "Just a moment, Andie. I'll let you talk to your brother. He's glaring at me, afraid we'll hang up before he gets to speak. It's been nice talking to you."

"Same here," Andrea replied politely.

Randy came on the line then, and they talked for perhaps ten minutes. Andrea was reassured more by the strength in his voice than his words when he said he was feeling fine.

"You'll have to come down to the farm sometime soon, sis," he told her. "I want you to meet Lisa."

"I'll do that," Andrea said breezily.

"Bill met her when he brought me home, and..." Randy paused to chuckle. "He said I've finally developed good taste in my old age. I know you'll just love her, Andie."

"I'm sure I will," Andie answered mechanically. But in her heart she didn't believe it. It seemed the fascinating Lisa had displaced her in the regard of the two men she cared most about in life. That wouldn't be an easy thing to forgive. Appalled at her thoughts, she rushed on, "Meantime, I'd better hang up before I have a long-distance bill I can't pay. I just wanted to let you know my schedule and check on your progress."

"Progressing by leaps and bounds," Randy proclaimed. "I think," he added in a stage whisper, "It's all this TLC I'm getting."

As passengers, loaded down with their belongings, straggled past customs at JFK Airport, he watched for her. Finally he was rewarded, just as he had begun to fear he'd somehow missed her.

There she was, walking between George and Kent. Her strawberry-blond hair was a bit tousled from long hours of leaning her head against a seat cushion, and even at a distance he saw that she looked tired. She was wearing blue slacks, a white blouse and a gray coat. Her shoulders were burdened by the straps of her handbag and a carryall bag, and in her hands she carried a suitcase and what looked to be a portable typewriter. The two men were similarly burdened.

As Bill moved to intercept the trio, Andrea abruptly looked his way and saw him.

Her eyes grew round with surprise...and an unexpected anxiety. Bill mentally kicked himself for that. He realized instantly that she feared he'd come to meet her with bad news again. Quickly he smiled, hoping to ease her mind.

"Hi," he said lightly when he drew near them. "How was the flight?"

"Long," George said succinctly.

"Too long," Kent seconded as Andrea remained silent. "It sure is great to be on firm ground again."

"I've got a limo waiting," Bill said as he reached out and relieved Andrea of both the suitcase and the typewriter. "Can I give you men a lift?"

George paused, then shook his head. "If you're going to Andrea's apartment, I'd be taking you out of your way. Thanks anyway, though."

"Kent?"

Kent grinned impishly. "If I wasn't so tired and was in the mood to be a devil, I'd take you up on it, since two's company and three's a you-know-what. As it is, I'll leave you two lovebirds alone."

Lovebirds? Andrea was startled. Is that what they looked like to others? Certainly she was delighted to see Bill, and she supposed it was there, in her eyes. For an instant, when she first saw him, her heart had leapt to her throat. Why should he have left Washington to meet her plane in New York unless it was to bring her more unpleasant news? Then, when he'd smiled, she'd known nothing was wrong, and she'd felt a flutter of happiness.

It was good to see him. Wonderful, in fact. Her eyes drank in the sight of him. Today, in dark slacks and a cream-colored heavy sweater, he little resembled the businessman he was. His hair tumbled across his forehead, his blue eyes sparkled and his smile was lazy and warm. He looked relaxed and content, like a man on vacation.

" . . . say goodbye. Andrea, I'll call you when I know the air date for the film," George was saying.

Andrea withdrew her gaze from Bill's face and nodded. "Fine. See you, George."

"I've got to run, too," Kent said as George left them. "If I'm lucky, I might be able to line up a date tonight."

Andrea grinned at him. "I thought you said you were tired."

"Never *that* tired," Kent said with a wink. "I'll call you next week. Maybe we can have lunch."

"All right. 'Bye, Kent," Andrea said.

The two men nodded their goodbyes, and finally Bill and Andrea were alone, at least as alone as two people can be in a crowded airport. Bill looked down at her, and this time his smile was soft and intimate. It turned her heart upside down.

"Hi," he said again.

Andrea smiled back. "Hi, yourself."

"How are you?" he asked.

"Stiff. I'll be fine once I stretch my legs a bit. How are you?"

"Can't complain." His gaze flickered across her face. "You look a little tired, but you're still the most beautiful woman in the world."

Andrea's heart skipped a beat. "Well, thanks," she said slowly. "You're looking pretty wonderful yourself."

"Thank you, ma'am." Bill grinned and said lightly, "Your chariot awaits, my lady. Shall we go? This suitcase is beginning to feel like a ton of bricks."

Andrea nodded, and they began walking toward the exit. "What are you doing here, Bill?"

He quirked a thick, black eyebrow. "What does it look like? I'm playing a porter."

She chuckled. "No. I mean, really."

"Really? I came to take you home."

"But why? Surely you didn't come all the way to New York just to take me home from the airport."

"There's a little more to it than that," he conceded.

"Now we're getting somewhere. What?"

"I'll tell you once we're on our way."

A few minutes later, they sat side by side in the back seat of the limousine while the driver manipulated the vehicle through traffic. Bill turned to Andrea, his eyes twinkling. "Glad to see me?"

"Oh, Bill." She sighed weakly. "When I left you in Atlanta, I thought I'd never see you again."

He took her hand and examined it with studied interest. "Is that a fact?" He paused, and said, "Actually, I thought the same thing. But you still haven't answered my question. Are you glad to see me?''

"Yes, damn it!" she snapped impatiently. "You know I am!"

Bill grinned. "So am I," he murmured. "Very glad to see you." He leaned over and brushed her lips with his in a fleeting kiss.

"You haven't told me yet why you're here," she said somewhat breathlessly. "Or," she added as a thought struck her, "how you knew my flight schedule."

"Randy called and told me. He wants us to spend a long weekend with him at the farm, so I came to get you. We'll fly to Washington tomorrow morning, pick up my car and drive down together. He's really looking forward to seeing you."

"You mean he's looking forward to my meeting his girl."

Bill nodded. "That, too, of course."

"Well, this just isn't a convenient time for me," Andrea said, "so you'll have to go alone. I've been away from home so long I've got a million things to do. Besides, I need some time to rest and catch my breath."

She knew she couldn't speak her mind and tell him the real reason—that she didn't want to meet Lisa. It would only prompt another lecture from him about jealousy, and she certainly wasn't in the mood for that. What was even more important, she didn't want to put herself back in the situation of being with Bill for an extended period of time. Her feelings were too chaotic. She'd been overjoyed to see him waiting for her at the airport and hadn't been able to hide it, but now she had to be sensible. Nothing but pain could come of their continuing to see each other. Better to cut things off before they happened.

"Of course you're going," Bill said mildly. "I can see you're tired and you need some rest, and that's why a few days at Randy's place will be good for you."

"I'm not going," Andrea declared obstinately. "You and Randy have no business making plans for me without consulting me first."

"Hmm, a little grouchy today, are we?" Bill teased. "I'm sure all that bucolic peace is exactly what you need."

Andrea stopped arguing. It seemed useless, anyway. She just closed her eyes and kept them shut until the limo stopped at her building.

Bill accompanied Andrea into her fifth-floor apartment. While she shed her coat and turned on the heat, he stood looking around with interest. It was even more stripped-down than his place. This was an expensive address, yet the living room had an incomplete look to it. There was a nice sofa, a couple of chairs, tables and lamps and a full bookcase and that was about it. There were no pictures on the walls, nothing on the tables except for a couple of magazines. In the adjacent dining area the table was bare.

"I see you still don't believe in being overly burdened with possessions," he observed.

"Is that so bad?" Andrea asked defensively.

Bill shrugged. "I'm sure it's preferable to the opposite extreme. Too many people think having as many things as possible is the be-all and end-all of life."

Andrea grinned in spite of herself. "And you believe there ought to be a happy medium in there somewhere."

He nodded seriously. "Yes, I do. I think your apartment, and mine, for that matter, are too Spartan. Making one's home as beautiful and comfortable as possible, without going overboard on ostentation, surely isn't unreasonable."

Again Andrea felt defensive. Bill had just intimated that her lack of interest or expertise in such matters was a defect. "If you feel that way," she said crossly, "then why don't you have your apartment done up by a decorator?"

"There doesn't seem much point in going to all that trouble just for myself."

"But you think married people should?" He was being subtly critical again, saying that she should have bothered about such things while they'd been married. Annoyed, she challenged, "They should have different values than single people? Be collectors of things? Be responsible for things? Be *owned* by things?"

He grinned. "Touché." There was a light tap at the door, and Bill went to open it.

The doorman entered and deposited the luggage—including, Andrea noticed, a duffle bag that didn't belong to her. Which could only mean that it belonged to Bill.

Suddenly she felt strange and nervous. Did Bill intend to stay overnight in her apartment? Or was he booked in a hotel room? She knew she couldn't send him away if he expected to stay with her. Not when he'd put her up in his apartment in Washington. Not when he'd done her so many kindnesses.

Nevertheless, if he stayed, it could be a dangerous, explosive situation. After Atlanta, she didn't trust either of them to keep a nice, divorced distance.

There was nothing to eat in the kitchen, so a short time later they walked the few blocks to a Chinese restaurant. Over the meal, it was like old times, being together, talking about anything that came into their minds.

"It's been a long time since we had such a carefree dinner together," Bill said at the end of it.

"I know. I was thinking the same thing," Andrea admitted.

"An evening like this makes you wonder why we ever got divorced."

"Yes. But we're forgetting the bad times."

Bill sighed. "I guess you're right."

It was after nine when they returned to the apartment. Bill paused near the door, by his duffle bag.

"Are you going to invite me to stay," he asked bluntly, "or do I go out and find a hotel room?" He saw the reluctance creep into her eyes, and in sudden fury he snapped, "I only meant the sofa, damn it!"

"Of—of course you can stay," Andrea said meekly. "I-I'll go get a blanket and pillow."

Bill was driven past all patience. As Andrea turned away from him, he grabbed her arm and swung her around to face him. There was nervousness...or fear...or both in her eyes, and this only infuriated him more.

Roughly he pulled her against him and his lips crushed hers with pitiless anger. No tenderness tempered him. His mouth stamped hers with the searing fire of possession. While his hands raked her body, her hips, her back, her breasts.

He felt Andrea squirm, trying to free herself from the assault, but that only incensed him further. He pressed her body to his more tightly, not caring if he hurt her. He could even feel her heart thudding. When she pushed his hand away from her breast, he merely brought it back, determined to have his way. When she tried to avert her face, to break the kiss, his teeth dug into her lower lip.

And to his shame, he felt himself becoming aroused.

Abruptly, he thrust her from him. He wiped his mouth while Andrea backed away from him. That, more than anything, stabbed him with a terrible remorse.

"I'm sorry, Andie!" he rasped. "I didn't mean to—to molest you! It's just that seeing you look frightened and nervous of me...*me*"—the word was filled with his agony—"I just went a little mad!"

"Yes." Andrea's eyes glittered with unshed tears. Her lips were a deep pink and swollen. They were also trembling. "Yes, you did go crazy. Don't ever touch me again, Bill," she ordered. "All I was afraid of was both of us messing up our lives again. We already did that once. Atlanta was a mistake, one I don't intend to repeat, so you'd better understand that."

"Oh, I do," Bill said bitterly. "Now, if you'll bring me that blanket, I won't be bothering you with any more unwanted attentions."

"That's fine," Andrea replied coldly.

Within ten minutes, the lights were out. Bill lay on the sofa, rigid with anger at Andrea and at himself.

In the bedroom, Andrea curled into a tight ball in the center of her bed and wished the lump in her throat would cease its throbbing.

Chapter Eight

The congestion of the nation's capital lay behind them now. Bill, relaxing from the tense alertness needed in heavy traffic, leaned back against the seat and shifted his long legs into a more comfortable driving position.

The midmorning sun blazing through wispy clouds had burned off the lingering chill, and the rest of the day promised to be exceptional. The countryside flew by in a blur as the car zipped along the interstate.

The sun's warmth did nothing to alleviate the coolness that existed inside the car, however. All morning Bill and Andrea had spoken little to each other, and then only polite civilities such as "More coffee?" or "We'd better get going so we won't miss our plane."

On the short flight to Washington, they buried their faces behind portions of *The New York Times*, but now there was no contrived barrier to shield them from the necessity of talking, and the silence grew heavier with every mile.

Bill hated the estrangement, but he didn't know how to put things right. Last night he'd behaved abominably, allowing his anger to get the better of him. He didn't blame Andie for despising him now: he didn't like himself, either. Yet he'd apologized, and there was little else he could do.

Ever since that morning in Atlanta, he'd nursed resentment over the abrupt change in Andie after they'd made love. One minute she'd been glowing, lively, teasing and fun. Then she'd regretted it all and frozen him out, so that the closeness they'd shared for a little while, both physically and mentally, had become only a distant dream. He'd felt cheated again, as he had during their marriage when she'd taken off on one of her trips or turned hostile whenever he'd spoken of establishing a real home together.

Sometimes it had seemed to Bill that Andie had only played at marriage, as though she'd been humoring him with a little game she couldn't take seriously. Never had she wanted the things out of the relationship that most people did—a home of their own, a family, a day-by-day sharing of life's experiences. She'd had no interest in domesticity whatsoever, no desire to entertain at home or to develop long-term mutual interests. She had wanted an intense personal relationship with him, but only up to a point. As long as everything was light and pleasant, she was pleased to be with him, but the instant he'd begun to press for the things most people took for granted, she'd withdrawn into herself, then spread her wings and soared away. Bill had never fully understood what made Andie tick. He supposed he never would.

She sat quietly beside him now, gazing out the window, so near that he could reach out and touch her, yet as far away in spirit as the sun. In some ways she was like the sun, peeking out, warm and healing, then blinding him with her brilliance. Then she'd pull away, hiding behind a cloud, remote and chilly. As distant as she was at that moment, Bill thought he might never reach her in any meaningful way again.

Anyhow, he asked himself disgustedly, why should he even want to? Andie had proved over and over again that she just hadn't loved him enough to stay with him. Now that they were temporarily back in each other's lives, what did he expect—that she would fall into his arms, say it had all been a mistake and beg him to take her back? Bill smiled grimly to himself. He'd have better odds entering politics and running for president.

Besides, he didn't want her back. She'd put him through enough agony the first time around. The *only* time around, he assured himself firmly.

Yes? Asked another silent voice. Then why had he accepted Randy's weekend invitation and gone to meet her in New York? Because he was a glutton for punishment, that's why! Because, much as he hated to admit it, Andie still fascinated him more than any other woman. She possessed some part of him yet, and he couldn't seem to break free.

You'd think, Andrea told herself as she stared blindly out the window, that after all these years you'd be free of any feelings whatsoever toward Bill Sheridan. You'd think that you'd put the past where it belonged and let it stay there.... She'd always been able to do it before, but somehow, this time, it was different.

She'd hurt Bill badly that morning in Atlanta, and last night she'd reaped the effects of his pain. His unexpected malice had shocked and horrified her. For a little while she'd actually hated him.

Physically, he hadn't really hurt her. But the antagonistic way he'd kissed and touched her was degrading and insulting. She'd never imagined that Bill was capable of such behavior.

Now that she'd had a night to calm down, she acknowledged to herself that she'd provoked it. Bill had accurately read her reaction to his desire to stay overnight, and her reluctance, coupled with the way she'd changed after they'd made love in that Atlanta hotel, had pushed him too far. His actions last night had been wrong, deplorable, in fact, but brought on by the figurative slap in the face she'd dealt him. Bill had only seen her rejection of him; he couldn't possibly know how much it had cost her.

Yet she was still convinced that she'd taken the right course. What was the use of drawing so close again, of indulging in the heady exaltation their lovemaking had always wrought? It would only lead to false hopes, baseless expectations, and sometime, somehow, the house of cards would once more come tumbling down.

All the same, it was going to be an impossibly long weekend if they were scarcely even speaking. Besides, she genuinely regretted the chill that had sprung up between them. She didn't want to be at odds with Bill.

Nothing could be worse than the situation as it was now, so, gathering her courage, she began hesitantly, "Bill?"

"Yeah?"

His curt tone was daunting, but she went on anyway. "About last night..."

"I've already apologized to you, Andie," he said coldly. "I'd rather not talk about it anymore if you don't mind."

"Well, I do mind!" she returned with a burst of spirit. "We have to talk about it, unless we plan to carry on this cold war all through the weekend, which wouldn't exactly be fair to Randy." She inhaled softly. "Look, I accept your apology. I apologize, too, so can't we please just put it behind us and try to be civil to each other while we're at the farm?''

Bill threw her a skeptical look. "What have you got to be sorry about?" he asked gruffly. "I'm the one who acted like a jerk."

Unexpectedly, Andie flashed a spectacular smile, and it just about knocked his socks off. It always had whenever her moods changed so abruptly. Here it was again, black anger dissolving into shimmering sunshine.

"Yes," she said pertly. "You did. A first-class jerk at that."

"Thanks," he said dryly. "I'd just as soon you didn't agree with me."

Andrea laughed at him and wrinkled her nose. "Poor, poor Freddie," she teased. "The truth hurts, doesn't it? Never mind. Your behavior last night sort of evens the score. In Atlanta I was a muddleheaded ninny who couldn't make up her mind what she wanted. Yesterday, too, come to think of it." Her face became pensive.

"How so?"

She shrugged. "I was very glad to see you waiting for me at the airport," she said frankly. "And over dinner I had a wonderful time being with you. But..."

"But?" Bill prompted.

"But when you wanted to stay, I was afraid."

"I know," Bill said grimly. "That's what drove me out of my mind. That you'd actually be afraid of me. And then I became a brute and only proved you had good reason."

"I wasn't afraid of you, Bill, don't you see?" Andrea said softly. "I was afraid of myself. And of us together."

"What do you mean?"

Andrea lifted her hands, palms up, in a gesture of helplessness. "Of our getting carried away and being hurt all over again." She clasped her hands and added in a soft whisper, "I'm still afraid."

Bill nodded. "I understand that. So am I, if you want to know the truth. I remember that when we're not together, but when we are, I keep forgetting it. It just seems so natural to..." He shrugged and broke off. "Let's forget it, okay? Friends this weekend?"

"Deal," Andrea declared.

Bill offered her his right hand and she placed hers in it. His fingers closed and tightened around hers for a moment, and then he released them.

They were both relieved and glad to be back on good terms. Now they could while away the time talking easily.

"So you visited John and Lydia, did you?" Bill asked. Andrea had just told him about bumping into John at Harrod's. "Did you enjoy it?"

"Very much. I fell in love with their son at first sight."

Bill's eyes widened with skeptical amazement. "You? Crazy about a baby? Now I've heard everything!"

Andrea giggled. "Well, I was for a little while, anyway, when he was being sweet and adorable. When he started crying and I didn't know what to do to stop it, my infatuation waned a bit."

"I'll bet." Bill grinned. "What'd you do, pinch him?"

Andrea drew herself up haughtily. "I did no such thing! It was a nature call. It was just that I didn't have enough sense to figure it out. Thank goodness Lydia knew what the problem was at once."

Bill laughed at her. "Good thing you weren't left in charge of the little fellow. He'd have had an unpleasant time of it."

"True," Andrea admitted ruefully. "What I don't know about babies could fill a book."

Bill was suddenly thoughtful. "Is that why you never wanted children?" he asked.

Andrea turned her face toward the window. "Partly," she replied. "I never did buy the theory that a new mother is automatically endowed with the wisdom of Solomon." She was still sensitive over the strange feelings she'd experienced when she'd held baby Christopher, feelings she couldn't share with the man to whom she'd denied children. Abruptly, wishing she'd never brought it up in the first place, she changed the subject. "Randy told me you liked his girlfriend when you met her."

"Yes, I did. She's a lovely person." The warm approval in Bill's voice was unmistakable.

"At least I know she's got charm." Andrea's voice hardened. "She seems to have won you and Randy over without any problem."

"You're still jealous of that girl, aren't you?" Bill exclaimed.

"Of course I'm not!" Andrea's denial was vehement—too vehement. "I talked to her over the phone," she added in what she hoped was a more reasonable tone, "and she sounded very nice. If she wants to spend her time playing nursemaid, who am I to object?"

"But you don't like her," Bill said flatly. "You're determined not to like her."

"I don't even know her! How can I like or dislike her at this point?" Andrea shrugged. "I'm just wondering what it is she has that seems to bowl men over, that's all. First Randy, now you. Is she a raving beauty? Well endowed? What's her great appeal?"

"You're being catty, you know that?" Bill snapped in exasperation. "It's very unbecoming, Andie. And unfair besides."

"Easy for you to say," Andrea retorted. "It's not your brother she's got in her clutches."

"Clutches? You make her sound like a gold-digger!"

"Well, maybe she is!" Andrea's anger spilled over. "Randy isn't exactly a pauper, as you well know! Both of us received very healthy inheritances when Daddy died."

"And you give Randy so little credit that you think he'd get involved with someone who only wanted to get close to his bank account?"

"It's been known to happen," Andrea pointed out coldly. "When a beautiful woman sets out to convince a man that she's really devoted to him, he can be blinded and not see the obvious. Lisa told me herself she's a bookkeeper. That's just fine, but you and I both know bookkeepers don't get rich off their salaries. And she *is* showing Randy how extraordinarily dedicated she is to him, taking care of him and all, since the accident."

"You're really something," Bill said in disgust. "My God, Andie, what a warped way of reasoning things! You've got it all figured out; you're the judge and the jury of the motivations of someone you haven't even met. In journalism school you were taught objectivity, but that must have been a subject you flunked!"

"Do you expect me to be objective about by brother's happiness? He means everything in the world to me."

"Don't I know it?" Bill snapped back. "He's the only person in the world you ever cared about! I know I sure came in a poor last."

"That's not true," Andrea cried. "How can you possibly say that? I loved you more than anything, Bill!"

He laughed harshly. "What a funny way you had of showing it! By constantly running away from me. Now you show it for Randy by wanting to tie sisterly apron strings

around him and prevent him from having a meaningful relationship with somebody of his own.''

Andrea crossed her arms and glared out the window.
''You just don't understand,'' she said in a brittle voice.

''You're right,'' Bill shot back. ''I sure as hell don't, and
frankly, I don't want to understand such selfishness.''

Exhausted by their outburst, they fell silent, and stayed
that way for the rest of the drive.

Randy's farm, while not large, was quite pretty. There
were gently rolling hills and flat valleys. One portion of it
was an apple orchard, while another was leased by a neigh-
bor who used it for cattle grazing.

Andrea had only visited the farm twice before, but she
could well understand its appeal to her nature-loving
brother. From the front porch of the house one could enjoy a view of the distant Blue Ridge Mountains. On a nearby
hillside was a thick stand of pines and poplar, interspersed
by mountain laurel and dogwood; and down in a valley lay
a pond stocked with fish.

The house itself, set atop a hilly rise, was old and plain.
Though it had only two bedrooms, a living room, kitchen
and one bath, it was spacious and comfortable enough.
When they arrived, smoke was curling from the chimney,
giving them an old-fashioned, country welcome.

Andrea got out of the car and breathed in the sweet,
clean, pine-scented air. Then, without waiting to see if Bill
was following, she squared her shoulders and marched toward the house. Now that she was here, she couldn't delay
meeting Randy's girlfriend any longer.

She knocked briefly on the front door before turning the
knob, calling out, ''Randy! We're here!''

''Come in, come in!'' Randy shouted back.

When Andrea entered the living room, he was rising stiffly
from a chair.

"You didn't have to get up," Andrea protested as she went toward him.

Randy grinned. "Wanted to show you how great I'm doing."

Andrea hugged him gently, mindful of his injured ribs. After he'd pecked her cheek, she backed away a step so that she could really look at him. His face was healing nicely. Most of the bruises had disappeared, and the few that remained were fading. Only one placed on his forehead was still plastered, and even that looked better because the large bandage he'd worn in the hospital was absent.

"You look terrific," Andrea said with delighted approval. "Much better than I'd have believed possible this soon!"

"I just have to remember not to make any sudden moves or lift anything heavy, that's all. Hi, Bill." Randy smiled as he glanced beyond Andrea's shoulder. "Glad you could make it."

"How's it going?" Bill shook Randy's hand.

"Not bad at all." Randy looked at Andrea again. "There's fresh coffee in the kitchen," he said. "Mind doing the honors?"

"Not a bit." Andrea went into the kitchen, and while she poured the coffee, she wondered where Lisa was. It was apparent she'd been here. The kitchen was spotless and neater than she'd ever seen it—obviously not Randy's doing. Even when he was in perfect condition, he was never this tidy. Grudgingly, Andrea approved of Lisa's contribution. Things were in their proper place for a change.

When she rejoined the men, she looked carefully around the living room. It, too, was clean and free of its usual clutter. Even Randy's small desk by the window, where he kept a typewriter and a novel he'd been working on in his spare time, was orderly.

A cheerful fire was blazing in the stone fireplace, and after she'd served the coffee to Bill and Randy, Andrea curled up on the floor to enjoy the warmth.

"Where's Lisa?" she asked, unable to contain her curiosity any longer. "I understood she'd be here."

"This is Friday," Randy pointed out. "She's at work. But she'll be here this evening."

"Do you manage all right during the day while you're alone?"

"Sure." Randy grinned. "I'm not completely helpless, you know. I can open a can of soup or put together a sandwich." He took a sip of his coffee, then asked Bill, "What's been going on at the office?"

Dusk was falling, when the front door opened and a petite young woman breezed inside, accompanied by a gust of cold air and a large shaggy dog.

The dog made straight for Randy, who was sitting in his recliner; the girl, her arms loaded with grocery bags, went toward the kitchen as she sang out, "Hi, all."

A moment later she reappeared in the living room, shedding a dark brown coat, and Andrea had her first real look at Lisa Weber.

To her surprise, Lisa was not at all like the person she'd imagined. She was small, with a perfectly proportioned body that enhanced her jeans and bright red sweater, but there was nothing of the sex bomb about her. Her dark brown hair was long and shining and swung loosely against her shoulders. But it was her face that captured Andrea's attention. Lisa was indeed attractive with large brown eyes, a pert nose and full lips that curved easily into a ready smile, yet no one would have called her really beautiful. Her nose was too small, her eyes too wide, her eyebrows too thick for that. She was neither stunning nor elegant, and she certainly didn't fit the pattern of Randy's usual dates. All the same, there was a refreshing wholesomeness about Lisa that gave her a special appeal. Slowly Andrea began to revise her preconceived notions.

"You're late. I was beginning to worry," Randy said.

Lisa clasped his outstretched hand and bent down to kiss him lightly. "I'm sorry. I didn't mean to worry you. I stopped off at the grocery store. I figured we might like to eat this weekend."

"Hmm. You have a point." Randy grinned. "I hope you bought plenty. Bill eats like a horse."

"Hey!" Bill protested. "Who enters whose office to swipe whose doughnuts every chance he gets?"

Lisa straightened and, laughing, said, "Stop squabbling, boys. Hi, Bill. Nice to see you again."

"Same here," Bill answered.

Lisa moved toward Andrea and dropped onto the sofa beside her. Her smile seemed to light up her entire face. "Since these two mannerless creatures haven't thought to introduce us, we'll just have to do it ourselves. I'm Lisa, and you can't be anyone else but Andie. You have Randy's eyes. I'm awfully pleased to meet you."

Andrea found herself smiling back. "Me, too. How are you?"

Lisa sighed and leaned back against the cushions. "Tired, actually. It's been a long day. But it's Friday evening, so I'll start feeling better every hour."

The dog lumbered over to lick Andrea's hand, and she scratched behind his ears. "Your dog's friendly to strangers, I'm happy to see. What's his name?"

"Mops," Lisa said with a grin.

"Fitting." Andrea laughed. "What breed is he?"

"Who knows?" Lisa shrugged. "I found him on the side of the highway one day, limping and bloody. He'd been hit by a car. But he's no descendant of an old, aristocratic Virginia family, I can tell you that much.''

"Ah, from the wrong side of the tracks.'' Andrea scratched behind Mops's other ear, and his tongue lolled in appreciation. "I bet you're a lot more fun to have around than those stuffy old purebreds, aren't you, pal?''

"Andie's a snob about snobs.'' Randy laughed. "She's been such a disappointment to Mother.''

She grinned back at him. "I don't recall you putting yourself out to make such a great impression on her highbrow friends, either.''

"I was too afraid they might actually like and accept me, and then I'd have been in a real mess!''

"You flatter yourself,'' Bill teased. "What is there to like?''

"Tell 'em, Lisa,'' Randy said.

Lisa grinned and shook her head as she swung gracefully to her feet. "You brought this one on yourself, my love, so you'll just have to bail yourself out. I'm going to cook dinner.''

"I'll help,'' Andrea offered, following Lisa toward the kitchen.

"Oh, no!'' Randy groaned. "Lisa, don't let her! It'll be inedible!''

"She's okay for setting the table and maybe even tossing a salad, but don't let her near the stove!'' Bill added swiftly. "We're hungry tonight!''

Andrea swung around to shake her fist at the two men while Lisa rushed to her defense. "Just for that, we ought to let you both go hungry.''

"You don't understand,'' Randy pleaded. "I love my sister, I truly do, but she's a disaster in a kitchen. There was this meat loaf once that—''

"Shame on you both!" Lisa exclaimed. "I never heard such rudeness in all my life! Apologize at once!"

Andrea suddenly realized Lisa seriously believed they'd hurt her feelings, so she grinned. "The problem is," she confided, "they're right. I'm terrible."

Lisa looked astonished. "You mean you really can't cook?"

"Afraid not. The worst days of Bill's life were the few times I tried when we were first married."

"Well, maybe not *the* worst," Bill conceded. He smiled slowly, and Andrea's heart did a little flip. He wasn't angry anymore.

Come to think of it, she wasn't, either. She smiled back and said, "Now you're being gallant, but truth is truth. Come on, Lisa." Andrea turned toward the kitchen. "You cook; I'll fetch and carry."

In the kitchen, Lisa began unloading a grocery bag. "I bought some steaks to grill because that's fast and easy. Tomorrow night we'll have lasagna, and if I get the time, I'll bake an apple pie. How is it you never learned to cook?"

Andrea unpacked another paper sack. "Living in boarding schools and college dormitories, I just never had the opportunity. Even when I was staying with Mother…well, she can't cook, either. I don't think it ever entered her head to try, and the cooks she employed never wanted me in their way. I hear that you're a fantastic cook yourself."

"I don't know about that," Lisa said modestly, "but I do know the basics. My grandmother made sure of that. She started teaching me when I was five years old." A wistfulness entered her eyes. "She died last year. I sure do miss her, and so does Mom."

Now it was Andrea who felt a little wistful. What was it like to be a part of a family like that, where even grandmothers took a hand in a child's training? Her own had tried for a couple of years, but then she'd gotten sick. The rest of the time, they'd lived so far apart that Randy and Andrea had only been able to visit her a couple of weeks out of the year.

"Hey, what's this?" She peered into another bag filled with Christmas decorations.

"Randy asked me to buy them. He wants Bill to cut a tree tomorrow. He's really excited about having Christmas here this year."

"I know. I'm looking forward to it, too. Do you think we might have snow by then?"

While Lisa prepared the meal and Andrea hovered nearby, they got acquainted. Lisa was interested in Andrea's career, while Andrea encouraged her to talk of her family. Lisa's father was a lawyer, and her mother an art teacher who was also very involved in community projects. Her brother, who was married and had two children, was a realtor in Culpeper. It was through him that Lisa and Randy had met when Randy had bought the farm, though they hadn't begun dating until a few months ago.

By midnight, when Lisa had gone home, Andrea's resistance had vanished. Andrea had never seen her brother look so happy and content, and it was evident that for Lisa the sun rose and set with Randy. Once, when they'd been discussing the plane accident, Lisa had shuddered so violently that she'd actually looked ill. That, more than anything else, had convinced Andrea of the sincerity of her love. That awful time of dread and fear had been as terrible for Lisa as for Randy's twin.

"I'm telling you, this is the one. It's perfect."

Bill tilted his head, looking upward. "I don't know," he said. "I still lean toward the one farther down the hill. It was nice and filled out. Also closer to the house."

"It was fat," Andrea declared. "It would take up half the living room. This one's taller and better proportioned. It's just crying out to be the one. Can't you hear it? It's saying, 'Take me! I'll make a wonderful Christmas tree! I'll look beautiful when I'm all decorated.'"

Bill looked at her. "Since when did you develop the ability to communicate with pine trees?"

"Oh, I've got all sorts of hidden talents," Andrea replied, grinning, "even if I can't cook!"

Bill grinned back. "Last night still rankles, hmm?"

"Well, you and Randy weren't very complimentary to me, you know." She eyed the tree and returned to the main subject. "Come on, Bill, let's take this one."

He sighed. "All right, if your heart's so set on it." He moved around her, into position to swing the axe.

A short time later, with a rope tied around the trunk so that Bill could drag the tree behind them, they started the journey down the hillside.

They were both dressed in jeans, boots and heavy jackets. The morning was sharply cold, so that their breath frosted on the air. When they inhaled, their nostrils filled with the heavy scent of pine. As they walked, their boots crunched over a thick layer of browned pine needles.

It was a wonderful day to be alive, Andrea thought. There was something about being in the woods, feeling the pulse of nature, that enhanced one's well-being. Maybe it was the peacefulness, the sense of sharing space with living creatures and other growing things, and the champagne sparkle of fresh, clean air. She didn't know. But she did know that it made her feel renewed, refreshed, rejuvenated.

Part of her happiness, she realized, was sharing it with Bill. She didn't dare analyze that. Better to accept the moment for what it was and just be pleased she had that much of him.

As though he sensed her thoughts, Bill suddenly looked down at her and smiled. His eyes were as blue as the deep sky, his teeth as white as the frost on the meadow. "Are you glad you came, after all?" he asked.

Andrea nodded. "I guess I did need a country weekend. I feel wonderfully rested. I think last night was the best night's sleep I've had in months."

"It shows. The tension in your face is gone. You look carefree and young, a lot like you did when we first met."

"So do you." Andrea smiled in approval. "I can hardly even remember you looking this relaxed. Certainly not since the day your father died. Running the *Patriot* is tough on you."

"It's not easy sometimes," he conceded.

"Maybe you should get away more often," Andrea ventured. "Find yourself a place like this, even." Her hand swept around, indicating their surroundings.

Bill shook his head. "I don't think it would be much fun all by myself."

"No," Andrea said thoughtfully. "I guess not. I wouldn't, either. We're not like Randy. And anyway, he's not alone when he comes here anymore, now that he's found Lisa."

"Still think she's a gold digger?" Bill teased.

Andrea wrinkled her nose at him. "Don't remind me of the awful things I said about her yesterday. I really am ashamed of myself."

"I thought you would be."

"I am." Andrea nodded. "Now I can see why Randy's so mad about her, and why you like her, too. She's so warm and kind and unpretentious. Not to mention very talented domestically. Do you think this might be the real thing? That they'll get married?"

Bill shrugged. "Time will tell, I guess. Would you mind?"

"No. I thought I would, but I really like her. I think she'd make a perfect wife for Randy."

"I agree."

"She's settled and quiet, content with her life. Not flighty and restless like me," Andrea went on. "Someone exactly like Lisa would be the right wife for you, too."

"Trying to marry me off, Andie?"

No, her heart cried. *Just trying to be fair.* She said as casually as she could, "That's up to you, of course. It's just that I wouldn't want you to make another mistake like me."

"Thanks for the advice," Bill said dryly, "but I think I'll have to make my own choices, even if it does turn out to be a mistake. Lisa's a sweet girl, but she's not my type. I was always a sucker for restless, flighty, hopeless cooks."

Andrea's heart fluttered. Did he mean it, or was he just teasing her? Anyway, what did it matter? The marriage hadn't worked. She had to remember that: it just hadn't worked.

"Bill . . ." she began uncertainly.

"I know," he growled. "I cared more than you did, and I came out the loser. I was a sucker once, but I don't intend ever to be one again."

It was as though he'd slapped her. Andrea inwardly reeled, suddenly realizing that he still carried a lot of hostility in him after all these years.

She deserved it, she mused. Maybe in the end this was best, their meeting again and Bill getting his feelings out in the open. Better for him to get rid of the bottled-up anger, so that when he did fall in love and marry a second time, he'd be free of it, free of her for good.

But how about herself she wondered dismally. Would she ever be free of her feelings for him now that they'd been reawakened?

Chapter Nine

The temperature was hovering at the freezing mark, but it felt good to Andrea. It had grown too warm inside the house, what with the blazing fire in the hearth, the heat of the kitchen and the crush of people.

Most of all, she'd felt a desperate need for a few minutes by herself.

Tonight she'd had a chance to see firsthand what it was like to be part of a real family gathering. Lisa and Randy had invited Lisa's family to come for dinner and to help decorate the Christmas tree. Mr. and Mrs. Weber had come, as had Lisa's brother, Warren, and his wife, Anne. Their two children were there as well, along with a cousin, Amy, her husband, David, and his brother and wife.

Andrea would have been appalled at so many people showing up expecting a meal if it had been her home, but Randy had seemed genuinely delighted. Not that it had been a hardship as far as food went. To Andrea's amazement, each group had arrived laden with dishes. The meal had run the gamut from Swedish meatballs and ambrosia salad to cheesecake and Christmas cookies; there had also been wine, apple cider, eggnog and coffee.

She had to admit to herself that the evening had been fun. Or at least, it would have been, if Bill hadn't so studiously ignored her. Everyone else had been friendly and cheerful, however, and within half an hour Andrea had felt comfortable with them all. The meal had been buffet style, of course. Decorating the tree had been a hilarious affair, with everyone getting in everyone else's way. When it was finished, except for the angel on top, Randy had insisted that Warren's three-year-old daughter, Kari, have that privilege. The little girl's father had lifted her onto his shoulders so that she could reach, and when the angel was in place, everyone had applauded. Then they'd sung Christmas carols to the accompaniment of David's guitar.

Andrea swallowed the lump in her throat marveling at the simple pleasure of it all. She'd never spent an evening quite like this in all her life. One thing was for sure: if Randy let Lisa slip through his fingers, he wasn't the intelligent man she thought he was.

A slash of light spilled over the porch as the front door opened. From where she stood, leaning against the oak tree in the yard, Andrea saw Bill step outside. He closed the door behind him, and all was in darkness once more, except for the lighted windows.

"Andrea?" he called softly.

"Here," she answered. "By the tree."

Though she couldn't see him in the heavy darkness, she could hear his footsteps as he came toward her. Then, by the faint glimmer of the moonlight, she saw his silhouette as he drew near.

For a time, neither of them spoke. Bill stood before her, hands thrust into the pockets of his heavy jacket, his head lifted as he looked toward the sky. Only a sprinkling of distant stars was visible tonight.

Finally, he broke the silence. "Aren't you cold? I saw you when you left. You've been out here a long time."

"I'm all right. You didn't have to check on me."

"I know. But I started worrying when you didn't come back." Andrea didn't reply, and another long silence fell between them.

After a time, Bill asked, "What do you think of Lisa's clan?"

He could almost hear the smile in Andrea's voice when she answered, "I think I'm envious of her. I really like them all, but I could love her mother without even trying."

Bill nodded. "She reminds me a little bit of my mother."

"Really?" Andrea replied eagerly. "You always spoke so fondly of her, but not having known her myself, I guess I couldn't possibly understand. Was she really as...as *comfortable* as Mrs. Weber?"

Bill chuckled softly. "That's a good word. 'Motherly' was what I would have said."

"Not a good word at all," Andrea said swiftly. "I have a mother, too remember? And she's nothing like that."

"No. She's not," he agreed quietly.

Andrea went on dreamily, "Mrs. Weber is my ideal of what one should be, though. A little plump, a nice smile, a little bossy, too, but in a sweet way that lets you know it's because she cares. Somehow, without even seeming to put out any effort at all, she had the food heated and on the table, organized all of us for cleanup detail, rocked little Jason to sleep, explained to Anne how to reupholster a chair she wants to do—and told me how easy it would be to make my own clothes!"

"You really did miss out on a lot of ordinary things most of us take for granted, didn't you, honey?" Bill's voice was sympathetic. "I guess I never realized quite how much that bothered you."

"Most of the time it doesn't," she told him. "It's only sometimes, like now, that I can't help wishing things had been different. That I was different. That family in there is *really* rich, and I'm not talking about money."

"Andie..." There was a catch in Bill's throat. "Do you ever wish things had been different for us, too?"

He felt her hand touch his arm, and her voice, too, was slightly unsteady. "Lots of times, Bill. Oh, so many times."

What restraint he'd had dissipated into the frosty night air. The other night in her apartment, Andie had told him never to touch her again, and he'd silently vowed to honor that wish. He'd reminded himself of that pledge this morning, when they'd been discussing marriage and he'd openly let her know he was still crazy about her. But then she'd turned white and nervous, and he'd been furious with himself for making such a fool of himself again.

God knows he was a fool, all right. Because he just couldn't quit caring, couldn't stop wanting her. He never had. Now, he groaned and gave in to the impulse to kiss her.

He wrapped his arms around her, pulling her close, and Andie didn't resist. Instead, she draped her arms around his neck and tilted her head up.

Her lips were as soft as dew on a flower petal, warm as the sunshine that dries it on a spring day; her breath was sweet as the flower's perfume and she tasted like nectar. Bill was intoxicated. All the pain within him melted as his frozen heart came to life once more.

He unbuttoned both their coats, then slid his arms around her slender waist. Andrea lowered her arms, too, so that she could snuggle closer to him with her hands pressed against his back. Suddenly they were on their own cozy island of warmth, sharing body heat, defying the cold, wintry night.

They kissed, and kissed again, each time more feverishly than before. Andrea's mouth was open to his, inviting him to explore the dark, moist secrets within.

His hands crept beneath her sweater, and when he cupped her breasts, she gasped softly with pleasure. She pressed closer to the long, hard length of him, and Bill's breathing grew ragged.

"I want you," he whispered finally. "I've never stopped wanting you like this." Andrea suddenly giggled, and affronted, he dropped his hands. "I didn't know I was being funny," he said stiffly.

Andrea burrowed close to him again and rested her head against his chest. "It's not funny," she said, stifling another laugh. "It—it's just p-pathetic, that's all. I want you, too, Bill," she went on more soberly now, "and our timing couldn't be worse if we tried. There's a houseful of people in there!"

Bill chuckled softly and ran a hand through her hair. "You're right. It is a hell of a situation." He wrapped his arms around her once more and rested his chin on the crown of her head. "We'll just have to be patient till later, that's all."

"Later?"

"After everyone's left and Randy's gone to bed."

Andrea pulled away this time. "But we can't!" she exclaimed.

"Why not? Surely you're not going to condemn me to another night on Randy's sofa, are you?" he asked in tender amusement. "When we could be cuddled close together, keeping each other warm?"

"I certainly do! Randy will also be in the house with us!"

"Well, what of it?" Bill demanded impatiently. "We used to be married. I'm sure your brother is well aware of the fact that we've slept together countless nights."

"Don't be an idiot!" Andrea pulled away from him and crossed her arms in front of her in a protective gesture.

"I don't understand, Andie." Bill's voice had grown cold again. "Do you think he'd be upset about it?"

"Quite the contrary. That's just it! He'd probably be delighted and leap instantly to the conclusion that we're back together again. For good."

"And that would never do, would it?" he asked in a dangerously calm voice.

"It would just entail a lot of explanations that would be difficult and awkward for us both."

Bill was silent for a long moment; then he said tonelessly, "I'm going back inside where the people aren't hypocrites about the way they feel toward each other."

As he began to walk away, Andrea called pleadingly, "Bill, don't go like this. Maybe I just didn't say it very well. Let me try, please."

But he kept on walking. Beneath the oak tree, Andrea watched as a shaft of light fell across the front porch once more before the man went inside the house and closed the door.

Andrea awoke because she was cold. Somehow during the night she must have tossed off all the covers. Her silky gown was like a river of ice that clung to her limbs, and her feet were freezing. Eyes still closed, she groped for the blankets. She waved her hand sideways and down, like a radar detector searching for buried treasure, but couldn't locate them.

Suddenly the feeling in her right foot returned. Somebody was tickling it.

So, the covers hadn't slithered away all by themselves after all! "Randall!" she shrieked. "Stop it this second, or I swear I'll murder you!"

She heard her brother's soft chuckle. "Wake up, lazy-bones. You're sleeping away the best part of the day. I brought you some coffee."

While Andrea sat up, tugging the covers back over her chilled body, Randy came around and gingerly sat down on the edge of the bed.

She noted the extreme caution with which he moved. She plumped her pillows, leaned back and accepted the mug of coffee he held out to her. "Lisa told me you still have a lot of pain but won't take the medication the doctor prescribed for it," she said. "Why?"

Randy grinned ruefully. "Because it might ruin my macho image, of course."

"Sure. Mr. Macho. The one who squealed and ran from a grass snake when we were ten."

"Now why'd you have to go and remember that?"

"The pain pills, Randy," Andrea pressed. "Why are you making things tougher on yourself than you have to?"

"Because they make me sleepy, and I don't like that. I usually do take one before I go to bed at night. The rest of the time, I manage okay. I don't really hurt. I'm just stiff and sore."

"And stubborn."

"That, too," he conceded. "But I didn't come in here to talk about that. What do you think of Lisa, sis? I mean the real-to-goodness truth," he added, using the term they'd devised as children for absolute, trustworthy no-holds-barred honesty.

"The real-to-goodness truth." Andrea solemnly held up her right hand, according to their ancient ritual. "I think she's a gem. She wins hands down over all your former girlfriends. She's pretty and fun, but she's also real and down to earth. I like that. But more to the point, how do you feel about her? Is this serious, Randy? Do you love her?''

Randy raised his right hand in a solemn oath, and his voice was quiet, yet vibrant. ''With all my heart and soul,'' he said.

Andrea had never heard her brother sound firmer or more sincere. He really meant this. It was there in his eyes as well as his voice. Thoughtfully, she digested his statement. ''What about her?'' she asked softly. ''Does Lisa feel the same way about you?''

Randy grinned. ''So she says. But she never actually admitted it until I went and almost got myself killed. Maybe she's just feeling sorry for me right now and saying things in the heat of the moment.''

Andrea smiled and shook her head, surprising herself by defending Lisa Weber. ''Not likely. If she says she loves you, I'm inclined to believe it. When she came so close to losing you, it made her realize how much she cared.'' She lowered her gaze to her coffee as she confessed, ''I wasn't prepared to like her, Randy. Bill said I was jealous, and I guess I was, at that. Your having someone else in your life to love more than me...well, it sort of put my nose out of joint, you know?'' She gave him a tremulous smile. ''But my honest opinion, for what it's worth, is that you're out of your mind if you ever let her get away. Or that wonderful family of hers. Strike while the iron's hot, brother. Pop the question and marry her as quick as you can.''

Randy shook his head in wonder. ''Somehow I didn't expect this wholehearted approval from you. I figured you'd tell me I hadn't known her long enough, or that all this was just an emotional reaction to a brush with death. Or that you'd even preach at me about the way most marriages don't last."

Andrea smiled ruefully and patted his hand. "Well, our parents' marriage certainly didn't. Or mine. But I have a strong feeling that if you marry Lisa, you'll break the family streak of bad luck. You've always wanted someone to settle down and raise a family with, and I believe she's the right someone. So if you're asking for my blessing, you've got it." She paused to take a sip of her coffee.

"Thanks. Now all I've got to do is get up the courage to ask her." Randy shifted his position. "As for your jealousy—" he was grinning now "—that's about the dumbest thing I ever heard. Do you honestly think anyone could change my feelings for you? Why, you're a part of my own self! I thought you were smart enough to know that! When you were married to Bill, I didn't let him shunt me out of *your* life, did I? Lisa understands that we're very close, that it'll always be that way. If she hadn't, I couldn't possibly have fallen in love with her." He chucked Andrea under the chin. "Don't ever let me catch you thinking such stupid nonsense again, you hear?"

Andrea smiled wanly. "I probably wouldn't have in the first place if I hadn't been so upset about you trying to get yourself killed. You gave me a bad time there, brother," she said shakily. "Don't you ever scare me like that again!"

"It's a deal." Randy's tone became brisk. "Now, there's something else I want to discuss with you. I've got a favor to ask."

"Shoot." Andrea took another swallow of coffee, but all of a sudden it seemed to disagree with her. She felt slightly queasy, so she set the mug on the table next to the bed. She decided she must be hungry.

When she leaned back against the pillows once more, she became aware of Randy's strange reticence. "Well? Is it that big?"

He nodded. "Elephantine."

"So are you going to ask me already?" she said impatiently.

"Okay. Here goes." He gazed at her intently. "I want you to take my place at the *Patriot* until I'm ready to go back."

Andrea stared at him. "Have you lost your mind?" she breathed at last. "I can't do that! Besides, Bill would never stand for it."

"I talked to him about it already this morning, and he said it's your decision."

"The answer is no."

"Look, Bill's been super about giving me a couple of months off, but much as I want this time, I feel guilty leaving him shorthanded for so long. You're a fine journalist, Andie, you've been with the *Patriot* before so you know your way around and you're free now since you finished that London project. There's no reason why you shouldn't do it, and it would really take a load off my mind."

"There's one gigantic reason why I shouldn't do it," Andrea said gruffly. "I'd be an employee of my ex-husband. It would never work, Randy."

"I don't see why not," he said reasonably. "Bill hardly ever goes into the Rumpus Room. Besides, you'd be out a lot, you know. Your dealings with him would be minimal to nonexistent."

"And how would everybody else feel about my being there? Their attitude is the reason I quit in the first place."

"True, but then you were Bill's wife."

"Yes, and now I'm his former wife. If things were awkward then, they'd be ten times worse now."

"You're just making excuses. Please do it for me, Andie. Otherwise, I'll have to go back in a couple of weeks."

"But Bill gave you a couple of months."

"I know, but I can't do that to him." Andrea groaned. "You do pick your times to be conscientious, don't you?"

"Please."

Sighing, she said at last, "I'll think about it. But I'm not promising anything! You're asking a lot this time."

"I know." Randy nodded and urged, "Talk to Bill. He'll probably be so pleased to have you back on staff, even temporarily, that he'll bend over backward to make things easy for you."

"Hmm," Andrea said dubiously. "Where is he now?"

"Outside. Chopping wood."

She nodded. "Okay. Scram so I can get dressed."

Last night, after Bill had called her a hypocrite, Andrea had pondered his words for hours. Alone and sleepless in the silence of the guest bedroom, she'd unhappily decided that he was right. As a result, she had thought she'd be reluctant to see him today. But her anger with him for giving Randy the idea that he didn't mind if she worked at the paper carried her boldly outside to confront him.

Bill was splitting wood into kindling, and Andrea paused for a moment to watch. He had discarded his heavy wool shirt and was working in a white T-shirt. The muscles in his back and arms rippled with every rhythmic movement.

Only when he paused to wipe his brow did Andrea speak, and he whirled around, startled at the sound of her voice. When he saw her, his eyes narrowed and his expression was far from welcoming.

"What do you want?" he asked curtly. "To tell me how comfortable your solitary bed was last night?"

"Stop it!" Andrea snapped back. "Maybe you're right about me. Maybe I am a hypocrite, but at least I'm smart enough not to want to borrow trouble, which is more than I can say for you! Randy just told me about his harebrained idea of my taking over his job until he's ready to go back. Why didn't you put your foot down and forbid it?''

"Why should I?" Bill countered. "I am short-staffed because he's out, and you are a damned good reporter, when all's said and done. What's the matter? Don't you think you could handle the pressure anymore?"

"I'm not worried in the least about that, and you know it! Bill, can't you see how insane it is? How awkward it would be for both of us, not to mention the gossip it would generate?"

Bill shrugged. "I don't care what people say. You're the hypocrite, remember? I figure if you're willing to do it so Randy won't come rushing back before he's really fit, I'm willing to give it a try. You know I don't hang around the Rumpus Room giving orders. That's Davidson's job. Probably the only time we'd even see each other would be at the weekly round table meetings."

"I don't know." Andrea shook her head. "I still think it's a rotten idea."

"If you don't have the courage to do it, then don't. I don't care one way or the other."

His words stung her and took the wind out of her sails. He went back to chopping wood, and she watched him as she mulled things over. Was she really that much of a coward? she asked herself. Or could she get through a few weeks at the *Patriot* to help Bill and give Randy peace of mind?

By the time she and Bill set out for the drive back to Washington, Andrea had come to terms with the situation. Randy rarely asked favors of her, and in the end she'd been unable to resist his entreaties. He'd suffered through a horrible ordeal recently, and she just couldn't refuse when it seemed to matter so much to him.

When she'd finally broken down and agreed to do it, he'd laughed gleefully. "I knew you wouldn't let me down, sis. I wouldn't have asked if you hadn't already been back on speaking terms with Bill, but since you seem to be getting along so well these days, I figured it wouldn't be a problem." For the first time he actually seemed to think about the ramifications of what he'd asked of her. More somberly, he ventured, "It won't be, will it? I'm not really putting you in a tough spot, am I?"

"No," she lied stoutly. "Maybe a little uncomfortable, but I'll manage."

Bill had taken the news with unnerving calm. Andrea didn't see how he could be so unaffected by their continually being thrust together. Then she finally figured it out. It was quite simple, actually: it just didn't matter to him.

That became even plainer on the trip back to the city. Andrea said, "I'll have to go home this evening and pack more clothes, but I ought to be able to start work by noon tomorrow."

Bill nodded. "I've been thinking. You'll need a place, and you sure can't stay at Randy's."

Randy shared bachelor quarters with two other newsmen, one employed at a rival paper, the other an anchorman at a local television station. "Hardly." Andrea laughed. "I like Al and Byran well enough, but not that much! Besides, from the stories Randy tells, about all they do over there is have one long, never-ending party. I don't think they ever sleep. I guess I'll stay at a hotel," she went on. "It seems ridiculous to rent an apartment just for a few weeks."

"There's no point in paying astronomical hotel bills, either. You can stay at the apartment."

Andrea's eyes rounded. "With you?"

Bill made a hissing sound beneath his breath. "Well, I'm sure not moving out!"

"That's not a—"

"It's only for a few weeks, like you said. I'm hardly ever there anyway, so for the most part, you'd have the place to yourself."

"Bill." Andrea's mouth was suddenly dry. She licked her lips and began again. "I . . ."

Bill glared at her. "Stop worrying! I won't bother you with undesirable or inconvenient attentions. You'll take the bedroom and I'll take the sofa bed in the living room. You're a beautiful woman, Andie, but you're also hard and cold. It just took me a long time to realize that. I still wanted you until last night, but you put out the fire yourself. You'll be perfectly safe, I promise you. The place used to be your home, so you may as well hang your hat there again as long as you're going to be helping me out of a bind at the paper. Let's just call it canceling out our debts to each other."

Andrea bit her lip. "If I accept your offer," she said hesitantly, "you won't tell anyone at the *Patriot*, will you?"

"That you're staying at the apartment?" Bill shook his head. "I won't tell anyone, period," he replied grimly. "I wouldn't dream of compromising your squeamishness about the truth. Since honesty is not the best policy in our case, I'll keep my mouth shut, if you do the same."

When she let herself into Bill's apartment the next day to drop off her luggage, Andrea still had reservations about the wisdom of staying there. But a stubborn streak urged her to go through with it. If she didn't, Bill would know she was indeed a coward. Worse, *she* would know she was a coward.

Cowardice had already caused her to run away from him once, from their marriage, from his desire to have a normal home and family. So she'd split. Couldn't she now, at least, prove to them both that she had what it took to stick out a difficult situation? She didn't ask herself why it seemed necessary to prove anything to him because she was afraid of the answer.

After a quick wash, she let herself out of the apartment again and took the metro to the office. Outside the building she took a deep breath, then reluctantly went inside to face whatever was to come.

She was welcomed back to the Rumpus Room more warmly than she'd expected. Davidson, the editor-in-chief, was upstairs in a meeting with Bill, but there were a few reporters in. As Andrea took Randy's desk, they stopped by to speak to her.

"Glad to have you aboard again, Andie," Charlie Crawford said. "Your being here will ease the load. Besides Randy, we're short another reporter because Sylvia's out on maternity leave."

"Thanks, Charlie. It's good to be here."

"How's Randy feeling?" asked Diane Lowell.

"Pretty good. He moves at a snail's pace because of the broken ribs, but he's doing fine."

"We were taking bets on how soon he'd push to come back," Frank Swanson said, laughing. "We never thought to bet he'd send you in his place."

"That's what you get for gambling, Frank," Andrea teased, then added seriously, "I've got to thank you all again for your prayers and concern when he was missing. And all the gifts and cards when he was found. It..." Her voice became husky, to her acute embarrassment, but she had to finish. "It meant everything to us both."

"Don't tell him I said this," Charlie replied with a grin, "or I'll deny it, but we think a lot of Randy around here."

Andrea smiled. "I think the secret's out. All those gifts and phone calls really lifted his spirits. I just want you to know that. You're a terrific bunch."

"Now, Andie, if you're gonna get soppy, we'll get Davidson to assign you to the society section."

"Like hell you will!" Andrea exploded.

They all laughed, and the tension eased.

"Welcome back," Diane said. "If you need anything, just yell."

One by one, they drifted away. Davidson soon came back, welcomed her briefly and sent her out to cover a homicide.

Andrea slipped back into the routine of newspaper work as though she'd never been away.

Bill was alerted that she'd arrived and been sent out on an assignment. He stood at his office window, gazing down at the traffic, and grudgingly gave her credit. Andie had come through after all.

It surprised him, actually. Until Davidson's call to say she was there, he'd doubted she would come. She'd been so reluctant to take on the job and so nervous about staying with him at the apartment, that he'd fully expected she'd chicken out once she was back in New York.

In a way, he was sorry she hadn't. Now that she'd committed herself, he was committed to seeing the thing through, too. Why hadn't he refused when Randy had first broached the subject?

Anger, of course. And pride. He'd wanted to see her squirm, and she had. He'd wanted, too, to demonstrate by his willingness to go along with the scheme that he was indifferent to her, that he could be unaffected by whatever she did.

So she'd stunned him by agreeing to take Randy's place on the staff. She'd called his bluff, and now he had to live with it.

All that was bad enough, but then he'd kept right on digging his grave by proposing that she move in with him for the duration. He couldn't imagine a more destructive, preposterous arrangement. Obviously, he'd gone right out of his head. And again she'd called his bluff!

What had possessed him to suggest such a thing? he asked himself grimly. Or her to accept, for that matter? He didn't know what had made him say it, except an urge to put her on the spot again, to prove his lack of interest.

That was the biggest joke of all! He'd been lying through his teeth when he'd told her he didn't want her any more. The fact was he couldn't be near her for five minutes without desiring her, and he despised himself because of it. So how in hell was he going to survive five or six weeks of living with her, of wanting her so badly that he was in pain half the time?

That evening, Bill couldn't bring himself to go home directly after work. Andie would be there, moving through the rooms they'd once shared as a married couple. She'd be hanging her clothes in the bedroom closet next to his, setting out her makeup and perfumes on the dresser, probably washing panty hose in the bathroom. Tonight he just couldn't deal with it.

He went to a nearby bar and nursed a few drinks for a couple of hours. Then he went to a restaurant for dinner and managed to stretch that out for a long while. Afterward, he went to another bar and brooded over a couple more drinks, drinks he really didn't want. But it was something to do to pass the time until it was late and he could safely assume Andie would be in bed asleep.

Andrea looked at the clock for probably the hundredth time. A quarter of midnight. Where on earth could Bill be this late?

She'd gotten back to the apartment around six-thirty and, since Bill wasn't home, had set to work unpacking her things.

By seven-thirty, she'd been starving. She hadn't known what Bill wanted to do about dinner, so she'd waited. When they'd been married, Bill would sometimes make a simple casserole or grill a steak while she tossed a salad; other times they'd pick up something to bring home; still other evenings they'd go out to eat.

When he hadn't come or called by eight, Andrea scrounged in the kitchen and found a TV dinner in the freezer. She put it into the oven and went to take her bath.

Later, dressed in a gown and robe, she'd sat in front of the television and eaten her solitary meal. Yet her attention wasn't really on the detective show she was watching. She kept stealing glances at the clock, wondering where Bill was and why he hadn't at least telephoned to say he'd be late.

She hadn't been really worried until around ten, but then she had begun to grow seriously concerned over his absence. True, she hadn't had one of her "knowing" feelings that something was wrong, but she'd fretted anyway. Maybe it was the recent crisis over Randy, but suddenly her imagination had conjured up all sorts of horrible things that might have happened. An hour and a half later she had become frantic.

She was literally pacing the floor when she heard his key in the lock. Bill came inside, looking slightly disheveled. He wore a business suit, but his tie was gone and his shirt collar was open, one side crushed beneath the coat collar. His hair was mussed and his face was flushed.

Instantly, she knew. "You've been drinking!" she hurled the words angrily in his direction. "I've been here worrying myself sick all evening, and you've been out getting smashed!"

"Why aren't you asleep?" came the counterattack. "You should have been asleep. I don't want any drowsy, incompetent reporters on my staff!"

"I'd have loved to have been getting some sleep!" Andrea snapped. "But I was too upset! Do you realize what time it is? I was scared to death something had happened to you! You could at least have had the decency to call and let me know you wouldn't be coming home!"

Bill glared at her. He might have been drinking, but she saw now that he was far from drunk. The look in his eyes was full of contempt. "Listen to yourself!" he snarled. "You're sounding like a wife! What I do or when I come home is my business, not yours! You never bothered to worry about my welfare when you *were* my wife because you were too busy running off to do your own thing, so don't start trying to play the part now! It's way too late for that."

Something froze within Andrea. For a moment she couldn't even speak. She was stunned, hurt that he'd take her concern and throw it back in her face.

Then, with as much dignity as she could achieve, she nodded and said, "I'll be very careful to remember that. Good night, Bill." Before she could fall apart in front of him, she went into the bedroom and closed the door.

Bill stared bleakly at the door for a long time. Finally, wearily, he brushed his hand across his face. "Oh, hell," he muttered in despair. "Oh, hell."

Chapter Ten

Mr. President, can you tell us if you think the talks next month with the Soviet Union will bring about any significant breakthrough for a reduction in nuclear arms?''

The president and his wife were crossing the White House lawn, returning from a weekend at Camp David. A few snowflakes drifted down as Andrea stood with other members of the press corps, hoping she'd get lucky and win a response. White House duty was Frank's job, but he was home today fighting a flu bug, so Davidson had sent Andrea in his stead.

The president lifted a hand in his familiar wave to the gaggle of reporters and cameras, and for a moment it seemed that he would move on without speaking. But he chose to stop after all.

"We certainly hope so," he said in reply to the question. As other reporters began a chorus of questions, he stepped closer to Andrea and smiled. "It's nice to see you're back with the *Patriot*, Andrea."

"Why, thank you, sir. It's nice to be back."

"Over the weekend I finished reading *Floods along the Rio Grande*. You showed remarkable insight into the illegal alien problem, both from their vantage point and ours. It's a complex subject without any easy answers, and you shed light on that. Congratulations on a good job."

"It's very kind of you to say so, Mr. President."

Andrea would have been less than human if she hadn't been flattered that the President of the United States had read her book and thought it had merit, or that he had told her so in the presence of her colleagues. But that evening, like every other in the two weeks since she'd been back in Washington, sitting alone in the apartment, she wished she could apply a little of that insight to herself and her relationship with Bill.

Or rather, the lack of one. After that first night, a pattern had been set and strictly adhered to. Bill stayed out late every evening until she was usually in bed and asleep. In the mornings they sometimes encountered each other briefly, but most days Bill had already gone by the time Andrea was dressed.

There'd been no talk of sharing rides or anything else. Each day, Bill took his car; Andrea rode the subway. She'd only seen him once at the office since she'd been back, and that had been at the round table meeting. They'd been in the company of the editors and other senior reporters while ideas for articles and features were tossed out for debate.

She told herself it was for the best, that this way they wouldn't end up hurting each other again. The only problem was that in her heart she didn't really believe it. She was lonely and found it emotionally difficult to be staying here where they'd lived together as man and wife. The apartment itself had changed little, but with each other nothing was the same. Devoured by the passage of time were the evenings they'd spent cuddled together on the sofa, sharing the day's events over a drink. Gone, too, were the times they'd laughed themselves silly over their own version of strip poker—the stock market. They'd both owned a good deal of stock when they'd married and had been keen on following the progress of their particular holdings; so sometimes they'd made a game of it. For every stock that fell that day, the owner had to shed a piece of clothing. It had been hilarious and fun, and of course it had always ended with them collapsing in each other's arms and making love.

These days, remembering, Andrea didn't even have the heart to follow the market. Or the energy, for that matter. The past couple of weeks she'd definitely not been herself. She felt listless and tired easily, and two or three times her stomach had been unsettled. Last week she'd taken to swallowing multiple vitamins. Then she'd tried antacids, wondering if perhaps she'd developed an ulcer. It wouldn't be surprising, she told herself ironically, after all the recent upheavals, what with her anxiety over Randy's plane crash and the lingering shock of Bill's resurfacing in her life.

As usual, Bill had not returned by the time Andrea crawled wearily into bed. If he were staying away simply to avoid her, he could save himself the trouble and come home much earlier, she thought with grim humor as she set the clock. It was only nine-thirty, but she could scarcely keep her eyes open.

Shortly before midnight, Bill inserted his key into the lock and let himself into the silent apartment. As usual, Andrea had left a lamp burning. She'd also opened the sofa and made the bed for him so that he had only to undress and turn in.

He shed his coat and shoes and tiptoed into the bedroom. He had no idea why unless it was to torture himself by the sight of her in his bed, in *their* bed. In the semidarkness he saw that she was lying on her side, curled into a ball. Her face was serene and relaxed in sleep; her hair tumbled over the pillow and one shoulder, riotous waves of glory. He could scarcely resist bending down and running his hand through it. What would she do, he wondered, if she awoke to find him watching her, longing for her? Would she invite him to bed or be angry?

Bill turned his back upon the tantalizing vision and returned to the living room. What did it matter? he asked himself. She was a bird he could never cage; even if she still loved him, she wouldn't stay. The old restlessness would come upon her, and she'd soon be flying away to some distant land. Away from him.

He locked the front door and began unbuttoning his shirt. Lord, he was tired. He was tired of staying out every night, of finding places to go, of spending endless hours in his office when he couldn't think of anyplace he wanted to go except home to Andrea. But he didn't trust himself to be here with her: the situation would be far too intimate. He would want her, ache for her as he did now, and he was afraid he wouldn't be able to keep his distance. So he had no choice but to stay on the same dreary treadmill, rising early every morning and trying to get away before she was up; hanging out every evening until he was heartily sick of it. He'd seen every new movie running; he'd checked out far more bars than he'd wanted, or were good for him; he'd stayed late at the office and dropped in on weekends so often that the guards were beginning to give him funny looks.

On top of everything else, he wasn't getting his quota of sleep these days, and it was beginning to catch up with him. Randy had called him today at the office to invite him to the farm for Christmas, but Bill had declined, saying he'd already promised his aunt in Miami that he'd spend the holiday with her family. The truth was he hadn't decided to go until that very moment. He'd only known he needed to be away from Andrea for a while. Now, the more he thought about it, the better the idea seemed. He hadn't seen his relatives in a couple of years, so it would be nice to visit with them again. And he'd be able to hit the sack early for a change.

When Andrea awoke to the sound of her alarm the next morning, she also heard the buzz of a second one through the closed bedroom door. Apparently Bill had risen before it went off and forgot to push in the button. Yawning, she padded barefoot across the room and opened the door. Still half-asleep, she bent over the clock on the table next to the sofa bed and turned off the alarm before she even noticed that Bill was still there. His head was half-buried beneath the blankets, and one arm was exposed as it stretched across the bed, cradling the second pillow.

A poignant tenderness swept over her. So many mornings she had seen him just so, burrowing his dark head deep into the pillow while one arm extended outward, across her own body. As she wished it were now.

Hastily she turned away from the enticing sight, suppressing the impulse to crawl in beside him. The way things were between them these days, he'd surely rebuff her, just as she had done that night at Randy's.

Andrea went into the kitchen and put on the coffee. Instead of rushing off to take her shower, she sat down on one of the bar stools, heedless of the chill morning and her skimpy nightgown. Quietly, without fireworks or the fanfare of rolling drums, she admitted to herself that she had never stopped loving Bill.

The revelation plunged her into a deep depression. It meant she'd made the gravest of errors when she'd lost his love by shying away from it. It meant she would never find happiness with any other man. Worst of all, it meant the contentment and satisfaction she'd been so earnestly seeking in her travels, in her independent life-style, would never be found. How could it be, when the only real satisfaction the world had to offer her was right here? Here, where she couldn't stay; here, with a man who now rejected her as she'd once rejected him.

The magnitude of it was staggering, and she slumped, one arm resting against the bar, as she tried to assimilate it.

Bill found her like that, ten minutes later, when the aroma of coffee awakened him. He'd glanced at the clock, realizing at once that he'd overslept, and immediately swung his feet to the floor. It was obvious that Andrea had been up before him since he smelled fresh-brewed coffee, but he stopped short when he found her in the kitchen, head bowed, shoulders drooping, wearing only a semitransparent nightgown.

In that brief moment, his hungry gaze would have given away his feelings if she'd happened to notice him. But she didn't. Bill's eyes feasted on the white, bent neck, the wild tumble of red-gold curls, the alluring curve of her breasts and the dusky hollow between them that vanished beneath the pale blue gown. Her body was starkly outlined by the silky fabric as it hugged the gentle flare of her hips, the shapeliness of her crossed legs. One small and dainty foot protruded beneath the hem of the nightgown.

He swallowed hard as desire instantly inflamed his blood. This was what he'd been trying so hard to avoid these past two weeks, yet here he was losing the battle of his will the first second he found her in such intimate circumstances.

He forced a jaunty note into his voice. "Since when did you learn how to sleep on a bar stool?"

Andrea's head shot up and her eyes widened in surprise. Within their depths was something more than surprise, though. Was it sadness? Unhappiness? He couldn't tell for sure, but she'd certainly been contemplating something serious.

"You scared the daylights out of me!" she gasped. "I thought you were still sound asleep."

Bill went to the cupboard, took down two mugs and poured coffee into them. "I must have been sleeping like the dead not to have heard the alarm," he said, handing her one of the steaming mugs. "Why didn't you wake me?"

"You looked so peaceful, I didn't have the heart," she replied. "I decided to wait until the coffee was ready."

She took a sip of the coffee and immediately felt that queasiness again. Grimacing, she set the mug on the counter.

"Something the matter?" Bill asked, eyeing her over the rim of his cup.

"Coffee doesn't always agree with me these days," she said lightly, thinking that a lot of other things didn't seem to agree with her, either. Still, she felt a need for food and got to her feet. "I think I'll have some juice instead. And some cereal. Want some?"

"I'm hungry, too," Bill admitted, "but I'd rather have something more substantial. Why don't I fix us a proper breakfast?"

Andrea peeped at the wall clock. "Fine," she said. "Except it might make us late for work. Will the boss be mad?"

Bill grinned. "I think I can smooth it with him," he replied as he opened the refrigerator.

While he started cooking, Andrea set their places at the breakfast bar, poured the fruit juice and dropped bread into the toaster. She located the salt and pepper shakers and was about to carry them to the bar when she turned abruptly and bumped into Bill, who'd turned once more toward the refrigerator.

The contact was electrifying. Andrea still wore only her thin nightgown; Bill wore white pajama pants, but his chest was bare.

Instantly, without conscious thought, they embraced. Andrea's heart skipped a beat as she gazed up into Bill's face. What she saw, despite his anger with her and his coldness, was not indifference.

Her lips parted as he bent his head toward her. His mouth, usually so stern and hard, was soft and gentle as it came closer to hers.

A sudden clanging jarred them, and they leapt apart. "My God!" Andrea cried. "What is it?"

Bill reached to the ceiling for the smoke alarm and flipped a switch that instantly silenced the racket. Then, in a fluid motion, he removed the skillet from the burner on the stove.

"Well," he said ruefully, "so much for breakfast."

Andrea moved beside him to get a look at the black, shriveled crisps of bacon floating in the smoking grease, and she burst out laughing.

Annoyance flickered across Bill's face. "What's so funny?" he grumbled.

"And you say *I* can't cook! You've got a nerve!" she gasped between giggles. "Even at my worst I never set off any fire alarms!"

"Touché!" Bill grinned. "Okay, now that I've demolished all the bacon, what do you say we get dressed and go out for breakfast?"

"Excellent idea." By now the toast was done. Andrea removed the slices from the toaster and tossed one to Bill. "Here. Something to munch on in the meantime." She started nibbling on the other slice.

"No thanks." Bill put his piece on the counter and looked at her with amusement. "Are you so starved you can't wait till we get to a restaurant?"

"I guess so." She'd discovered that dry toast eased her upset stomach. She swallowed it now for that reason more than from actual hunger, although she didn't say so.

By the time they were seated across from each other at the restaurant, Bill had come to the conclusion that the burnt bacon had been his salvation. He'd come *that* close to succumbing to the heat of the moment when they'd practically fallen into each other's arms. Now, he mentally kicked himself for being such putty in her hands. If that alarm hadn't gone off, they'd probably have ended up in bed together. The trouble was, Andie only wanted him as long as it was a secret between them. She didn't want the world to know; she didn't want Randy to know. That way, when she left him this time, as she inevitably would, there would be no awkward explanations to make to anyone.

As though a shutter had been lowered, Andrea knew that once again the brief time of intimacy was over. Now they were both fully dressed with a table separating them.

A lot more than clothes and tables separated them, though, she couldn't kid herself about that. Especially when it was her fault. She'd been the one who'd kept running away from the marriage, the one to retreat that night at Randy's. If he were reluctant to let her back into his life now, there was no one to blame but herself.

And she still loved him.

Her throat tightened painfully. She wished she could just reach across the table, touch his hand and tell him so. But she couldn't. The emotional barricade he'd thrown up wouldn't let her. She felt near tears, vulnerable somehow. If he were to scorn her love, she couldn't bear it.

When they finally arrived at the office, Andrea was over an hour late for work. In the elevator, Bill asked, "Want me to go in with you and square things with Davidson?"

Andrea smiled and shook her head. "No, of course not. Let him rant and rave. He can't fire me, can he?"

Bill grinned wanly. "All right."

The elevator jolted to a halt. The door slid open and Andrea stepped out into the corridor.

"Andie?"

She turned back as he pressed the button to hold the door open. "Yes?" There'd been a haunted quality to his voice; it was in the smoky-blue fathoms of his eyes as well, as though he were being pursued by demons. Andrea yearned to free him of the torture, but she could not. She had her own demons to contend with. All she could do was wait. "Yes?" she asked again.

Bill gazed at her an instant more, then shook his head. "Nothing." He pressed another button and the elevator doors closed.

The next afternoon, Andrea crossed the echoing marble rotunda in the Capitol, dodging clumps of sightseers, finally reaching the long wing of offices that had been her objective.

"Andrea! Andrea Sheridan!"

She whirled around. The tall, good-looking man who came toward her wore the same youthful, easy smile that won him much trust and admiration with the voters of his state.

"Well, hi, Doug. How are you?"

Senator Douglas Rogers grinned broadly as he clasped both her hands in his. "Couldn't be better," he replied. Then, in a low, almost intimate tone of voice, he added, "Except that I've missed you."

"Is that a fact?" Andrea's eyes twinkled. "Last time I saw your picture in the newspapers, you were escorting a lovely lady to some big benefit."

"Only because you weren't available," Doug countered swiftly. "Don't you *ever* stay home? I tried to call you three or four times last month, hoping we could get together."

"I was in England."

Andrea tugged her hands free of his, and he asked, "So...what're you doing here?"

"There's a press conference with the Senate Majority Leader in a few minutes. I'm back on the *Patriot*."

"You are?" Doug sounded astonished.

"Don't you ever read the papers?" Andrea teased.

"Not thoroughly enough, apparently. Does this mean you're back with Sheridan?"

"No. I'm just helping out until Randy's able to return."

"Oh, yes. I heard about his accident. I hope he's all right now."

"He's fine. Just a few broken bones still mending." She glanced at her watch. "I'd better get a move on, Doug, or I'll be late."

"Sure. How about dinner tonight?"

Andrea was sorely tempted to accept. She was so tired of being alone every evening. She'd dated Doug a few times during the past year whenever he happened to be in New York, but the last time he'd become rather insistently amorous. When she'd refused to go along, their parting had been less than cordial on both sides. She didn't think it would be wise to give him fresh encouragement, nor did she want to, now that she'd faced up to her feelings for Bill, hopeless as they were.

"Thanks, but I can't. I'm tied up."

Doug frowned. "I'm leaving town tomorrow. Christmas recess, you know. Where are you staying? I'll call you after the holidays."

"With a friend," Andrea replied vaguely. "Look, I've really got to run." She moved away.

"Then phone me," Doug called after her retreating form.

"Sure," Andrea shouted back, and waved casually. But she knew she would never make that call.

By four o'clock on the afternoon before Christmas Eve, all work except the most essential had ceased at the *Patriot*. The staff bustled about in the Rumpus Room, preparing to celebrate. Some covered desks with red paper tablecloths; others set out food. Andrea helped string crepe paper and hung festive red and white paper bells. Gag gifts had already been placed beneath the huge decorated tree in the corner.

"Wish Randy had been able to make it up for the party," Frank said as he steadied the ladder Andrea was perched upon.

"He thought about it," Andrea said, "but he decided the round trip would be too jolting. He can't sit in one position too long without the ribs starting to bother him."

Frank nodded. "You going to his place for Christmas?"

"Yes. You going anywhere?"

"I'm flying to Missouri in the morning. Haven't seen my folks in two years."

"That ought to be nice. I hope you'll have a good trip."

"Oh, I intend to," Frank said with a grin.

At that moment Bill entered the room, spotted Andrea immediately and came toward them. She felt herself tense as she balanced on the ladder, arms upraised while she taped a streamer to the ceiling. Since that morning at breakfast a few days earlier, she'd only had brief glimpses of him and even fewer words.

From his vantage point on the floor, Bill had an intriguing view of Andie. With her arms stretched above her head, the dark blue blouse she wore hugged her breasts and rib cage, outlining them in stark detail. Neat black slacks skimmed her hips and legs, showing off her lovely shape to advantage, and a narrow gold belt circled her waist. He swallowed hard, wishing she didn't look quite so alluring. It was so difficult to pretend indifference.

"Looking good," he said lightly, approving the decorations. "Except that the white bell's a little crooked."

"I know, but I can't seem to get it straight, so it'll just have to list." Andrea glanced down at Frank. "Hold it steady. I'm coming down."

"Hey, Frank, come see this!" someone shouted from across the room.

"Go ahead," Bill told him, placing his own hands on the ladder. "I'll help her."

Frank departed and Andrea descended. When she neared the bottom rung, Bill put one arm around her waist until she was safely on the floor, but then the hand fell away with haste.

Though they'd both intended to play it casual, since each was acutely aware of the presence of others, something happened when their gazes met. All pretence was stripped away, and their hearts were laid bare. Their eyes spoke what neither dared say.

"Well," Bill said at last with a forced heartiness, "you must be planning a trip to Randy's."

Andrea nodded. Her throat was scratchy as she, too, tried to speak naturally. "Tomorrow afternoon. Are you staying in town?"

"No, I'm going down to Aunt May's," he replied. "I'll be away about ten days."

"I see." Andrea slowly digested the news. Disappointment welled inside her, but she was careful not to let it show. "Then you won't be back until after the New Year?" she asked in a steady voice.

"That's right. I wanted to offer you the use of my car while I'm gone. You'll need it to get to Randy's."

"I've already rented one, but thanks anyway."

They were both stiff, awkward with each other. That one long, meaningful glance had left them shaken, eager to pretend it hadn't happened.

"Say hello to Randy and Lisa for me."

"I'll do that. Have a safe trip."

"Merry Christmas, Andie."

"Merry Christmas, Bill," she said softly.

Merry Christmas, Andrea told herself ironically on Christmas night as she crawled into the same bed she'd used before in Randy's house. She could scarcely recall a Christmas when she'd been less happy or felt more alone.

Yet she had no one to blame but herself: she simply was not in a holiday mood. In reality, everything should have been wonderful. Fresh snow covered the ground, giving the countryside a pristine sparkle. Christmas dinner had been held at the Webers' rambling home, where there had been plenty of good food and drink. Andrea had been swept into the bosom of Lisa's warm, boisterous family and treated as one of their own, and even Randy and Lisa, who were now formally engaged and might understandably have preferred a little privacy, had done their best to make her feel wanted. Still, she'd felt cut off, isolated and alone.

The problem was that she missed Bill, ached for him, and wished with all her heart that she could be with him.

But he hadn't wanted to be with her. He had made that crystal clear by going to Florida instead of accepting Randy's invitation. He'd made it clearer still by keeping a rigid distance between them these past few weeks. Only that one morning had he let down his guard, and then but momentarily.

Andrea went back to Washington the day after Christmas and plunged herself into work. With all the politicians away, however, the city was practically dead, and there was little news to be gathered. Even crime was down. The weather was too cold, and she supposed the criminals were still in a benign holiday spirit themselves.

On New Year's Eve, she found herself at loose ends. Everyone else, it seemed, had big plans for the evening. Andrea toyed with the idea of going to New York. She'd only managed to get home for one weekend since she'd gone back to the *Patriot*. But most of her friends probably had plans for tonight, and the idea of sitting alone in her own apartment was no more appealing than sitting alone in Bill's. Even if she did get herself invited somewhere for the evening, she wasn't in much of a party mood, so why bother? It all seemed like more trouble than it was worth.

In the end she ushered in the New Year alone, watching the trumped-up celebration on television. She felt very sorry for herself as she sipped at a glass of cola—the strongest thing there was to drink because she'd even forgotten to buy herself a bottle of wine, and she couldn't find the keys to Bill's liquor cabinet.

She slept late the next morning, but it didn't matter. There was nothing to do, nowhere to go. She ate breakfast, then wandered into the living room. Bored, she flipped on the television and sat down, still in her robe, to watch the Rose Bowl Parade.

Half an hour later she heard a rattle at the front door, and Bill walked in looking as astonished to see her as she was to see him.

He dropped his suitcase by the door. "Hi. I didn't expect to find you here," he said.

"Where did you think I'd be?"

Bill shed his coat and shrugged. "I don't know. New York. Randy's. Someplace. It's New Year's."

"What about you? I thought you weren't coming back until tomorrow."

Bill dropped onto the sofa beside her. "I was able to get an earlier flight on standby, so I took it." He sighed. "I love Aunt May, but a week of hearing about her arthritis pains got to be a little tedious."

"I see. I envisioned you out dancing last night with some southern beauty."

Bill grinned impishly. "Well, I could have had a date last night, but I wouldn't call her a beauty. Earlier in the week Aunt May fixed me up with a dinner date one night, and I couldn't get out of it without hurting her feelings. The woman wasn't bad-looking, I guess, but she's a divorcée whose sole purpose in life, I gather, is to stick her ex for as much alimony as possible, and then hang on to it by getting as much for her money as she can." Andrea could hear the disgust in his voice.

"How so?" she asked in amusement.

"She made sure I took her to a really elegant restaurant. When we got there, she told me what to order so I'd get the most for the least, she overruled my choice of wine for the house brand, and then, long and loud, embarrassingly loud," he added, wincing at the memory, "she argued with me because she thought I was leaving too generous a tip for the waiter."

Andrea choked with laughter. "Sounds like a lady who knows what she wants."

"That's a lady?" Bill grimaced. "She also wanted a date for last night. She very pointedly hinted that I should take her out to celebrate the New Year. She knows this place where we wouldn't have to pay a cover charge, you see. I told her I already had other plans and couldn't possibly get out of them."

Andrea giggled. "At least she's conservative. You should have snapped her up."

Bill glowered at her. "Are you kidding? I couldn't get away from her fast enough." He sighed again, heavily. "That was the highlight of my week. How was yours? Did you have a nice Christmas?"

Andrea nodded. "Randy and Lisa are now officially engaged."

"How about that!" Bill looked at her with interest. "How do you feel about it?"

"Great. Lisa's the best thing to happen to Randy since he landed a job with your father."

"You really mean that, don't you?"

Andrea was suddenly annoyed. "Of course I do. You know I got over my little streak of jealousy as soon as I met her."

Bill leaned back against the cushions and took in the robe, her lack of makeup. "Are you sick?" he asked.

Andrea shook her head. She'd had her usual bout of queasiness this morning, but it had soon worn off. "Just being lazy," she said. "Besides, I didn't think anybody would see me like this." She touched her hair. "I must look awful."

"You've never looked awful to me," he said quietly. "Not even that time I nursed you through the flu."

Andrea's mouth went dry. The intensity of his gaze was deeply disturbing. She didn't know how to answer him; in the old days there would've been no question, but now...Maybe he was kidding, or worse, just being kind.

She decided to keep it light. "I really *must* look awful if you're comparing the way I look now to then," she said with a little laugh. "Maybe I'd better go play with the pots of paint." She unfolded her legs, about to get up.

Bill put his hand on her arm. "Stay," he said softly. "I always liked you best this way—your hair a little wild, like a siren's, your face scrubbed clean, like an innocent, and dressed as though you were just waiting to go to bed with me."

"Bill..."

"Hush," he murmured as he drew her to him. "Don't you know the real reason I came home early?"

She shook her head, not daring to speak, to spoil the moment.

"Because I had a rotten Christmas without you. Because I couldn't enjoy anything for thinking about you, for missing you, for wanting to see you again."

His lips crushed hers fiercely, demandingly, and Andrea responded with equal fervor. Her heart began to pound. Joy flooded through her, wild, hot, recklessly undisciplined. At last, she was coming alive again.

Bill's hand slid between the folds of her robe, beneath the fragile lace of her nightgown, where it encountered the soft, smooth fullness of her breast. He heard Andie's whispered sigh before she buried her face against his neck.

"I don't know whether I hate you or love you, Andie," he said softly.

He felt her stiffen. "Why do you say that?" she asked.

Bill smiled and brushed her hair away. "I can't bear being around you when I can't touch you, so I go away and get mixed up with shrewish tightwads. Then I come back to find you sitting here, seductive and beautiful, and I forget all my resolutions."

"You don't see me objecting, do you?"

He pulled back so that he could look at her. "No. No, I don't, at that."

"I missed you, too," she said, smiling. "Not that I ever seem to see you anymore, anyway, but I guess it was just knowing you were so far away. And it being Christmas. It was nice at Randy's, fresh snow and everything. Lisa's parents welcomed me with open arms, just as though I were a part of the family. Yet I . . ."

Bill's lips, so close to hers, parted in a teasing smile. "Yes?"

"I moped around the whole time, pretending to enjoy myself and hating every minute. And last night I sat here all alone with the TV and felt good and sorry for myself, especially when I thought of you with the beautiful southern belle."

"Miss Pennypincher herself, eh?" Bill chuckled. He continued in a serious vein, "I sat alone in a hotel bar last night brooding over my beer and thinking you were probably out with some man. It drove me crazy." He paused, and his eyes glowed with desire. "Andie, if you still don't want me, I don't think I can stand it."

Andrea's eyes were shining. "Oh, but I do, Bill. So much."

Chapter Eleven

Andrea dropped her gold hoop earrings onto the bedroom dresser. "Umm," she purred with satisfaction. "The dinner was exquisite."

She wore the black designer dress she'd had on the night in London when she'd first seen Bill again. It had seemed fitting to wear it tonight, now that things were so wonderful between them.

"So are you." Behind her, Bill's voice was low and sensual. They were both reflected in the mirror as he bent his dark head and kissed her creamy throat. "In fact, you taste sweeter than the dessert we ordered."

Andrea smiled at their reflection and tilted her head back, raising a hand to caress his cheek. "You always did have a golden tongue," she said.

Bill laughed softly as his hands snaked around her and slid up to her breasts. He lifted his head and met her gaze in the mirror. "Only when I was seducing you," he replied.

Andrea turned in his embrace and encircled his waist with her arms. "Is that what you're doing?" she teased. "Seducing me? I'd have thought you'd be tired of me by now."

"Never!" Bill declared. To prove it, he pulled her closer and kissed her ready lips.

Andrea felt as though she were floating. New Year's Day, and she'd been given a new lease on life. After the despair of the past few weeks, it seemed like a lovely dream—hazy, foggy, not quite real, but oh, so beautiful.

They'd spent all afternoon in bed, getting up only long enough to forage for something light to eat before making love again. Afterward they'd slept, wrapped in each other's arms, until dusk.

Finally they'd forced themselves, groggy from loving and sleeping, to get up, shower, dress and go out into the cold, clear night.

They'd gone to one of the finest restaurants in Washington and had a perfect meal, enhanced by flickering chandeliers, soft music, attentive waiters, champagne and each other.

Now, Bill wanted her again. Andrea glowed with the knowledge.

They undressed each other slowly, touching, caressing, kissing. The urgency they'd experienced earlier was gone; tonight they had all the time in the world to savor each other with leisurely appreciation.

The lamplight cast a soft golden glow over them as they embraced once more, their shadow a single form as it fell across the carpeted floor.

Bill was mesmerized by the silkiness of her skin. He was enchanted by the scent of her, by the billowing cloud of her hair, by the luminescence of her eyes, enthralled by the magic that was Andie. His lips moved on hers with renewed hunger as his hands roamed over the curve of her hips, the incline of her narrow waist, the delicate perfection of her breasts. He was filled with unspeakable delight because she was his again. His need for her was insatiable; he couldn't seem to get enough of her—nor, to his immense gratification, she of him.

They stood thus for long minutes, clasped in each other's arms. He smothered her face with kisses, and she did the same to him. His body hardened with urgency, and Andrea laughed huskily out of sheer exultation.

"Think it's funny, do you?" he said, trying to sound stern. "You find it amusing to torment me like this?"

She nodded, her eyes shining. "Yes," she admitted in an unsteady voice. "It's only fair, because it's what you do to me. I honestly don't think I've been alive at all the past three years, Bill," she whispered, suddenly very serious.

"Neither have I." His lips widened in a self-mocking smile. "But if I die tonight from too much loving, at least I'll die a happy man."

She laughed with uninhibited joy. "Oh, don't do that!" she exclaimed. "Because I'll want you again tomorrow and the next day and the next and—"

She broke off, gasping, as Bill bent to take a rosy nipple into his mouth. Andrea's fingers dug into his bare shoulders as his tongue teased this pleasure point.

"Ah, Bill, Bill," she murmured. "Oh, darling..."

A moment later he lifted her up and carried her to the bed, where he could make love to her properly. As he came down to her, his heart skipped a beat at the expression in her eyes. They were brilliant with a fire of urgent desire, of excited expectation. For him. All for him. Bill groaned and lost all coherent thought.

The swell of her breasts allured him; the round, marble smoothness of her hips enticed him; the red-golden triangle between her legs hypnotized him. He became lost once more in the wonder of her beauty, the glory of her femininity, the thrill of her wanton, provocative movements. This was Andie, marvelous Andie, his precious love.

He teased and excited her until she was in a wild frenzy, writhing and moaning, clutching and grasping. She was all woman, hot-blooded and unashamed of it, openly enjoying the pleasures of mating as a full and equal partner. Bill reveled in the ability to unleash such passion in her. She met the demands of his own sexual arousal, but she demanded her own satisfaction as well, and he adored her because of it. Andie was no shrinking violet, afraid of her own needs.

Neither of them could be easily or swiftly appeased tonight, as had been the case earlier in the day. The rhythmic music of the blood coursing through their veins, accompanied by the beating of their hearts, played on, primitive, earthy, inciting them still further. They were being swept away by the dance of love as turbulent passions throbbed, swelling, rising, quickening the beat of their untamed music.

At last the dance was over, the music ended, and they came together. Then, reverberations of the crescendo shuddered violently through them. Bill's arms tightened around Andrea as she clung to him, kitten-soft and sighing. Perspiration dampened their skin, and their breathing was harsh.

"I love you, Bill," Andrea whispered, still holding him close. "I want you to know that. I never stopped."

Bill ran his fingers through her moist curls. "I love you, too, Andie," he said softly. "I always have."

A few minutes later, sighing one last time with utter contentment, Andrea floated off to sleep still cushioned in Bill's arms. For a time, he watched over her slumber, feeling tender and protective. Finally he reached over and switched off the lamp.

Tired as he was from the long flight and an afternoon and evening of lovemaking, Bill slept fretfully. With the gray light of dawn, he slipped quietly from bed so he wouldn't disturb Andrea, grabbed his robe and left the room.

She found him, an hour later, sitting in the semigloom of the living room, sipping coffee. His dark hair was still tousled, his unshaven jaw a smoky blue.

"Morning, love." Andrea smiled, morning bright and lively, and bent to kiss him briefly. Then, tracing an affectionate finger along his raspy overnight beard, she went into the kitchen.

When she came back, carrying a glass of milk, she sat down on the sofa beside him and nestled close to his shoulder. "I slept like a log, but I guess I must have sensed when you weren't there anymore because the past hour or so I've been waking up off and on. What're you looking so serious about, darling?"

Bill glanced at the glass she held. "Milk? What happened to your morning coffee habit?"

Andrea shrugged lightly. "I told you before. It doesn't seem to agree with me anymore. You didn't answer my question. Why so serious? Is something wrong?"

Bill's eyes were cloudy and intense. Something in his gaze sent a jolt of fear and warning through her even before he nodded.

"We're wrong," he said finally.

The fear spread icy fingers along her spine, and her mouth went dry. "What—what do you mean?"

"You. Me. Us together," Bill said grimly. "It's just all wrong, Andie. It's no good."

Andrea felt as if a fist had just slammed into her stomach. "How can you possibly say that?" she asked faintly. "After last night? After yesterday? We were so happy!"

Bill rose and began pacing the room. "Sure we were!" His voice was suddenly harsh. "We were reliving the good old days!"

"What's so bad about that?"

He stopped in front of her, and his face, it seemed to Andrea, had the chilling look of implacability. "Nothing would be wrong with that," he told her, "if that were the whole story, but it's not. We had a hell of a lot more bad old days than good ones, and yesterday we forgot that part."

"Bill, what are you saying?" Deep inside, with sickening dread, Andrea already knew. "That it's over?"

He sighed heavily. "That's exactly what I'm saying. Yesterday we let ourselves stray off the track, but it's time we got back on our individual, separate paths again. There's nothing between us worth reliving or trying to preserve."

Andrea swung to her feet, and her eyes glittered with pain and humiliation. "How can you say this?" she demanded. "Bill, we love each other!"

Bill began pacing the room again, but after a moment he paused a few feet away from her, nursing his brow as though he had a headache. "Yes, but that's wrong, too. What does it change? We loved each other the first time around, and our marriage didn't work, so what's the difference now?"

Andrea licked her dry lips. "We—we could try..." Her voice faded completely as Bill shook his head decisively and turned his back, physically and symbolically rejecting her plea.

"I tried before, Andie," he said in a muffled voice. "God knows I tried. I didn't want to lose you, but it happened anyway." Abruptly he swung around, and his eyes were dark and piercing. "I just can't go through all that again. I kept waking up and thinking about it all night. About what might happen if we got married again, or even just tried living together. But I always came up against the same brick wall. You'd grow restless and leave again, and I'd never have the sort of life I really want. I'm not blaming you, please understand that. It's just the difference between how you are and how I am."

"Maybe we learned something from the first time," Andrea ventured. "Maybe this time, since we already know how easy it is to lose what's important, we'd try harder to hang on to it. I—I'm willing to try, Bill. Really try."

Bill shrugged. "Maybe we could compromise. Maybe you wouldn't stay away so much of the time, and maybe I'd learn to give you the freedom you need. Maybe you'd put up with a house and dinner parties and such on my account, and I'd take more vacations so I could travel with you. But there's just no way to be fair all the way around. I still want children someday—with a woman who wants them as much as I do. I'm grateful now that we never had a child together. In that respect, you were a lot smarter than Carrie: at least you had better sense than to bring children into the world and then reject them the way she did." He sighed. "We should never had gotten involved again, Andie. You were right about that when we were in Atlanta. The sad truth is we're still crazy about each other, and maybe we always will be to a certain extent, but we're just not right for each other. Somewhere down the line we'd end up hating each other."

"I . . . see." Andrea choked back tears and struggled to keep her voice from breaking. "I'll go pack my bags." She turned and stumbled toward the bedroom.

"I didn't mean that!" Bill said sharply as he grabbed her arm and swung her around. "Of course you'll stay here until Randy's back. I'll just stay out of your way as much as possible."

Andrea nodded listlessly, too miserable even to argue. If he wanted her to stay, she'd stay; if he wanted her to go, she'd go. It made little difference. The important thing was that he didn't want her anymore; the pain of that would be with her whether she saw him again or not.

By the time she was ready to leave for the office, Bill had dressed and gone. Andrea smiled grimly. Back to the original setup, she thought—to being strangers who lived in the same apartment and worked in the same office building.

That afternoon after work, Andrea went shopping instead of going straight to the apartment. She knew that if she was to get through more long, solitary evenings the next few weeks, she'd have to find something to distract herself. She'd never been a hobbyist, but now she decided to take up needlepoint and cooking. There would probably never be a better time to practice the latter: whenever she traveled there was no opportunity; whenever she was at home in New York she went out most evenings with friends. Here in Washington she was isolated.

There were old friends in Washington she could have seen, of course, but she'd been reluctant to call them. They were Bill's friends, too, and she hadn't wanted to create any embarrassing, awkward situations. The fact that her byline was appearing in the *Patriot* again had elicited enough curiosity, and now that Bill had rejected her, she was doubly glad she hadn't let anyone know they were sharing the same apartment.

That evening she created a disaster in the kitchen. The spaghetti sauce scorched on the bottom of the pan so that when she stirred it there were black globs floating around in the thick, red liquid. It was inedible and she threw it down the disposal. The spaghetti, too, was unpalatable. It came out gummy and stuck together in a huge, stringy mass. Andrea stared at her ruined efforts with tears stinging her eyes. But as they slid down her face, she realized she was crying not for the spaghetti, but for herself. The disaster she'd created had nothing to do with food: it had come years ago, when she'd destroyed her marriage out of fear. Now she'd discovered just how much she still loved Bill—but he no longer wanted a life with her.

Andrea threw out the remainder of the meal, put the dishes in the dishwasher and went into the living room. Its silent walls mocked her. *You had your chance. You had your chance.*

When she and Randy were growing up, no one had seemed to want them for more than a couple of months at a time. At the end of that time they'd worn out their welcome and been shipped off somewhere else. Andrea had soon concluded that to keep the affection of those you loved most, you never clung. You smiled and went away on schedule, and when you came back a few months later, they'd be happy to see you again. That had been the pattern with her parents, aunts and uncles and friends. She'd naturally believed the rule held true for marriage, too.

She'd been afraid of marriage from the start: it seemed to lead inevitably to arguments, anger, separation and, finally, divorce. Nevertheless, she'd loved Bill so much that she'd been willing to try—until they'd started to have problems. Then her instinct had been to escape, to get away before he grew tired of her. Instead, he'd grown tired of her leaving and it had only caused more dissension.

Three days later Andrea was summoned to Bill's office. It was the first time she'd seen him since he'd told her they were through. He'd been coming home at some point during the night, she knew, but he was always gone by the time she woke up in the morning. As she walked into the room, he was hunched over the desk, scribbling something on a piece of paper. When he lifted his head, she was startled at how haggard he looked. Evidently he wasn't sleeping any better than she.

"Yes?" she managed to say coolly.

Bill stood up. "It's time for the round table meeting."

Andrea's eyes widened. "Didn't Davidson tell you I wouldn't be there?"

"He told me. That's why I sent for you. Whatever our personal problems, this is business, and I expect you to be present at the meeting just like every other senior reporter."

"Sorry, but I can't make it today. I have an errand to run."

His eyes narrowed. "In connection with a story you're doing?"

"No," she answered truthfully. "It's personal."

"Then it can wait until after the meeting," Bill said decisively.

"No, it can't."

"What the devil is so important it can't wait a couple of hours?"

"I told you," she said, shrugging. "It's personal."

Bill glowered at her. "You mean you won't tell me."

"That's right."

"I'm warning you, Andie. You'd better be in that meeting room in exactly ten minutes."

Andrea smiled and asked sweetly, "And what'll you do when I don't show up? Fire me?" She went to the door and waved. "Have a nice meeting."

"Andrea, don't you dare—"

Softly, she closed the door on his tirade and hurried away. She had no time to waste on Bill's temper today. Her appointment was important, and she had no intention of missing it.

Andrea did get to her appointment, and missed the meeting. She didn't hear anything more from Bill on the subject—in fact, she didn't see him at all on the following day. Surprisingly, she hardly noticed his absence. She was preoccupied with her thoughts and it took all her attention simply to get through the day.

Then, just as she was about to leave the office to cover a news conference two days after her confrontation with Bill, she received the telephone call she'd been anxiously awaiting. She listened to the voice at the other end, but had no time to mull over the message. After she hung up, she went to the press conference and, in robot fashion, asked her share of questions and jotted down the replies. All the while the news she'd been given over the phone was demanding her attention, its impact far more earthshaking than any world crisis.

When she was at last free to go, she hurried to a telephone and called Davidson, dictating her notes and telling him to get somebody else to work on the story. She would not, she said, be returning to work today. When he tried to press her for a reason, she told him what she'd told Bill a few days earlier: it was personal business.

A cold, misty rain was falling as Andrea crossed Constitution Avenue and headed toward the Lincoln Memorial. Even in the rain there were tourists milling around. She didn't join them in viewing the statue but turned instead toward the reflecting pool. Today, dotted with thousands of raindrops, it reflected a slate-gray sky.

Damp air gusted across the Potomac, but Andrea was scarcely aware of its chill as she moved aimlessly in the direction of the Mall. Ahead were the Washington Monument, the complex of Smithsonian buildings, the Capitol dome in the far distance, yet she saw none of it. She was centered utterly and completely within herself.

A baby. The words swirled around in her mind, by turns frightening, exquisitely beautiful, wondrous, and frightening again. She was going to have Bill's baby.

It explained why she was so easily fatigued these days, why certain foods or coffee didn't agree with her anymore, why she so often felt queasy. The doctor who had examined her several days ago had been almost certain at the time, but Andrea had refused to accept even the possibility. Now the test results proved conclusively that she was pregnant. Somehow she would have to accept it.

She found a park bench and sat down weakly not caring that it was wet, not caring about the cold rain lashing her face. Her legs simply wouldn't carry her any longer. She was in a state of shock, trying to absorb this unbelievable turn of events.

Obviously it had happened that morning in Atlanta when she and Bill had made love; she'd been so glad he was with her, so thrilled that Randy was safe, that she'd let down her defenses. Now she tried to sort out her emotions, but she couldn't decide whether she was happy or sad. Having a baby was something she had never planned for herself.

For the next two weeks Andrea's moods swung from one extreme to the other. One moment she was ecstatic over the life inside of her; she would go about her work feeling bubbly, almost giddy with joy over her precious secret. Other times she sank into depression because the one person she wanted to share it with, *should* share it with, couldn't be told.

She wasn't sure he would even believe her. Sometimes she didn't believe it herself, it seemed so incredible. But Bill had said he didn't want to renew their relationship. He loved her, he'd said, but not enough to try again. He'd also said he still wanted children, but not with her. Her memory of that was painfully clear.

Andrea cringed with humiliation just thinking of that morning. She'd opened up to him, expressed her willingness to try to change, to be what he wanted this time. But it hadn't made any difference: Bill hadn't believed her. So if she told him of her pregnancy, he might think she was faking it just to get her way. Even if he did believe her and asked her to come back to him, it would only be for the baby's sake, not because he wanted her. And that she would never allow. What possible sort of relationship could they carve out of that?

Sometimes when she thought about the baby, the sweetest tenderness came over her, she felt so protective of it, wanted so much for it. Fortunately, she'd started to take better care of herself nutritionally several weeks ago, when she'd begun to feel squeamish. Now that she knew why, she was even more careful. Her unborn child's health was of the utmost importance, and she intended to do everything in her power to guard its well-being.

But how well would she care for it after birth? The thought of raising a child, of being totally responsible for it, filled her with misgivings. She had no experience with children, no real family background. She was totally inept, and that was most frightening of all. Her child deserved the best, and she knew she was emotionally ill-equipped to provide it.

One of the first and last great arguments she'd had with Bill after their marriage had concerned children. She'd adamantly opposed having any, while he'd been first incredulous, then furious over her attitude. What he had never realized was that her implacability had stemmed from fears, not selfishness or indifference. She'd been deeply afraid that she'd turn out to be like her mother, and she never wanted to subject a child to such unconsciously cruel indifference. Yet surely this protective feeling she had toward the tiny living creature in her womb, this melting tenderness, were characteristics of love and devotion. Maybe, a small voice whispered, just maybe, it would be all right.

It *had* to be all right! She told herself this daily. It had to be all right because there was no one else to make it right. Certainly not Bill, who didn't want her, who now rejected her love as she'd once rejected his. But it saddened her that his attitude made it impossible for her to share this with him—the most important event that had ever happened to either of them.

"It'll be very simple," Randy said, "since we decided to do it so soon, but we couldn't see much point in waiting months on end just to make a lavish event of it. So...what do you say? Will you be my best man?"

Bill leaned back in his swivel chair and gazed out his office window at the swirling snowflakes. "I'd be honored," he said into the telephone. "How does Andie feel about all this?"

"She doesn't know yet," Randy replied. "I tried to reach her first, but she's out on an assignment. She probably won't even go back to the office, so will you tell her for me when you get home?"

Bill grimaced. Randy was asking a lot more than he knew. But then, he had no way of knowing that Bill stayed away from the apartment until late every night, that when they did accidentally meet, he and Andie had nothing meaningful to say to each other. Now Randy wanted him to go home and tell her that her twin was getting married on Saturday.

"I really think you'd better do that yourself," he said. "Andie won't be very happy to hear your news through me."

"I know, but she'll be more upset if she isn't told right away. Lisa and I have an appointment with the minister in about an hour, and then we're going out to dinner with her brother and his wife. I won't be back until late tonight, so it'll probably be tomorrow morning before I can talk with Andie. You'd better tell her tonight, Bill."

"All right," Bill agreed after a slight pause. "I'll tell her."

"Thanks," Randy said. "Talk to you later."

"Okay. Oh, by the way, Randy. Congratulations. You're marrying a great girl."

Randy chuckled. "That's not news!"

They rang off and Bill went on staring thoughtfully out the window, wondering how Andie was going to take his announcement. She'd seemed happy enough about Randy's engagement, but this sudden wedding might be a different story. He hoped for Randy's sake that she wouldn't be upset.

At six-thirty he let himself into the apartment. From the kitchen came enticing scents and the sound of Andie singing above the rattling of cooking utensils.

Bill shed his overcoat and suit jacket and loosened his tie. Andie's voice was sweet and clear, not strong, but certainly on key and melodious. It occurred to him that he had not heard her sing like this since the early months of their marriage. Suddenly he was filled with a wistful longing for the past and for a future they'd never had.

In the last couple of weeks, both Andie and the apartment had undergone a strange, almost revolutionary metamorphosis. Bill had been vaguely aware of it during his comings and goings, but now he gave it more consideration. Like Andie's singing, the other changes were so unusual that he felt he hardly knew her or his own home anymore.

Lately there'd been a great deal of evidence in the kitchen of her attempts at cooking. He'd found dishes in the refrigerator, and one evening he'd discovered a cake. When he'd eaten a piece, he'd been impressed because it had actually been delicious.

There were other things, too. Andie had always been neat and orderly, but the sudden interest she was taking in the apartment was truly odd. Recently, fluffy new towels had appeared in the bathroom; there was an attractive painting now gracing the living room wall, as well as a new bedspread and lamp in the bedroom. Colorful place mats now adorned the breakfast bar in the kitchen, and new curtains hung in the windows. A mass of green plants had also arrived and were brightening up every room.

The changes were definitely an improvement. The apartment had a cozy, friendly look it had never had before, but what puzzled Bill was why Andie bothered. During their marriage she hadn't exhibited the slightest bit of interest in such things. Why now, and for a home she would not be living in much longer?

He walked into the kitchen, where he found her stirring something on the stove. She looked up swiftly, and her face mirrored her surprise. "Bill! What are you doing here?"

He shrugged. "I live here, remember?"

"Sure, but I didn't think you did." She turned back to her stirring.

Bill watched her in silence. She had changed from her work clothes into sneakers, a pair of jeans and a gray sweatshirt with an orange smudge on it. The tip of her tongue was thrust between her lips as she leaned over the counter and peered at a cookbook in deep concentration. He couldn't help but be amused at how earnest she looked, and how delightfully domesticated.

"Something smells good," he said.

"Umm." Andrea kept on studying her recipe.

"What're you cooking?"

"Chicken cacciatore and noodles. Now I'm making a cheese sauce for the asparagus."

"Sounds fabulous. Do you have guests coming?"

She looked up in astonishment as she lifted the saucepan off the stove. "Here? Why would I do that? It's your home, not mine."

"You could have people over if you wanted," Bill protested. "Surely you know that?"

It was her turn to shrug, and another silence fell between them.

Finally, Bill spoke. "Well, if you're not having guests, do you have enough to share with me? I'm starving."

"There's plenty," Andrea said briefly, spooning sauce over the asparagus.

It wasn't the most gracious of invitations, but Bill pretended he hadn't noticed her curtness. "Fine," he said easily. "Why don't I fix us each a drink while you finish dinner?"

"Nothing for me, thanks," Andrea said.

Bill was suddenly furious. He slammed his hand on the counter, and the sound of it got her attention. "Damn it, I'm trying to get along here, and you're not helping a bit."

As they stared at each other in a silent tug-of-war, Bill became aware of something in her eyes, a wariness that he'd never seen before. It was as though his presence alone made her nervous. He glanced down and noticed something else: her hand was actually trembling.

That made him explode again. He strode to her and placed his hands heavily on her shoulders. "Are you *afraid* of me?" he demanded incredulously.

"Of course not!" Andrea denied. All the same, she squirmed until she was free of his touch. Then she swung around and opened the refrigerator, putting the door between them.

"Then what's the matter?" Bill asked as she emerged with the makings for a salad. "You're sure acting strange."

"So are you," she replied swiftly. "You came home tonight. Why?"

This time her gaze met his directly, assessing, demanding.

"Can't I just come home without a reason?" he countered. Bill reached into a cupboard for a glass, then walked over to the liquor cabinet.

"No, I don't think so," Andrea said. "You've avoided me like the plague for two weeks, so there must be a reason why you've come home early when you know you'll find me awake. What gives?"

Bill sighed and turned to look at her. "Andie, if I've been avoiding you, it's only because I think it's best for both of us."

Andrea went rigid, and her face hardened. "Right."

Bill stepped toward her. "Believe me, I don't want to hurt you—"

"Stop it!" she said harshly. "Don't you dare be patronizing and condescending to me! Believe me, I can get along just fine without you! I've done it before and I will again, so you don't have to feel *sorry* for me! You made your choice and I don't care to discuss it any further."

"Right!" Bill snapped back, equally angry. "So if all this—" his hand swept in a wide arc "—the cooking and the decorating bit are supposed to impress me with how much you've changed, it won't work! There's absolutely nothing you could say or do to convince me that a second time around with you would be worth the effort!"

Chapter Twelve

At noon on Friday, Bill and Andrea left the office together and headed for Randy's farm. Besides their overnight bags, the trunk of the car was loaded with wedding
gifts from Randy's coworkers. When Andie had spoken
with her brother, he'd instructed her to issue a general invitation to all. The few who could make it on such short
notice would be at the ceremony tomorrow.

Bill had seemed surprised at her pleasure over the news of
Randy's imminent marriage, but Andrea had long since
gotten over her doubts and sisterly jealousy of Lisa. She
hadn't seen Randy or Lisa since Christmas, but she had
often spoken with them on the telephone. Several times,
when she'd been experimenting in the kitchen, she'd called
to ask Lisa for advice. Those chats had extended far beyond cooking pointers; in fact, the two women were becoming solid friends. Andrea suspected that she was going

to benefit from this alliance almost as much as her twin, and she liked the idea of having a sister.

On the drive she and Bill kept strictly to impersonal topics of conversation and were able to pass the time with little tension. Fortunately they had the *Patriot* to talk about as well as Randy's marriage. They seemed to get along fine when they were concerned with any subject other than themselves. Andrea found that as long as she didn't think about her feelings for Bill, or the baby, or the hazy, frightening future, she could get through whatever was at hand. By the end of the trip, they were joking and laughing like the best of friends.

They found the usually unflappable Randy in a tizzy. Healthwise, he looked marvelous. He'd regained his color and the bit of weight he'd lost during his ordeal. Two days ago he'd had a checkup and the bandages had come off his ribs. He was back to normal except for the state of his nerves.

"I've been trying to call the travel agency to confirm our flight to Nassau and I keep getting a busy signal," he greeted them distractedly. "And Lisa's gone shopping with her mother and the caterers just called to find out how many to expect at the reception and I didn't know what to tell them. The number keeps changing by the minute. Tonight Al and Byran are bringing down the rest of my clothes from the apartment, but they can't find my tan sportjacket and I don't know where else it could be."

Andrea laughed and kissed his cheek. "Hello to you, too. Calm down, Randy. Everything will work itself out, you'll see."

"I'm not so sure," he said morosely. "Everything seems to be conspiring against me."

"Not getting cold feet, are you, pal?" Bill teased.

"Not on your life." Randy flashed him a grin. "But why does getting married have to be a three-ring circus?"

"To make you suitably impressed with the seriousness of the occasion." Bill chuckled.

"Did you get our tuxedos?" Randy asked anxiously.

"I got them," Bill assured him.

Randy sighed. "Then at least something's going right." The telephone rang, and as he turned to answer it he said, "I just made some coffee if you want any. Maybe this is the travel agency calling *me*."

Bill and Andrea went into the kitchen. She felt really well today, so Andrea decided to risk some coffee herself. She poured two cups while Bill got the sugar and cream.

They sat down at the table across from each other and their eyes met. Both of them suddenly burst out laughing.

"Do you think he'll survive the ordeal?" Bill asked.

"I wouldn't place any bets on it," she replied. "I believe this is harder on him than the accident was! I wonder if Lisa's as bad?"

"If she's anything like you were, she's probably coming apart at the seams along about now."

Instantly they were transported back in time. On the day before their wedding Andrea had created a huge argument with Bill over the most trivial thing. They'd met for lunch that day, knowing it would be the last time they'd really be alone until afterward. Andrea had ordered soup, which she couldn't eat because her stomach was tied up in knots. Bill had made a casual comment about how she'd better try to eat to keep up her strength, that he didn't want a fainting bride at the altar. She'd taken it as a personal attack on her eating habits and had been angrily defensive. Then she'd attacked his driving. In no time at all they'd started arguing about the wedding itself, his friends, her friends, the honeymoon, a tennis game they'd lost the previous week. It had all been so silly, so stupid. Of course they'd laughed about it later, but it hadn't been funny at the time.

Andrea grinned at him now. "Maybe it's a good thing Lisa's shopping today instead of having lunch with Randy."

"It's probably why her mother decided to keep her occupied," Bill answered with a matching grin. "I don't think there's anything we didn't fight about that day."

"I came that close—" Andrea laughed, holding her thumb and forefinger a fraction of an inch apart "—to calling the whole thing off right then." She sobered and turned abruptly to gaze out the window. "Looking back, I guess it would have been the best thing for both of us if I had."

There was a short silence, and then Bill said heavily, "Yeah. I guess you're right."

Another silence fell, and this time it lasted until Randy joined them. "That was Mom on the phone, Andie. I asked her if she wanted to talk to you, but she was in a hurry to go somewhere. She said she'd call you next week to find out how the wedding went."

Andrea swung around in the chair. "She's not coming," she said flatly.

Randy shook his head and poured himself a cup of coffee. "She said it was too short notice. They're vacationing at the house in Saint Moritz and they have guests this weekend. She can't—"

"—Possibly just abandon them, darling!" Andrea quoted along with him.

Randy grinned and straddled a chair as he joined them at the table. He looked at Andrea's pinched, angry face and patted her hand. "Now come on, sis, don't let it get you down. You know I didn't really expect her, and it *was* short notice. Besides, as long as I've got you both here for moral support, that's all that counts. I don't think the wedding would be legal if my twin wasn't with me, would it? Not to mention my all-important best man.''

Andrea mustered a smile. "I have a feeling you're going to have a very happy marriage, Randy.''

"I have a feeling you're right.'' Randy looked from Andrea to Bill, then back to Andrea. "Of course that's what I thought about you two at one time.''

Andrea couldn't meet Bill's eyes across the table, though she could feel them on her. "Some things just weren't meant to be, that's all,'' she said lightly. She got to her feet and added, "I think I'll take a walk down to the pond.''

The following afternoon, as Andrea was dressing, she heard a soft knock at the bedroom door. Before she could call out, it opened. Startled, she froze with her hand in the air, fingers gripping her comb, as she looked toward the door.

Bill came in, not even seeing her as he bent his head over his right cuff. He kicked the door closed behind him, still preoccupied with inserting the cuff link through the hole. He wore a snowy-white shirt with a pleated front, black tuxedo pants and a cummerbund. A black bow tie hung open around his neck.

"Randy's in the shower and I can't get this cuff link to...'' He lifted his head at that moment, and the words died away.

Andie stood before the dresser mirror in a strapless bra, half-slip and panty hose, looking as beautiful as a bride herself. Her face seemed to have an exceptional glow to it; her skin looked dewy fresh. Her hair was a river of shimmering red-gold as it spilled over her creamy shoulders. She wore pearls at her throat and on her ears, and Bill knew at once they were the same pearls he'd given her on their wedding day. There was a rich, satiny luster to them that indicated they'd often been worn.

Bill swallowed with difficulty and moved toward her, his eyes drinking in every detail of her appearance from the ripe swell of her breasts to the sensuous curve of her hips beneath the paper-thin slip. Her shapely legs were smooth and enticing in sheer stockings, and her beauty was enough to drive any man insane.

He tried hard to resist. Offering his arm, he grinned ruefully and said, "Do you mind? I really can't seem to get it myself."

"Sure." Andrea bent her head over his hand, and her slender fingers worked at the cuff. "How's Randy doing?" she asked conversationally.

"Holding on for dear life," Bill replied. "Two more hours and the worst will be over."

Andrea laughed softly. "Or at least his jittery nerves won't be our problem any longer. It'll be Lisa's. There!" she exclaimed, sounding satisfied. She dropped her hands and raised her head. "All done, except for your tie. Do you want me to do it for you?"

"Would you?" Bill asked.

Andrea took hold of the tie and deftly fixed the bow. But when she started to move her hands away this time, Bill caught them in his. Andrea lifted her eyes to his face, and once again he saw a wariness there, as though she were half-afraid of him.

"You're so beautiful today, Andie," he said because he couldn't help himself. "You remind me of the way you were on our wedding night."

Andrea looked startled at his words and shook her head. "Bill, don't say things—"

"How can I help it?" he demanded huskily. "You do look like you did then. You're even wearing my pearls. It makes me wish it were that night again." Without realizing he was losing control, he traced one finger down her cheek. "Do you remember it, too, Andie? How we made love all night long and yet the next day we were both rested somehow, even though we hadn't had a wink of sleep?"

"And caught a plane at dawn. Ah, those sunny Caribbean beaches! And now—" Andrea sighed "—it's Randy and Lisa's turn."

"I want it to be our turn again, too," Bill said gruffly. His arms closed around her, and his hands caressed her bare back as he kissed her.

He felt Andie stiffen, and that made him all the more determined. His mouth was rough and demanding as it moved on hers, silently insisting she match the sudden burst of fire that streaked through him.

Andrea placed her hands on his arms and leaned back, trying to break free. The kiss ended, but Bill would not let her go. He bent his head to her shoulder, then to her white throat, and he heard her soft gasp.

"Bill! Don't!"

"You don't mean that," he murmured as his head lowered still further until his lips were gently caressing the alluring fullness of her breasts above her bra. "You know you don't mean that, darling. You make me crazy with wanting."

"Stop it!" With one hard push, Andrea broke free. Passion had hazed Bill's eyes, but now his gaze cleared and focused. Andrea's breasts were heaving, and she lifted a trembling hand to her lips, as though to wipe away his kisses.

Bemused and shaken, Bill said, "Andie, I thought you—"

Andrea cut through his words in a voice as sharp and painful as a knife. "The morning after New Year's you told me plainly enough that you didn't want to be involved with me anymore, Bill. That my love meant nothing. Well, your desire for me now means nothing! Nothing, do you hear!" Her voice rose, shrill and ragged. "I can't handle this type of relationship, hot one day and cold the next! I just don't have the emotional stamina for it."

"Andie, you know I still love you! God help me, I've tried not to, but I do!"

"Yes?" Her voice was soft now, her green eyes dull with sadness. She shook her head. "You're still attracted to me sexually, though sometimes you fight it. That may be flattering, Bill, but it's just not enough for me because it's not really love. It's not a complete relationship."

"No?" He tilted his head, and his eyes narrowed. "You're an expert now on what love is? Love is deserting a husband whenever the mood strikes?"

"Maybe not," she conceded. "Maybe I don't really know what it is, either, but I do know it has to be more than just physical desire. There has to be something between the bursts of passion."

"That's really a joke, coming from you!" Bill snapped. "The one who never stayed home long enough for anything else to develop!"

Andrea winced. "I'll admit I ran away from that something before, but now you're doing it."

Bill sighed heavily. "Can you blame me?" he demanded. "You took my love and threw it back in my face. I keep thinking sooner or later it will happen again."

"I know. But what can I say except that I love you and I'm truly sorry? You're afraid I'd hurt you again, and maybe I would, though I'd try my hardest not to."

Bill rubbed the back of his neck and shook his head. "I want you, Andie. And I do love you. That's what makes it all so damned hard. But I won't lie to you. I just can't bring myself to believe you've changed, that you care enough to make a real marriage out of it this time, and I sure can't stomach the idea of going through a second divorce with you."

Andrea's eyes were dark and somber. "Then there's nothing more to say, is there?" she said huskily.

"No," Bill answered bleakly. "I guess not."

He left the room, and Andrea turned back to the dresser. The mirror reflected a haunted, tormented face...the face of a woman who had loved and lost.

Later she sat in the church pew and witnessed her brother's marriage. To anyone who might have glanced at her, she appeared serene. But inside Andrea was broken, and her emotions were turbulent when she saw the tenderness in Randy's eyes as he gazed at his glowing bride. Her throat tightened, and tears burned her eyes. There was so much love between them, so much promise and devotion.

Her gaze moved to the tall man at Randy's side, his face serious as he listened to the couple exchanging vows. Andrea wondered if he were thinking about the vows they'd once made to each other, vows she'd broken because she had lacked the courage to uphold them. Vows he now feared to make again.

February roared in with a vicious snowstorm, and Washington lay shivering beneath an icy blanket. For several days traffic was minimal, and those who didn't have to get out stayed indoors. Sightseers, usually so abundant, were nowhere to be found.

By Thursday the sun had reappeared, dazzlingly reflected by the white confection covering the ground. The temperature climbed, and gradually the lively activity typical of the nation's capital resumed.

The daily-newspaper business had ground on without letup in spite of the weather. Deliveries, however, had been delayed, giving Bill and his circulation manager a lingering headache.

On the morning the storm began, Bill had bumped into Andrea in the kitchen. As they'd exchanged pleasantries, he'd noticed that she looked wan and peaked. But when he'd asked if she were ill, she'd denied it. Then, not five minutes later, she'd rushed off to the bathroom and been sick.

Bill hadn't let her go to work that day, though she'd been quarrelsome about it. The following day she'd still seemed pale and tired. He'd suggested she stay home again, but that time she'd flatly refused, insisting she was perfectly fine.

This morning he hadn't seen her at all because she'd been up and gone by the time he awoke. Bill wondered how she was. She'd seemed so unwell lately that he was concerned, in spite of her angry assertions to the contrary. He promised himself that he'd find an excuse to drop into the Rumpus Room later and see for himself how she looked. If she still appeared under the weather, he decided, she was going to see a doctor if he had to drag her there.

In the end, he didn't have to manufacture a lame excuse to see her: he was handed a legitimate one.

At midmorning his phone rang and Sara said, "Randy Wade's on line three."

Bill punched the lighted button and leaned back in his chair, his mouth curving into a smile. "Well, well, how goes it, pal?" It had been almost two weeks since the wedding. "Marriage still agreeing with you?"

"You bet," came the cheerful reply. "You ought to try it again yourself sometime."

Bill let that pass. "How was Nassau?"

"Sunny and warm. We've both got gin-you-wine tans," he said, drawling it out for effect. "I saw in the papers that you poor suckers have been making like polar bears, though it doesn't look so bad today."

"The worst is over," Bill said. "Say, where are you?"

"Still at the airport waiting for our luggage."

"Are you going to the farm today, or are you staying in town tonight? If you're going to be here, maybe Andie and I could see you at dinner."

"We'll be here, but I think we're going to be too pooped to do any socializing. We're planning to spend the day apartment hunting. How does tomorrow night sound instead?"

"Fine with me. I'll check with Andie."

"Okay, I'll call you tomorrow," Randy said. "By the way, I'm putting you on formal notice that I'll be back in harness Monday morning."

The news ought to have pleased Bill, but instead it filled him with dismay. "That sounds great," he said quickly, trying to sound glad. "But aren't you rushing things a bit? I mean, since you don't even have a place to live yet? Maybe you'd like another week or two to get things squared away."

"I've abused a good thing long enough already, Bill," Randy said. "Thanks for the offer, but I'm looking forward to getting back to work. Lisa and I figure we'll be able to find an apartment today or tomorrow and do a lot of the moving in over the weekend. If not, we'll just stay at the hotel and she'll keep searching during the week. I'll definitely be at my desk Monday morning."

"All right. Suit yourself." Bill could offer no other arguments to delay Randy's return, and he knew it.

They hung up, and desolation swamped Bill. Monday. Randy would be back Monday. And Andrea would have no further reason to stay.

Why couldn't he be happy about it? And relieved? It would make things so much easier. Once Andie was gone he wouldn't constantly be fighting this aching desire for her. Or would he?

He lifted the telephone receiver once more and told Sara, "Ask Andie to come in here, please."

Andrea was not surprised to receive Bill's summons. She'd been expecting it ever since she'd talked with Randy ten minutes ago.

So this was it, she thought dully as she stared at the computer terminal in front of her. She'd been working on a story, but since Randy's call she hadn't written a single word. She'd lost all thought of everything except that the time had come to leave. And in doing so, she'd be leaving behind the only man she'd ever loved. The father of her child.

Bracing herself, she went upstairs. When she entered Bill's office his back was to her as he gazed out the window, one hand thrust in a pocket. He seemed deep in thought, but he must have heard her come in. He sighed heavily and, without turning around, said, "I guess you've spoken to Randy, too."

"Yes," she answered hollowly.

Bill turned around, and his gaze was frankly unhappy as it met hers. "So...this is it," he said.

Andrea nodded. "End of the line," she replied, trying to inject a lightness into her voice that she didn't feel.

"I appreciate your taking Randy's place all this time, Andie. You're a marvelous reporter."

"Thanks."

"There's always a permanent position for you here, you know," he ventured. "If you ever want it."

Andrea shook her head. "It's kind of you, Bill, but we both know it's better if I go."

He nodded and gazed at her silently for a time. "When do you intend to leave?"

Andrea shrugged. "Saturday, I suppose. I'll start packing tonight."

She waited breathlessly, hoping he would object, praying he would ask her not to go. But Bill said nothing. Andrea knew then that he was determined to cut the bond that had linked them ever since that July day several years ago when he'd bumped into her in his father's office. Divorce had not severed it; but his will—his implacable will—would achieve what judges and lawyers and decrees had been unable to accomplish.

"I invited Randy and Lisa to have dinner with us tomorrow evening. Do you mind?"

"Of course not. Naturally I want to see them before I go." In truth, she dreaded it. She hadn't been lying about wanting to visit with her twin and his new bride, but she wished it didn't have to be with Bill. It was already hard enough, knowing she had to leave because he didn't want her, because he'd rejected her overtures of love. Having to spend her last evening in Washington with him was almost more than she could bear.

Bill nodded briskly. "Good. I'll make dinner reservations." He paused, and his eyes searched her face. "How are you feeling today?"

"Terrific!" Andrea forced a bright smile.

Bill frowned. "You still don't seem to have all your color back. Why don't you see a doctor this afternoon? Just to make sure nothing's wrong?"

"Don't be silly. It was just a virus. I'm fine." She went on breezily, "Well, until tomorrow afternoon I'm still on staff, and I'd better get back to work. I have an ogre of a boss, you know."

Bill grinned and said, "How about letting the ogre take you to lunch?"

Andrea raised her eyebrows. There was an odd expression on Bill's face, as though he had surprised himself by the invitation. She thought it must have been impulsive and that he was already regretting it.

"For old times' sake?" she said quizzically, then shook her head. "Thanks, but I think not. See you, Bill."

She moved toward the door, and he did not try to stop her.

Randy and Lisa were in high spirits when they met the other pair at the restaurant. There were hugs and kisses and handshakes before they all settled down around the table.

"Lisa, you look positively radiant," Bill said, smiling at his friend's wife. She wore a bright-red silk dress, and her dark hair was piled with artful grace atop her head. Her eyes flashed with happiness, and her lips seemed quirked into a permanent smile.

She laughed at the compliment. "That's sunburn," she said gaily. "I'm cooked all over and it glows."

"It glows all over, too," Randy added with a wicked gleam in his eyes. "*Especially* in the dark!"

Lisa blushed, then playfully punched her husband's shoulder. "Behave yourself, tiger," she ordered sternly. "We're with civilized people here tonight. Try to pretend you fit in."

Randy answered by gnashing his teeth at her.

Andrea and Bill both laughed, but Bill felt a sharp wistfulness as he watched them. The fullness of their love emphasized the emptiness in his own life. He shifted in his chair so that he could see Andie without being obvious.

She held herself rigidly, shoulders back, hands out of sight beneath the table. She was smiling at the other couple, but to Bill it seemed slightly forced. The newlyweds' lighthearted bantering appeared to be hard on her, too.

Andrea was extraordinarily lovely this evening. Her dress was soft velvet, a turquoise that was spectacular with her coloring. The restaurant's gentle lighting and the flicker of candlelight on the table cast burnished copper highlights on the golden sheen of her hair. The pallor of the past few days was gone, and there was a heightened rosiness to her cheeks that was entirely natural and alluring. Tonight her skin looked vibrant and luscious, like a ripe peach, and her green eyes seemed darker. They glittered mysteriously, as though concealing a great secret. Bill couldn't remember ever having seen her more beautiful.

As though she felt his eyes upon her, Andrea slowly turned her head. Their eyes met and locked for a long moment, during which all else was shut out. Bill could hear his heart beating.

Then Andrea broke the contact. Her lips trembled for a moment before she turned back to the others and asked, "Did you have any luck finding an apartment?"

They had, and Lisa proceeded to describe it to them. The waiter arrived to take their orders for drinks. The evening, the last one Bill and Andrea would spend together, had been launched, for better or worse.

Now why had he thought of it in those terms? Marriage vow terms. Their marriage had deteriorated swiftly, even though they'd gone right on loving each other.

Bill wondered if he weren't being a bigger fool now than the first time around. Andie had told him she loved him still; she'd made it clear enough that she wanted to reestablish their relationship. Ironically, this time it was he who had backed away, but a strong instinct for self-preservation had made him cautious and reluctant to commit himself. He'd suffered the tortures of the damned when their marriage had broken apart, and he never wanted to go through such a thing again. His love for her then hadn't been enough to keep her at his side, so what made either of them think it would be enough this time?

All the same, as he smiled and talked, ate and drank, he was keenly aware of time sliding away; bringing the morning closer, the moment when Andie would walk out the door for the last time. He knew that if he but said the word, even hinted that he wanted her to stay, she would. But he couldn't do it.

Though his resolve was strong, Bill found the evening incredibly difficult. He made small talk and played the part of gracious host, but always his thoughts returned to Andie. Though she sat beside him, it was as if she were already gone, leaving his life flat and meaningless.

Having honeymooners as dinner companions did not make the situation any easier. Bill was excruciatingly aware of the contrast between them—Randy and Lisa, wrapped in a happy cocoon of marital bliss; he and Andie, tortured by a love that seemed destined to destroy them whether they were together or not.

He ordered champagne to fete the bridal couple and noticed that Andie took a single sip during the toast, then left her glass untouched. Earlier, when the rest of them had ordered cocktails, she'd asked for sparkling water.

When the evening was finally over, Bill and Andrea drove home beneath a sky powdered with stars. On the way, they struggled to make conversation. Andie had grown silent and withdrawn as the evening had progressed, as though she, too, were suffering from an awareness that time was running out.

"They seem happy enough," Bill said inanely, simply to break the thick, tense silence.

"Yes."

"Now that you're free again, I guess you'll be starting some new project that'll take you off to some distant point on the globe." He glanced at Andie and saw her shrug listlessly.

"I suppose," she said.

"Have you decided where to this time?"

"No. Actually, it's been so long since I've spent any time at home, I think I just may stay in New York for a while. Maybe write a few magazine articles that I can research easily without making any major trips." She stirred restlessly and changed the subject. "It was a lovely dinner. It was nice of you to welcome Randy and Lisa home that way."

"Speaking of dinner, I noticed you didn't drink anything."

In the darkness of the car, Bill felt Andie's surprise. "I didn't know there was a law against not drinking," she said irritably. "Who appointed you watchman over what I eat or drink, anyway?"

"I just happened to notice, that's all," Bill said mildly, wondering why she sounded so defensive. "You always liked champagne before, and we were drinking a toast to your favorite brother, after all. Andie, are you feeling sick again? I really think you should have a checkup."

"Stop worrying about me! I've told you and told you, I'm fine. I just wasn't in a party mood tonight, that's all. I've got to get up early tomorrow morning, remember? I want a clear head."

Somehow the explanation didn't ring true, but Bill didn't press her further. Her reminder that she was leaving in the morning plunged him once again into despondency.

His depression intensified when they entered the apartment. The first thing he spotted were her suitcases, packed and waiting near the door, and he was overcome by a feeling of emptiness.

Andrea slipped out of her coat and turned to smile at him, but she avoided his eyes. "Tomorrow night you'll finally get back the bedroom. You must be looking forward to that."

"I'm not!" he declared vehemently, and took an involuntary step toward her. "Andie..."

Andrea quickly shook her head. "Don't!" she gasped huskily. "It's late and I'm tired. Let's not get into another one of those long heart-to-heart discussions that only end up making us both feel wretched."

Bill stopped and gazed at her unhappily. "I wish there were an easy way to say goodbye," he said at last.

Andrea smiled sadly. "Maybe it's best just to say it straight out." She paused for the space of a heartbeat, then said softly, "Goodbye, Bill."

"Goodbye, Andie. Take care of yourself."

Andrea hurried into the bedroom and closed the door just before the first teardrop fell. The pain of parting was almost more than she could endure, but she'd managed to get through it without breaking down. As she undressed for bed, she knew that the goodbyes had been final. Bill would not be here in the morning to see her leave.

A couple of times, including tonight, she had come dangerously close to telling him about the baby. Now she was glad she hadn't yielded to that temptation. Bill didn't want her in his life anymore, and she would do nothing to make him feel as though he owed her something. If he was aware of her pregnancy, he'd feel responsible for her. She didn't want him that way—not motivated by obligation and conscientiousness. He had to come to her of his own free will and out of love, or she wanted no part of it.

Admittedly she didn't know very much about real families, given her own background, but Andrea knew for certain what a real family *shouldn't* be. It shouldn't be a mother who's more interested in partying with the rich and famous than in spending even the most special occasions with her children. It shouldn't be a father who thinks that if he shells out enough money and sends you to the best schools, he's done his job. Above all, it shouldn't be a home where the parents don't love each other. Until their divorce, her parents had argued and fought and belittled each other in front of her. Even now, all these years later, she shuddered at the memory. She could not, would not do that to *her* child.

She would do her best to provide as loving and normal a home life as was possible for a single mother. After all, millions of other women did it. But something else bothered her: Was she capable of being the sort of mother her child deserved, or would she turn out like Carrie—indifferent, uninvolved, too self-absorbed to give her child the emotional security it needed? It terrified Andrea to think that she might follow the pattern established by her mother.

Finally, there was the nagging voice that kept whispering that despite her rationalizations, her child also needed a father's love. Andrea ignored it for now. After the baby was born, there would be time enough to tell Bill. She wouldn't keep it a secret from him then, nor would she ever deny him the privilege of knowing and spending time with his child. By then, however, the turmoil of these last couple of months would have subsided, and she'd be able to face him calmly, without awkwardness or uncertainty, confident that she'd made the right decision in not telling him earlier.

But she was far from confident now, as she huddled, frightened, alone and confused, in "their" bed...for the last time.

Chapter Thirteen

W e'll leave around the first of May and be gone about three weeks. Of course the accommodations will be a bit primitive, tents and all, but you can handle that, I know. What do you say, Andie? Want to come along?'' George applied himself to his steak while he waited for her reply.

"Of course she'll come!" Kent said with an easy grin. "Andie wouldn't turn down a story like this!"

The three of them were having lunch in a Manhattan restaurant. Andrea had seen Kent a few times in the six weeks she'd been back in New York, but this was the first time she'd seen George since they'd all returned from London.

The British documentary had aired two weeks ago, and now George was proposing a new one that was so poignant and compelling it was hard for Andrea to refuse. The plight of the poor starving refugees in Africa had touched her deeply, and to do an in-depth documentary on the situation would be a great opportunity, not to mention a humbling experience. Any other time she would have jumped at the offer, but she knew she had to refuse. It would be an arduous trip, and she just couldn't risk it. She had to think of her unborn baby.

"Much as I hate it, I have to turn you down, George," Andrea said at last.

"But this sort of thing is precisely your forte, Andie. You can weave all the pieces together in a compassionate style without being maudlin, and that's essential to a story like this. We'll be covering everything, the drought, the ignorance, the politics, the pathos. We need you to handle the human interest side—families, personalities, the real people involved. You've got to come!"

Andrea shook her head. "I want to, honestly, but I can't." She groped for an excuse. "I'm already committed to another project at that time. I'm really sorry."

George heaved a sigh and stared gloomily down at his steak. "Not as sorry as I am," he said. He stroked his bushy beard. "Who else am I going to get who'll even come close to doing as good a job as you could?"

"Lots of people." Andrea smiled wanly and named a few.

George had some objection to each person she mentioned. "Couldn't you try to rearrange your schedule?" he asked. "Maybe if I give you a week or so to think it over and see what you can do?"

"It's just not possible this time, George," she said firmly.

Immediately after lunch, George hailed a taxi and left to keep an appointment. Kent wandered along the street beside Andrea. A blustery March wind was blowing, but the sun was shining and it was a beautiful day with the promise of spring in the air.

"Okay," Kent said. "Now tell me the real reason you turned George down, and don't feed me the line about being committed to some other project. Last week you were working on a magazine article about nutrition for pregnant women. That can't possibly run you into May."

"No." Andrea inhaled deeply and asked, "If I tell you something, will you swear not to repeat it to anyone?"

"Sure." Kent eyed her curiously.

Still, Andrea hesitated. She'd told no one about the baby, not even Randy. Except for not telling Bill, that had been hardest of all. But Randy was Bill's friend as well as her brother, and she wasn't certain she could trust him to keep quiet. Yet she simply had to tell someone, and there were few friends she felt closer to than Kent.

"I'm pregnant," she blurted out.

Kent stopped so abruptly that a man walking behind him on the sidewalk bumped into him. "Sorry," Kent mumbled. He looked intently at Andrea. "Did you just say what I thought you said?"

She nodded. "You heard right. So, now you know why I can't accept George's offer." She had stopped walking, too, but now she began to move again.

Kent caught up with her. "Okay, I can understand that. But... damn it, Andie, what gives? Who's the man?" She merely looked at him, and after a moment he whistled beneath his breath. "Your ex."

"Yes."

"Does he know about this?"

"No."

Kent took her arm and drew her to a halt again. "I don't know what the problem is," he scolded in a firm voice, "but this is wrong. You've got to tell him."

"I will. After the baby's born."

"Don't you think you're being unfair?"

"Probably," she admitted. "But it has to be this way. If I told him now, he'd insist we get married."

"And you don't want that?"

"I want it more than anything on earth," she said with a catch in her throat, "but not like this. What was it you said in London? That I must still be in love with Bill since I never got romantically involved with other men? Well, you were dead right. I love him so much that it's like a sickness, and I'd give anything if he'd only let me prove it to him. But I blew that chance years ago. He doesn't trust me anymore, and looking at it from his point of view, I can't blame him. I was a lousy wife."

"But surely with the baby coming, that changes things," Kent said. "Bill seems like an honorable man and—"

"Oh, he is!" Andrea exclaimed. "That's the problem. He'd marry me, but only because he felt pressured, backed into a corner. That wouldn't be any good for either of us, or for the baby." There was earnest concern in her friend's eyes, and suddenly she gave him a weary smile. "Thanks for caring, Kent, but don't look so worried. I'll be okay."

"I'm not so sure," he replied. "Maybe I ought to marry you myself to make sure you're taken care of."

She laughed. "And ruin a perfectly wonderful friendship? I wouldn't dream of it!"

Kent grinned. "It would sort of spoil things, wouldn't it? Having to face each other over breakfast every day? Especially after all the secrets we've shared. We know too much about each other. Still, if there's anything I can do for you . . ." He broke off and shrugged.

"I know," she said huskily. "Thanks."

They parted, and Andrea returned to her apartment building. Carl, the doorman, opened the heavy glass door for her and said, "Good afternoon, Mrs. Sheridan. Your mother arrived about an hour ago, but since you weren't here, she went out to lunch. She should be returning soon."

"My mother? Here?" Andrea stared at the man in disbelief. "Are you sure?"

"Yes, ma'am. It was the countess all right. She said she'd be back around three."

"Thank you." Andrea went inside and took the elevator to her apartment. It was just like Carrie, she thought, to breeze in without warning.

Thirty minutes later her mother joined her. "Hello, darling," Carrie greeted. She hugged Andrea and kissed the air beside her cheek. "Are you surprised to see me?"

"Very. How are you, Mother?"

"Marvelous, dear, simply marvelous!" Carrie tilted her head, looked critically at her daughter and said with disapproval, "I believe you've put on some weight since the last time I saw you."

"Maybe a little," Andrea conceded.

"Now's the time to go to work and get it off," Carrie said emphatically, "before it gets out of hand. I know this wonderful new diet that can actually help you lose up to ten pounds in..."

Andrea tuned out, not about to admit that there was a reason for the small amount of weight she had gained. Carrie would definitely not be pleased to hear she was about to become a grandmother—especially under the circumstances. Better to let her find out later by mail. It might be cowardly, but Andrea was in no mood to argue with her mother. So for now, she nodded in the right places, pretending to absorb the diet information because it was the path of least resistance. To her mother, there was no sin greater than being overweight, so the lecture was sure to be lengthy.

Carrie was a walking advertisement for any diet book. Pencil slim, she was stylishly turned out in a dramatic black suit trimmed with springtime white. Her expensive French perfume cloyed the air, and not a single hair on her blond head dared to be out of place. Her makeup was impeccable, and her manicure was as flawless as the diamonds she wore on her hands. As always, her appearance was perfection itself, down to the tiniest detail.

At last Carrie exhausted the subject of diet. "What brings you here, Mother?" Andrea asked as they sat down together on the sofa. "Is Carlos with you?"

"No. He'll be joining me in Palm Beach at the end of the week. I came ahead so that I could see you and Randy and do a bit of shopping."

"How nice. How long will you be here?"

"I'll go to Washington in the morning to see Randy."

"So soon? But what about your shopping?" Andrea asked in surprise. She knew Carrie loved New York's stores.

"I did that yesterday and the day before." Carrie smiled. "I picked up the most *precious* little dress, Andrea. Shell-pink chiffon. Just the perfect thing for a party I'll be attending this weekend." She named the wife of a multimillionaire and added, "It'll be her sixtieth birthday and she's *quite* depressed. Naturally as one of her *dearest* friends, I must be there to help cheer her up."

Again, Andrea found herself shutting out the flow of chatter. Carrie could go on for half an hour about her new clothes and the socially prominent guests who would be attending the party. But to Andrea, her mother had already said the most significant thing.

She'd been in New York for at least two days, and only now had she found the time to look up her daughter.

In that moment, Andrea lost forever the fear that had haunted her. Now she knew with absolute, unshakable conviction that she was nothing like Carrie and never would be. By some biological accident they were mother and daughter; physically they even resembled one another, especially around the eyes and mouth, but in personality and character, in all the things that really counted, they were light-years apart.

Why had she never seen that before? Andrea wondered. What other mother who lived an ocean apart from her child would visit the same city and spend two whole days shopping, and probably seeing social friends as well, before contacting that child? Nothing could better emphasize Carrie's lack of interest in her own flesh and blood. Here she was, chattering away with girlish excitement about a sixty-year-old woman's birthday party, yet not once had she been present for Andrea and Randy's birthdays. Even when Randy's plane was missing, and later, when he'd been married, she hadn't come.

But Carrie was the only role model Andrea had had, so she'd always been secretly afraid she'd turn out just like her, vain and selfish, neglectful of her children as she pursued an endless round of dinners and parties and vacations. After all, it was in her genes.

Now Andrea knew it couldn't happen. Already she felt such enormous love for her baby that sometimes it threatened to overwhelm her; she intended to savor this precious gift of life to the fullest. Surely the joy of motherhood lay in being an important, integral part of a child's life. Andrea wanted to be the first one to see her baby smile; to be the one who rocked it to sleep when it was ill; to be watching proudly when it took its first independent step. She wanted to guide and educate her child, be the source of comfort when things went wrong, an enthusiastic supporter when encouragement was needed. She wanted to be there for birthdays and Christmases, the first day of school, graduation night. In short, she wanted to give her baby the loving, secure childhood she herself had been denied, and no power on earth, short of death itself, was going to cheat her of that goal!

Strangely, with that resolution, and the self-confidence it engendered, came a feeling of forgiveness toward her mother. As Carrie rambled on about the Côte d'Azur, Andrea suddenly saw her as she really was—a pitiful woman without any commitment to life. Her hands fluttered nervously, conveying an insecurity her daughter had never noticed before, blinded as she'd been by her own resentment. Now she realized the truth: Carrie had been unable to give of herself to her children in any meaningful way because there was, quite simply, nothing there to give.

Her children had tried to compensate for this by always being there for each other, creating a semblance of family feeling and stability. Thus, they had kept each other's feet on the ground as best they could. Randy had decided when he was a child that he would someday have a country place and a family of his own. He'd accordingly had little use for travel as an adult, and then only for business. Andrea, on the other hand, had traveled a great deal, trying to escape her self-doubts; but now that she was to be a mother, she knew she'd come home at last.

Carrie, however, would float through the rest of her days, never realizing that beneath the surface glitter of her life, there was nothing substantive, nothing of value. Or maybe she did know, Andrea thought with sudden insight. Maybe she knew and as Andrea had once done, was running from herself.

That evening the two of them went out to dinner. Over the meal, Carrie surprised Andrea by inviting her to Palm Beach. It seemed a friend's eligible son, a Grand Prix race car driver, was to be there. "He's utterly charming, darling," Carrie said. "I know you'd really hit it off."

"No thanks, Mother," Andrea said. "To be honest, I'm not in the mood to be charmed."

"It's that Bill Sheridan, isn't it? Now that you've seen him again? He never was the right one for you, darling. Imagine resenting your travels and your career! Why, he wanted to turn you into some ordinary little housewife!" Carrie shuddered.

"Bill never minded my having a career," Andrea said calmly. "He just didn't like the fact that his wife was away all the time, and he was right."

"How can you possibly defend him?" Carrie demanded.

"It's easy," Andrea answered. "He was right and I was wrong, and I made the worst mistake of my life when I didn't stay put and fight to save my marriage."

Later, when Andrea was home alone once more, she found herself moving restlessly from one room to another. The walls seemed to close about her; the silence screamed at her. Here there were no familiar mementos of her marriage; here Bill would not be coming in sometime during the night; here it was not possible to see him occasionally over breakfast; here she would never see him at all.

A lump swelled in her throat. She missed him desperately; she ached for him relentlessly. She had to get over him.

But she had no idea how.

The round table meeting was over. As the staff filed out of the room, Bill remained at the table. He brushed a hand across his face and closed his bleary eyes. He felt drained and listless. He hadn't slept well in weeks—in fact, not since the day Andie had left Washington.

"Bill?"

"What?" Bill came out of his reverie and met Randy's sharp green eyes, so like his twin's.

"Care to talk about it?"

"About what?" Bill hedged.

"About whatever it is that's making you look like hell." Randy pulled out a chair and sat down facing him.

Bill grimaced. "Do I really look that bad?"

"Worse," Randy said cheerfully. "But you know me...I'm a polite sort of guy, so I tend to approach things tactfully." They both chuckled, then Randy went on seriously, "What's the matter? You're not sick or anything, are you?"

Bill shook his head. "No, I'm fine. Just not getting any sleep to speak of."

Randy crossed his arms behind his head and tilted the chair back. "So...what's keeping you awake nights? Business problems? Nightmares? Andie?"

Stunned, Bill stared at him. "Boy, did you ever slip that one in nice and slick." He expelled a long sigh. "How'd you know?"

Randy laughed shortly. "It doesn't take a genius. I could see which way the wind was blowing ever since you showed up at my bedside in Atlanta. You were trying too hard to pretend casual indifference to each other. And that night you took us to dinner, when Lisa and I got back from our honeymoon, you both had your hearts in your eyes."

"Yeah," Bill said heavily. "I guess it would be hard to fool you."

"A bit. I know you both too well. Besides, ever since she left you've kept asking me if I've heard from her and how she is, and when she calls she asks the same things about you. Lisa says I should write a column for the lovelorn."

Bill smiled wanly. "No point in it," he said, "unless you can solve other people's problems."

"I was hoping this time you'd work them out for yourselves. I tried to give it a little boost by coming up with the idea of Andie taking over my job."

Raising an eyebrow, Bill gave him a menacing look. "So that was really a setup?"

"Of course!" Randy chuckled. "At least give me credit for my brilliance. You were shorthanded without me, and Andie was between jobs. What could be better than to throw you together a few extra weeks so you could try to work things out? Only it doesn't seem to have worked out the way I'd hoped."

"No," Bill said. "I guess it didn't." Suddenly he met Randy's eyes and said frankly, "I love that woman, Randy. Unfortunately I'm afraid I'll never stop loving her. But you know Andie—she's not the type to settle down, and I just can't survive a long-distance marriage."

"You want to know something?" Randy said. "As kids, hopping around from place to place was the normal routine whenever anyone got tired of us. It just seemed natural to Andie to keep on doing it later, before you could get tired of her."

"Tired of her?" Bill roared. "I never saw her long enough to get tired of her!"

Randy nodded. "That was precisely the point."

"That's absurd," Bill said flatly. "I was tired of her leaving, not her staying."

"True, but Andie believed if she stayed, you'd eventually grow bored and lose interest in her."

"That's the silliest thing I ever heard!"

Randy swung his feet to the floor. The chair legs crashed down with a thud, as he stood up. "It may be silly, but it's the truth. Somehow Andie always needed to be loved and accepted a little more than I did, but she never felt secure enough about herself with anybody except me. So whenever she felt her welcome was wearing thin somewhere, or that somebody was annoyed or angry with her... why, then she just ran. She didn't know what else to do. I never will forget what she told me when we left the courthouse after the divorce. She said, 'I just lost the most important person in the world to me. I loved him and loved him. But nobody ever taught me how to be loved back.'" He gazed at Bill intensely as he added, "Maybe you should have tried harder to teach her. Or maybe some things just can't be learned at all." He shrugged, glanced at his watch and went on, "I've got to get back to the Rumpus Room and finish a story before I pack it in for the day."

"Sure," Bill said vaguely. "Sure. See you, Randy."

Randy was almost at the door when he paused and turned back. "Want to hear something odd?" he asked. "Mother was in town a couple of days ago, and she told me Andie had just turned down an opportunity to do a documentary in Africa."

Bill looked up in surprise. "Why'd she do that?"

Randy shrugged. "Beats me. Do you suppose she's finally through running?"

An hour later Bill headed out to the parking garage and got into his car. He couldn't seem to get Randy's words out of his mind. Or rather, Andie's words. Had she really said that...and meant it...that nobody had ever taught her how to accept love? And if she had, did that include him? Had he been just one more in a long parade of people who hadn't had the patience to teach her that she was lovable?

Soon he had to concentrate on the car instead of his thoughts. It was skipping and knocking, chugging along sluggishly exactly as it had a couple of weeks ago. The repair shop was supposed to have fixed the problem; they'd certainly charged enough.

Bill's temper had been short for weeks now, ever since Andie had left, but he'd tried hard to control it around the office. Now, as the car rattled and shimmied like an old jalopy, he blew up in frustration. He intended to give those mechanics at the garage a chewing out they'd never forget. Such shoddy workmanship was little short of criminal.

As always these days whenever he entered the empty apartment, the dead silence was like a physical blow. He saw Andie everywhere...in the painting over the sofa, bending over a cookbook in the kitchen, asleep in "their" bed, her red-gold curls spread across the pillow. The now familiar pain of loneliness spread through him, though he tried, as always, to battle it with noise and activity. He turned on the TV, intending to listen to the evening news, and then he mixed a drink and flipped through the mail. He thought with annoyance of the car and decided that he'd better find the garage receipt now, while it was on his mind. When he went down there tomorrow, he wanted to have proof that they'd already been paid a small fortune for a carburetor that still knocked and clanged and spit.

He couldn't find the receipt in the usual places, and finally, in desperation, he went into the bedroom and pulled open the bottom drawer of the bedside table. It was a catchall drawer, harboring the odds and ends he rarely needed but was reluctant to throw out. He doubted the receipt was there, but on the other hand, once when he'd lost a—

Bill's thoughts froze as he pulled out a paperback book and stared at the photograph of a baby on the cover. It was a book about pregnancy and childbirth.

Where had it come from? He shook his head and looked at it blankly. *He* certainly hadn't put it here, and except for Andie and his cleaning woman, no one else had been in the room. The cleaning woman was pushing sixty, a widow with no children; it was unlikely she was expecting a baby at this late date.

A baby! *Andie!* Bill felt as though someone had punched him. He gasped for breath, and sank to the edge of the bed, surprised to see his hands trembling.

Surely it wasn't true, he thought, dazed. Not Andie, who had never wanted children. There had to be another explanation.

Andie was a writer, he rationalized as he calmed down. Maybe she'd decided to take on some project concerning pregnancy and had only been doing research. Now that made sense; that was more like it.

Bill returned to the living room, freshened his Scotch and soda and slumped in a chair. No, the research explanation was too pat, too easy.

And dead wrong.

A chill raced up his spine. That glorious morning they'd spent together in Atlanta...The timing was right—she could have found out while she was still here in Washington. Now he recalled all the little signs that, taken singly, had pointed to nothing in particular: the frequent upset stomachs Andie had blamed on coffee; a heartier appetite, her abstinence from alcohol, the vitamin pills, even her attempts to learn to cook. One morning she'd been violently ill, and he himself had diagnosed it as a virus and made her stay home from work! Finally, there'd been the day at the office when she'd refused to be bullied into attending a round table meeting. Personal business, she'd said, and had refused to give him a more precise explanation. Could that have been the day she'd gone to see a doctor?

But if all this were true, why hadn't she told him? Why had she taken such pains to conceal it from him? For this, he thought furiously, he might just throttle her!

Suddenly he knew the answer: He had turned away from her. Bill felt sick as he realized what he had done. At the time, Andie had pleaded with him to try once more, but he'd been too bullheaded, too worried about the possibility of her walking out on him again. So he'd left her no choice but to go it alone.

He tried to phone her, but she didn't answer. Bill sat down, raking his fingers through his hair, half-demented with every emotion known to man from self-loathing to wild surges of joy: from a dread that it was too late to put things right to a melting tenderness as he thought of Andie, his Andie, bearing his child.

For hours he kept trying to call, but she never answered. At last, stretching out on the sofa, fully dressed, he fell asleep, partly from drinking too much, partly from emotional and physical fatigue.

Andrea had slept unusually late. She seemed to do that a lot these days, but the doctor had said it was perfectly normal.

She yawned and stepped into the shower. Her midsection was now a round little mound. She patted it affectionately before she turned on the water.

Last night she'd made dinner here for Kent and his new girlfriend, and then the three of them had gone to a movie. Afterward they'd stopped at a small all-night restaurant and talked for hours over a midnight snack. Andrea had enjoyed it and was glad she'd gone, but though they'd invited her to attend an art exhibit with them tonight, she'd refused. She didn't want to be a hanger-on.

Which meant her social life was severely limited these days. Most of her friends were either married or involved with someone, and dating was certainly out of the question. For the time being, at least, she was going to have to get used to being alone.

Not that she didn't have enough to keep her busy. Yesterday she'd bought her first maternity dress, thought it was still worlds too big. Tomorrow the painters and paperhangers would come to begin transforming her spare bedroom into a nursery. She was practicing her cooking and needlepoint and had begun taking knitting lessons once a week.

And she still had her work, thank goodness. Andrea finished her shower, dressed in a brown-and-gold sweater and a pair of beige slacks with a comfortable elastic waist and went to the kitchen for her breakfast. She was currently working on an article concerning exercise for pregnant women, and while she ate she read over what she'd written so far.

With a red pen she edited the work and made notes in the margins. There was a doctor in Los Angeles who'd been an excellent source of information, and now she found that she had a few more questions to ask him. She would call him later. There was also the doctor here in the city who— The buzzer sounded, interrupting her train of thought. Andrea went to the speaker. "Yes?"

"Mrs. Sheridan," Carl said, "there's a Mr. Sheridan here to see you. Can I send him up?"

"Of—of course." Andrea found that she was trembling as she stared at her reflection in the foyer mirror. Bill, here! But why? Why now, when she'd been trying so hard to convince herself that it didn't matter if she never saw him again?

Her heart hammered crazily when the bell rang, and she opened the door.

Instead of his usual business suit, he wore dark casual slacks, a pale-blue shirt and a deep-blue sweater. A corduroy jacket was flung carelessly over his shoulder. His face was strangely colorless, but the blue of his eyes was intensified by his piercing gaze.

Andrea tried to smile. "Hello, Bill," she began cordially. "This is a nice surprise."

"Is it?" he said, tight-lipped. Without waiting for an invitation, he brushed past her and strode into the living room.

Andrea had no choice but to close the door and follow him. Puzzled, she asked, "Are you angry with me about something?"

A sneer curled Bill's lips. "Now why on earth would I possibly be angry with you for keeping secret from me the fact that you're having my baby?"

Andrea felt faint as his words burned into her mind. Her knees grew rubbery, and she groped her way to the sofa and sat down. All she could think of was that the doctor must have contacted Bill and told him. Or Kent. Either way, the game was up. Someone had betrayed her.

"How did you find out?" she croaked.

Bill reached into a pocket of his jacket and tossed a paperback onto the sofa beside her. Andrea recognized it at once; she'd been wondering where she'd misplaced it. Now she knew—she'd betrayed herself by her own carelessness!

Before she could gather her wits, Bill knocked the book to the floor and sat down beside her. He took her clammy hands in his, and his voice broke as he asked, "Why, Andie? Were you really going to keep me from my own child?"

The pain in his voice was unmistakable. "Of course not," she assured him quickly. "I always intended to tell you. When the time was right."

"Meaning you didn't want me storming in here demanding that you marry me immediately."

Andrea nodded, astonished that he understood.

Bill released her hands, stood up and paced to the window and back. "How are you?" he asked abruptly.

"Fine."

"No problems?" he asked anxiously. "Other than the morning sickness that I was too foolish to recognize?"

Andrea smiled. "Why should you have? I didn't recognize it myself at first. Anyway, that part's about over and there are no other problems. The doctor says the baby and I are models of disgustingly robust health."

"Thank God!" Bill exclaimed fervently. He sat beside her again and clasped one of her hands, gazing at her imploringly. "I know if I insist that you marry me, you'll only refuse, but I'm asking you, Andie. Please."

He felt her grow rigid before she withdrew her hands and clasped them in her lap. "Thank you, Bill," she said as politely as though he'd offered tea, "but the answer is no."

"Andie!" he groaned. "Do I have to beg you?"

"No!" Her eyes darkened, flashing with sudden lightning. "I don't want you to feel you must sacrifice your life on my account, or for the baby!"

Bill stared at her blankly. "Sacrifice?" The very word sounded foreign—the last thing he was feeling was noble and self-sacrificing!

Before he could say so, Andrea went on. "It's awfully funny—ironic, really—that when you wanted children, I was so determined not to have them. Now that it's going to be a reality, I'm overjoyed. I was afraid, you see, that I might be like my mother, but now I realize I'm not in the least like her. I'm going to be one terrific mother, Bill, I promise you that. So you needn't feel that you've got to step in and take on the burden, because to me it's not a burden at all!"

"Burden! Sacrifice! What drivel, Andie!" Bill snapped angrily. "I want this baby as much as you do. I want to be a part of its life, but that's not the only reason I'm here today. Since you left, I've regretted letting you go. It was my pride, but more than that, it was my fear that if we did marry again, you'd soon grow bored and hit the road again."

"It was never boredom," Andrea murmured.

"No." Bill took possession of her hands again and said quietly, "Instead you were afraid *I'd* grow bored or lose interest if you hung around too long. If we had an argument, you figured if you skipped out for a while, I'd cool off and be glad to see you again."

Andrea's eyes widened. "Well," she gasped. "You sure are getting wise all of a sudden."

Bill shook his head and said ruefully, "No. I just had a long chat with somebody who knows you better. I should have had that talk with him three years ago."

"He'd been sworn to keep his mouth shut back then." Andrea looked severe. "I don't remember giving him leave to open it."

"Andie, don't you know, didn't you sense it back then, that I love you more than my own life? So what if we have a fight sometimes? I just want you there beside me to fight *with*! I can't imagine ever growing tired of you or bored. I just want you, period. It's not that I don't want you to be free to take trips. I don't want to own you or your time, or to hold you down in what's become a spectacular career. It's just that I don't want it to be so often or for such long spells, because I miss you so much when you're not with me. Please come back, let me try again, because I need you so very, very much."

Andrea was so moved that for a long time she didn't trust herself to speak. "Bill," she asked at last, "do you really mean this?"

He bent his head and kissed her hand. "With all my heart," he said huskily.

"It's not just because of the baby?"

"I'd be lying if I didn't say the baby's important. Of course it is. And you know how much I've always wanted children." Andrea nodded, but her eyes never left his face. "Andie, the minute I saw you again that night at the London theater I knew then why no other woman could ever satisfy me. Because she wasn't you. You're the only one I've ever loved or ever will love. I can't help it, darling. That's just the way it is, whether you like it or not."

Andrea smiled, and all at once, for Bill, the sun came out. "I still can't cook very well," she said.

He smiled back. "It didn't stop me from marrying you the first time. Anyway, you're trying, and I'll eat whatever you cook."

"That's mighty brave," she said, laughing softly. "Maybe you do love me more than I thought, at that."

"I do." Bill wasn't laughing.

"I've taken up knitting, too," she went on. "You might get some irregularly shaped socks for your birthday."

Bill grinned. "I solemnly pledge to wear them."

Andrea became serious. "I love you so, Bill. On New Year's Day, even before I knew for sure about the baby, I'd already made a vow to myself that if you wanted me back, I wouldn't make any more prolonged trips. Ever. That I was through with running, with not having the courage to stick out the rough spots and try. But the next day you'd changed your mind."

Bill winced. "Darling, please forgive me. I had my own insecurities just like you. It wasn't because I didn't love you."

"I believe you," she said softly. "So what I'm trying to say now is that you'd better be very sure about this, because you'll have more than enough time to get tired of me...like the rest of our lives. If you marry me again, I give you fair warning that I don't plan ever to leave you. Or our child."

"Children," Bill corrected, grinning.

"I beg your pardon?"

"Plural. This is only the beginning of the happy, closely knit Sheridan clan, you know."

"Umm," Andrea murmured, savoring the words. "The *large*, happy, closely knit Sheridan clan," she amended. "I want at least four or five children."

"Sounds reasonable to me." Bill smiled. His lips were so close to hers that his breath caressed her skin.

"In that case, maybe we ought to follow Randy's example and find ourselves a country place," Andrea suggested. "So the children will have a place to play."

"First thing after the wedding," Bill promised. Then he gave her a wicked, teasing grin. "Well, maybe the second thing." He crushed her to him and whispered, "I've missed you so. You know how you said I'd be glad to get my bed back when you left?" Andrea nodded, her eyes shining, and he continued, "I haven't been able to sleep a wink in it. I don't think I ever can again unless you're there beside me."

"I will be," she assured him.

Suddenly Andrea found herself being soundly kissed, and she nestled happily within Bill's strong arms. At last she knew that she need never fly away again in search of a place to belong.

She belonged with Bill. Forever.

AMERICAN TRIBUTE

**Where a man's dreams count
for more than his parentage...**

*Look for these upcoming titles
under the Special Edition
American Tribute banner.*

LOVE'S HAUNTING REFRAIN
Ada Steward #289—February 1986
For thirty years a deep dark secret kept them
apart—King Stockton made his millions while
his wife, Amelia, held everything together.
Now could they tell their secret, could they
admit their love?

THIS LONG WINTER PAST
Jeanne Stephens #295—March 1986
Detective Cody Wakefield checked out
Assistant District Attorney Liann McDowell,
but only in his leisure time. For it was the
danger of Cody's job that caused Liann to
shy away.

Silhouette Special Edition

AMERICAN TRIBUTE

AMERICAN TRIBUTE

RIGHT BEHIND THE RAIN
Elaine Camp #301–April 1986
The difficulty of coping with her brother's
death brought reporter Raleigh Torrence
to the office of Evan Younger, a police
psychologist. He helped her to deal with
her feelings and emotions, including love.

CHEROKEE FIRE
Gena Dalton #307–May 1986
It was Sabrina Dante's silver spoon that
Cherokee cowboy Jarod Redfeather couldn't
trust. The two lovers came from opposite
worlds, but Jarod's Indian heritage taught
them to overcome their differences.

NOBODY'S FOOL
Renee Roszel #313–June 1986
Everyone bet that Martin Dante and Cara
Torrence would get together. But Martin
wasn't putting any money down, and Cara
was out to prove that she was nobody's fool.

MISTY MORNINGS, MAGIC NIGHTS
Ada Steward #319–July 1986
The last thing Carole Stockton wanted was to
fall in love with another politician, especially
Donnelly Wakefield. But under a blanket of
secrecy, far from the campaign spotlights,
their love became a powerful force.

Silhouette Special Edition

COMING NEXT MONTH

THIS LONG WINTER PAST—Jeanne Stephens
Cody Wakefield was a temptation that Assistant District Attorney
Liann McDowell vowed to resist. He was intelligent, charming
and attractive . . . but he was a cop.

ZACHARY'S LAW—Lisa Jackson
Zachary's law partner was against him taking the case, but when
Zachary looked into Laura's eyes and saw the pain that so closely
mirrored his own soul, he knew he had to help her.

JESSE'S GIRL—Billie Green
Ellie had always been his "Little Peanut." Even when the trouble
started and Bitter, Texas, turned against him, Jesse didn't realize
that the girl standing beside him was becoming a woman—and
she was in love.

BITTERSWEET SACRIFICE—Bay Matthews
While searching for the surrogate mother who was now denying
him his child, Zade Wakefield found Lindy. Neither of them
knew that the bond they felt was the child they shared.

HEATSTROKE—Jillian Blake
Ten years had passed since Carey had been introduced to rock
star Tony Miles. Now she could discover if the sparks ignited that
night meant love, or were merely a flash in the pan.

DIAMOND IN THE SKY—Natalie Bishop
Taylor couldn't just walk away. Jason had transformed her from
an ex-model into a box-office smash. Now he needed help, and he
was going to get it . . . whether he wanted it or not.

AVAILABLE THIS MONTH